PET WHISPERER P.I.

Books 7 - 9

MOLLY FITZ

Editor: Megan Harris
Proofreaders: Alice Shepherd, Tabitha Kocsis & Jasmine Jordan
Cover Designer: Lou Harper, Cover Affairs

Whiskered Mysteries
PO Box 72
Brighton, MI 48116

AUTHOR'S NOTE

ABOUT MOLLY FITZ

While USA Today bestselling author Molly Fitz can't technically talk to animals, she and her doggie best friend, Sky Princess, have deep and very animated conversations as they navigate their days. Add to that, five more dogs, a snarky feline, comedian husband, and diva daughter, and you can pretty much imagine how life looks at the Casa de Fitz.

Molly lives in a house on a high hill in the Michigan woods and occasionally ventures out for good food, great coffee, or to meet new animal friends.

Writing her quirky, cozy animal mysteries is pretty much a dream come true, but sometimes she also goes by the names Melissa Storm and Mila Riggs and writes a very different kind of story.

Learn more, grab the free app, or sign up for her newsletter at **www.MollyMysteries.com**!

PET WHISPERER P.I.

Angie Russo just partnered up with Blueberry Bay's first ever talking cat detective. Along with his ragtag gang of human and animal helpers, Octo-Cat is determined to save the day... so long as it doesn't interfere with his schedule. Start with book 1, ***Kitty Confidential***.

PARANORMAL TEMP AGENCY

Tawny Bigford's simple life takes a turn for the magical when she stumbles upon her landlady's murder and is recruited by a talking black cat named Fluffikins to take over the deceased's role as the official Town Witch for Beech Grove, Georgia. Start with book 1, **Witch for Hire**.

MERLIN THE MAGICAL FLUFF

Gracie Springs is not a witch... but her cat is. Now she must help to keep his secret or risk spending the rest of her life in some magical prison. Too bad trouble seems to find them at every turn! Start with book 1, **Merlin the Magical Fluff**.

THE MEOWING MEDIUM

Mags McAllister lives a simple life making candles for tourists in historic Larkhaven, Georgia. But when a cat with mismatched eyes enters her life, she finds herself with the ability to see into the realm of spirits... Now the ghosts of people long dead have started coming to her for help solving their cold cases. Start with book 1, **Secrets of the Specter**.

THE PAINT-SLINGING SLEUTH

Following a freak electrical storm, Lisa Lewis's vibrant paintings of fairytale creatures have started coming to life. Unfortunately, only she can see and communicate with them. And when her mentor turns up dead, this aspiring artist must turn amateur sleuth to clear her name and save the day with only these "pigments" of her imagination to help her. Start with book 1, **My Colorful Conundrum**.

SPECIAL COLLECTIONS

Black Cat Crossing
Pet Whisperer P.I. Books 1-3
Pet Whisperer P.I. Books 4-6
Pet Whisperer P.I. Books 7-9
Pet Whisperer P.I. Books 10-12

CONNECT WITH MOLLY

You can download my free app here:
mollymysteries.com/app

Or sign up for my newsletter and get a special digital prize pack for joining, including an exclusive story, Meowy Christmas Mayhem, fun quiz, and lots of cat pictures!
mollymysteries.com/subscribe

Have you ever wanted to talk to animals? You can chat with Octo-Cat and help him solve an exclusive online mystery here:
mollymysteries.com/chat

Or maybe you'd like to chat with other animal-loving readers as well as to learn about new books and giveaways as soon as they happen! Come join Molly's VIP reader group on Facebook.
mollymysteries.com/group

To anyone who wishes she could talk to her animal best friend… Well, what's stopping you?

RACCOON RACKETEER

Pet Whisperer P.I.

ABOUT THIS BOOK

My crazy old Nan loves making decisions on a whim. Last week, she took up flamenco dancing. This week, she's adopted a trouble-making Chihuahua named Paisley. This wouldn't be much of a problem were it not for the very crabby tabby who also lives with us.

Man, I never thought I'd miss hearing Octo-Cat's voice, but his silent protest is becoming too much to bear, especially since we just opened our new P.I. business together.

Things go from bad to worse, of course, when Nan and I discover that someone has been embezzling funds from the local animal shelter. If we can't find the culprit soon, the shelter may not be able to keep its lights on and those poor homeless pets won't have anywhere to go.

Okay, so I just need to find the thief, rescue the animals, and save the day—all while trying to find a way for Octo-Cat and Paisley to set aside their differences and work together as a team. Yeah, wish me luck…

CHAPTER ONE

Hey, my name's Angie Russo, and I own one-half of a private investigation firm here in beautiful Blueberry Bay, Maine.

The other half belongs to my cat, Octavius—or Octo-Cat for short. It may not seem like his nickname keeps things short, but trust me on that one. Every time he tells anyone his full name, he always adds at least one new title to the end. The most recent version is Octavius Maxwell Ricardo Edmund Frederick Fulton Russo, Esq. P.I.

Like I said, it's a mouthful.

And he's kind of a handful, too.

While my spoiled tabby is undoubtedly my best friend, he does have a way of making my life harder. For instance, he's been catnapped, ordered to court for arbitration, and even repeatedly threatened to kill our new dog.

Did I mention that all happened in the span of just one month?

But that's Octo-Cat for you.

Love him or hate him, there's no denying he's a true individual.

And even though he's just about as stubborn as they come, he does occasionally change his mind about things.

That new dog we adopted? She's a sweet rescue Chihuahua

named Paisley. She liked him from the start, but it took Octo-Cat much longer to warm up to her. Now I am proud to report that the two have become close friends. In fact, one of my cat's favorite hobbies has become stalking and pouncing on his dog and then wrestling her to the ground.

Yes, his dog. That's how much the tables have turned these past few weeks.

Together, the three of us live with my grandmother, Nan. Although she's the main one who raised me, she lives in my house.

And I live in my cat's house.

Yup, Octo-Cat is a trust fund kitty, and his stipend is more than generous enough to pay the mortgage on our exquisite New England manor house.

It's a bit ridiculous, I'll be the first to admit that. But, hey, when life gives you lemonade, it's best if you drink up and enjoy!

Speaking of, I've been dating my dream guy for about seven weeks now. His name is Charles Longfellow, III, and he's my dream guy for good reason. Not only is he the sole partner at the law firm where I used to work, but he's also incredibly smart, kind, attentive, handsome—and, okay, I may as well just admit it—sexy.

Not that we've…

Anyway!

I can talk to my cat. I probably should have mentioned that earlier, seeing as it's the most unusual thing about me.

I can talk to my dog, too, and most animals now.

Long story short, I got electrocuted at a will reading, and when I regained consciousness, I heard Octo-Cat making fun of me. Once he realized I could understand him, he recruited me to solve his late owner's murder, and the rest is history.

From there, we realized two things. One, we make a really good crime-solving team, and two, we were stuck with each other for better or worse. Usually, things are better, but he still has his hissy fits on occasion—and so do I, for that matter.

And I guess that brings me to today.

Today marks the two-month mark since we first opened our P.I. outfit for business, and in that time, we've had exactly zero clients.

Even my normally optimistic nan can't spin this one in a positive light.

No one wants to hire us, and I'm not sure why.

I'm well-liked in town, and it's not like people know I can actually talk to animals. They think including my cat as a partner is just a gimmick, and I prefer it that way, honestly.

But I'm starting to worry that we'll never bring any business in.

At what point do we give up on our entrepreneurial enterprise?

Octo-Cat is pretty happy sleeping in the sun most of the day, but I prefer to have more in my life. I even quit my former job as a paralegal to make sure I had enough time for all the investigative work I felt certain would fall into my lap the moment we opened for business.

Yeah, I was more than a little wrong about that one.

I need to figure out something, and fast, if I want to keep my operation afloat, but how can I trust my instincts when they were so wrong before?

Here's hoping Octo-Cat has a bright idea he'd be willing to share…

It was Wednesday morning, and I'd spent the better part of the last two days handing out flyers to any person, business, or animal who would take one. Out of desperation, I'd even visited parking lots and shoved the brightly colored papers touting my credentials under the windshield wipers of each car in the lot.

Still, not one person had called to share a case with me.

Not one.

Nan had left the house early to serve a volunteer shift picking up litter around town. We'd both agreed the animal shelter, while in need, wasn't the best place for her to share her generous heart— because we both knew she'd end up adopting almost every dog and cat in that place.

Our house was already full enough, thank you very much.

I sat in the front room of the house, sipping a can of Diet Coke.

The coffee maker still scared me silly, given that the last time I'd used one I'd been electrocuted, and tea just wasn't the same without Nan to keep me company.

Paisley and Octo-Cat scampered around the house in their perpetual game of tag, and I wracked my brain for any kind of idea that would help get us some clients.

The electronic pet door buzzed, and both animals ran outside.

I smiled and watched them zigzag through the yard. Mid-autumn had hit Maine, and now most of the fire-colored leaves had fallen from the trees. While I tried my best to keep up with the raking, it wasn't easy given the fact that an enormous forest flanked my property on two sides.

Leaves blew into our yard all the time.

Like right now.

I sighed as a gust so strong I could practically see it swept through the trees and deposited at least five landscaping bags full of leaves on the front lawn. Leaves of every color carpeted the greenish-yellow grass—red, orange, yellow… turquoise?

"Mommy! Mommy!" Paisley cried from outside, and I went running. The sweet and innocent Chihuahua got upset fairly easily, but her small size also made her incredibly vulnerable. I never took any chances when it came to her safety, and neither did Nan or Octo-Cat.

One of us was always with her whenever she ventured outside.

And even though I knew Octo-Cat was out there now, I still needed to make sure nothing had happened to frighten her.

Both Paisley and Octo-Cat were waiting for me on the porch when I stepped outside. Paisley even had a turquoise piece of paper clamped within her jaws.

"What's this?" I asked, taking it from her.

"It's one of your papers, Mommy!" the little dog cried proudly.

I glanced at the bright paper in my hands and then back out to the yard where dozens, maybe even hundreds, more had mixed with the autumnal leaves.

She was right. This was my paper. In fact, it was the flyer for our P.I. firm that I had so painstakingly distributed the last couple of days. I'd handed out every single one that Nan had printed for us—I'd made sure of it.

So why had they all followed me home?

And how?

A squeaky laugh underneath the porch gave me a pretty good idea.

"Pringle!" I yelled, stomping my feet as hard as I could to try to force the raccoon out of there.

I knew he was mad at me ever since I'd banned him from entering the house, but to sabotage my business? Really?

CHAPTER TWO

"Pringle! Show yourself!" I cried, stomping so hard the impact raced up my foot and all the way through my calf. I tried to be fair to the animals that had made themselves part of my world, to accept them for their unique selves. Most of the time that was easy...

But this particular raccoon was driving me straight in the direction of the nearest asylum.

His laughter continued from under the porch, but Pringle made no move to answer my call. I had half a mind to widen the hole he used as a doorway and climb under there myself when Octo-Cat graciously intervened.

"Angela, that's not how this is done." He paced the edge of the porch with tail and nose held high. Whatever he was about to suggest, he was obviously very proud of it.

I stopped stomping and placed a hand on my hip, widening my eyes as I waited for Octo-Cat to enlighten me.

"Paisley, stay," he said to the Chihuahua, then trotted down the stairs and approached the edge of the raccoon's nearly hidden burrow. "Sir Pringle, would you kindly give us the distinct honor of your presence?"

I heard the raccoon before I saw him. "At your service, dear Octavius."

When I peeked over the railing, I saw him making a deep bow toward my cat. For whatever reason, he idolized the tabby. At least that was his excuse for stealing so many of Octo-Cat's things. I still didn't know where his occasional fairytale knight mannerisms came from, but he clearly enjoyed this particular brand of make-believe.

Normally, I'd play along, but I was too angry to play by the raccoon's ever-changing rules today.

"What's this?" I demanded, waving the brightly colored flyer in the air.

Pringle bared his teeth in irritation. "I'm not at your beck and call, you know."

I bared my teeth right back, just barely holding in an irritated scream. I'd never hurt a hair on his thieving head but hoped I could at least scare him into good behavior with the threat of it.

"Pray, answer the fair maiden's question," Octo-Cat intervened yet again. Oh, jeez. I'd have to block whatever medieval fantasy channel he was watching on TV when I wasn't around to supervise. Even though I realized he was trying to help, this whole thing was turning into one giant migraine.

The raccoon ran up the porch steps, climbed the railing, and plucked the paper from my hands. "That's mine," he said then tucked it under his armpit before running back to the yard and out of my reach.

I placed both my hands on my hips and narrowed my eyes at him. "Actually, it's mine."

"Finders, keepers." The smile that crept across his face now was far worse than his earlier show of aggression.

"What? No!" I cried. Just as I'd never hurt him, I knew Pringle would never cause me physical harm. At the moment, I was feeling rather emotionally attacked, however.

"Mommy, do you want me to chase the big bad raccoon away?" Paisley wagged her tail in excitement, refusing to take her eyes off the masked thief for even a second.

"Oh, no, sweetie, you don't have to…" My words trailed away

as I watched Pringle dive into the newly distributed leaves and gather up the remaining flyers.

"Actually," I said, changing my mind in an instant. "Go for it."

The little tri-color dog took off like a shot, barking at the top of her lungs. "Hey, you! Nobody messes with my mommy!"

Pringle lowered himself to all fours and shook his head. "Call off your hound. Let's discuss this like the civilized creatures I know at least one of us is."

Paisley ran a wide arc around the yard and then returned to my side. "He's still there," she pouted, then instantly brightened again. "Should I try again, Mommy?"

I smiled and bent down to pet her silky fur. "You did great. Thank you." Rising again, I marched straight over to Pringle. "Okay, let's hear it. Why did you take all my flyers?"

"They're pretty," he explained, hugging the disheveled stack to his chest. "I like pretty things."

"But they weren't here. I put them up all over town. How did you even…?"

He shrugged. "So I hitched a ride. Sometimes I like to go on adventures, too, you know? It would be nice if I didn't have to invite myself, but since you're not doing the job." He shrugged again. If I wasn't mistaken, the beginnings of tears had formed in the corners of his giant black eyes. Strange how sometimes my animal friends seemed more human than any of the people I knew.

"I'm sorry if I hurt your feelings." I squatted down to face him head on. "I didn't know you wanted to come, too."

"Of course I wanted to come!" he shouted. "I like adventures just as much as the next forest animal, you know."

I chose not to mention that distributing flyers begging for work was hardly an adventure. "Tell you what, next time we'll invite you along, too. Deal?" Or at least the next time after I'd had a chance to cool down. As it was, he'd wasted a day and a half of hard work when I'd have given him colored paper had he just asked for it.

Pringle shook his head and eyed me warily. "Not quite."

I waited, refusing to add fuel to his flaming theatrics. I got enough of this from Octo-Cat, and frankly I liked him far more than this nuisance raccoon who'd become a frenemy at best.

Pringle sighed. "I'm keeping the pretty papers."

"Why do you even need them?" I asked with a groan.

"I'm taking up origami, and these will do very nicely." Pringle turned his nose up so high I could only see chin, then he marched straight back to his under-porch apartment.

How did he even know origami was a thing?

And how did he know enough to want to attempt it himself?

What an odd animal.

"See, Mommy! I scared him away!" Paisley sat proudly on the edge of the porch, shaking so hard with excitement that I hadn't the heart to tell her that Pringle had played us rather than other way around.

"That guy..." Octo-Cat plopped himself down beside the Chihuahua. "He's getting way too big for his britches."

I couldn't agree more, but for the moment I was done discussing the masked menace. We had too much else we could be doing with our day.

"C'mon, you two," I said with a sigh. "It looks like we need to come up with a new advertising plan."

As the three of us filed back indoors, a new determination overtook me. My P.I. business would succeed or fail based on its own merits. I would not let an egotistical raccoon with delusions of grandeur stand between me and the role I just knew I was meant to play in this world—or at least in my small corner of it.

"I know that look," Octo-Cat said with an open-mouthed smile that showed off his pointy teeth. "Nobody puts Angie in a corner."

I snorted at that one, picturing myself in the classic 80s romance opposite Patrick Swayze. Even though he used to watch only Law & Order, he'd greatly expanded his viewing habits in recent months. Largely, thanks to my nan.

And while I appreciated my cat's support, I definitely needed to start limiting his television time.

CHAPTER THREE

As it turned out, my cat wasn't the only one watching too much television these days. Normally, Nan would spend most of her mornings in the kitchen as she did the food prep for the day and whipped up treat after delectable treat for us to enjoy with our daily tea. Today, however, the kitchen sat empty, pristinely clean, and completely abandoned.

"Nan?" My voice felt disturbingly loud as it echoed through the empty manor.

When no response came, I raced to the garage to check if her little red sports car was still parked snugly inside. She often left after lunchtime to volunteer or take a community class, but she generally informed me before heading off. Besides, if she'd left the house early today, I should have seen her from my place on the front porch.

Well, her car sat waiting in the garage, right where it belonged.

So then where was my nan?

Paisley stood on her hindlegs and padded my leg with her tiny clawed feet. "I can still smell her close by. Want me to show you where she is?"

As soon as I nodded, the little dog bolted up the stairs and began scratching at the door to one of the bedrooms we didn't use.

"Nan?" I called cautiously before pushing it wide open.

Paisley raced in before me, and Octo-Cat slinked in after.

Nan, however, was still nowhere to be seen.

"Paisley, are you sure she's here?" I asked, seriously beginning to worry now.

"Oh, yes! Up there!" She ran over to the closet and began to jump and do clumsy side flips, not stopping until I looked up and noticed the open attic hatch.

I craned my neck to try to see inside. "Nan?"

She appeared in a cloud of dust. The bright silk scarf on her head featured an emoji print, and she wore cat-eye sunglasses, presumably to protect her eyes from all the floating dust motes. "Oh, hello, dear."

"What are you doing up there?" I demanded, not any less worried now that I'd found her in a potentially dangerous situation. "How did you even get up there?"

"Just sorting through some things. I started with my bedroom but wasn't quite ready to call the whole thing quits for the day just yet." She turned away and crawled out of view.

"Call what quits?" I shouted after her.

"I didn't know we had a higher place," Octo-Cat remarked, then dropped low and wiggled his butt, making an impressive leap toward the hatch.

His front paws grazed the entrance but couldn't get a grip.

"Ouch," he moaned after he fell clumsily back to the ground.

"Are you hurt?" I asked, attempting to stroke and soothe him.

He flinched and slinked away from my hand. "My poor pride," he whined. "What kind of a cat can't stick the landing? Ouch."

"Oh, Octo-friend. Can I kiss your ouchies?" the dog offered, licking her lips in anticipation.

"Insult to injury," my cat muttered.

Both animals ran out of the room, leaving me on the ground and Nan somewhere above.

"Nan?" I called again. "What are you doing up there?"

She popped into view again, laughed, and shook her head as if this should have all been obvious. "Why, Mission Marie Kondo, of course!"

"Marie Kon—Wait… Is this from that book everyone's talking about?" If memory served, there were also memes aplenty.

Nan scrunched her face up. "A book? Hmm, well, I don't know about that. It's a show on Netflix. I binged the full first season the other day. I do hope there will be a new season soon."

I knew for a fact it had been a book first but kept mum.

Her eyes lit up as she explained, "It's the new Feng Shui. Everyone's doing it. If something doesn't spark joy, then it doesn't belong in your home. Fun, right?"

"Yeah… Fun," I muttered. Already we had far more house than possessions to put in it. Sometimes I felt like we lived in a museum with all the antiques we'd inherited as part of the estate. We could do with more personal items to fill it out, not fewer.

"Well, are you coming up or am I coming down?" My grandmother tilted her head to the side in a gesture that reminded me very much of her Chihuahua sidekick. "You know what? I'll come down."

A moment later she'd scurried out of the crawl space and dropped the rest of the distance to the carpeted floor below. Her knees bent a little on impact, and I worried she'd broken something.

Racing to her side, I gently pulled her back into a standing position. "Oh my gosh! Nan! Are you okay?"

"Of course I'm okay. What do you take me for? Some kind of invalid?" Both her knees and her voice shook, but shockingly she wasn't any worse for the wear. Not like Octo-Cat and his poor, damaged pride.

What do I take you for? A seventy-something woman, that's what! But I didn't push it since she appeared to be perfectly okay. Maybe one day I'd be in as good of shape as my grandmother, but somehow I doubted it—not when she was part Betty Crocker, part ninja.

"Do me a favor, because you know I worry," I begged. "Next time you want to go in the attic, grab me first—or at least grab a chair."

She waved my concerns away. "No need to worry. I'm done for now."

"Did you get rid of lots of stuff?" I asked, only now noticing the two large trash bags that sat to the side of the closet.

"A good chunk of it. What have you been up to this morning?"

I filled her in on the reappearing flyers and the confrontation with Pringle, ending with the most unbelievable part. "And get this? He says he needs them so he can do origami!" I exploded.

"Oh, good," Nan said with a pert nod. "I was worried he wouldn't be able to find any craft supplies."

"Wait. Are you the one who turned him on to the Japanese art of paper-folding?" Why was I even surprised?

She shrugged. "I had an old book. It wasn't sparking joy for me, but it seemed to spark joy for our raccoon friend, so I handed it right over."

"But a book? Does he know how to read?" How could he read if Octo-Cat, who'd lived much more closely with humans, couldn't?

Nan chuckled. "Well, that's a question for him, dear. Not me."

I rolled my eyes hard and let out a long, extra breathy sigh.

"No need to get snippy now," Nan scolded as she charged toward the door.

I followed her down the stairs and into the kitchen. "Sorry. I didn't mean to take it out on you. It's just I'm trying so hard to find clients for Octo-Cat's and my business, but nothing seems to be working."

"Oh, you need clients?" Nan raised an eyebrow my way while filling our tea kettle at the sink.

"Of course we do. It's been two months, and still we have zero clientele to show for our efforts." Talk about depressing.

My grandmother set the kettle on the stovetop and turned back to me with a giant grin. "Well, why didn't you say so? I happen to know someone who is in desperate need of your services."

"What?" I gasped. "And you didn't tell me?"

Nan hit me gently with a hand towel. "Calm down, you. I just found out yesterday, and I was quite busy at the time."

With her Marie Kondo-ing, right. I rearranged my features into a placating smile. Even though I loved my nan more than anyone else in this entire world, sometimes her roundabout methods could be a bit infuriating.

"Well," I said when she still hadn't said anything after a full minute. "Who is it?"

She crossed her arms over her chest and turned her face away. "Apologize first. That's twice you've snapped at me in the space of five minutes."

"I'm sorry." And I was. I loved Nan's quirkiness and wouldn't change her for the world. For all her faults, my grandmother was still my best friend and my idol.

As soon as that final syllable left my mouth, she whipped back toward me to make her big reveal. "I prefer to let you be surprised, but I'll ask your new client over for dinner tonight so she can give you all the details. I feel quite sure she'll hire you on to help her out."

"Thank you, Nan!" I sang, wrapping her in a solid hug. At the end of the day, it didn't matter that she was playing coy with the details. Nan had found a client, a real, honest-to-goodness client!

Finally, things were looking up for Octo-Cat's and my P.I. business.

CHAPTER FOUR

W hen the doorbell chimed a spirited rendition of the Village People's YMCA, I knew two things. My first client was on the other side of that door, and Nan had obviously been having some fun at my expense.

Nan, of course, had refused to divulge any details pertaining to the case or the client, preferring not to shade my judgment, or so she said. I personally believe she just thought it was more fun that way—well, at least for her.

So when I pulled open the door to reveal our mail lady Julie, I was completely taken by surprise. "Julie, hello! How are you today?" I asked cautiously, not quite sure whether she was the client or simply here on urgent US Postal Service business.

"I've been better, that's for sure." The normally smiling woman stood uncertainly on the porch, a giant frown marring her cherubic features. She wrung her hands and let out an enormous sigh.

"Well, invite our guest in already!" Nan called from the bottom of the staircase. I hadn't even heard her approach. I'm telling you, she's part ninja.

"Thank you, Dorothy." Julie nodded and moved to stand awkwardly in our foyer. She was one of the few people around town who knew and used Nan's God-given name rather than her preferred nickname.

"Well, I'll leave you two to discuss business in private." Nan swept away, hips swinging as she made her way toward the kitchen.

"Oh!" she cried as she twisted back to face us from across the room. "Be a dear and take the cat with you. He has a horrible habit of getting in my way lately." She paused, opened her mouth, and then shot me a giant, exaggerated wink that Julie surely couldn't have missed.

Octo-Cat growled as he hopped onto the lowest step. "Just because she can't understand me doesn't mean I don't understand her, and that was hurtful."

I wanted to comfort him but simply couldn't with Julie watching us both so closely. "Let's head up to my office," I said instead.

What had been a mere guest room when we'd moved in was now my favorite room in the entire manor. Brock Calhoun—who now went by Cal for short—had done a fantastic job converting the space into a luxury library and office, but the crowning feature was the six-foot-long window seat that overlooked the estate's back gardens. The huge vaulted ceilings and antique crystal chandelier weren't so bad either, nor were the built-in bookshelves that took up two entire walls from floor to ceiling.

"Wow," Julie whispered in reverence as she took it all in. "I bet you hardly ever leave this room."

"Not if I can help it," I said amicably, even though that wasn't entirely true. While I definitely spent a few hours reading in my library each week, the fact I hadn't managed to book any clients to fulfill the office function of the space depressed me. Most days I found it easier to read in my bedroom rather than face my own inadequacy as a private investigator.

Well, that all changed right here, right now, and all thanks to the blessed woman before me.

"Nan says you have a case," I started once Julie had settled onto the leather fainting couch opposite my large walnut desk and swivel chair. "Catch me up."

Octo-Cat paced the perimeter of the room, trying—and failing—to act naturally. We'd have to talk about that later.

"I do." Julie glanced toward the tabby, then turned back to me and cleared her throat. "For the past couple of weeks, mailboxes on my route have been getting vandalized. And mail I know I delivered is also getting reported as never having reached its destination. I know I'm not making any mistakes, but I'm on thin ice at work. The office is blaming me and threatening to put me on administrative leave or even dock my pay to cover the cost of replacing the mailboxes."

I reached forward and touched her knee sympathetically. "That's horrible."

If I wanted to be a good investigator, I needed a good rapport with my clients just as much as I needed my sleuthing skills. Luckily, I'd always adored Julie and considered her—if not quite a friend—a well-liked acquaintance.

Even Octo-Cat appeared moved by her story. He stopped patrolling and jumped up beside her on the couch, then rubbed his head against her hand asking for pets.

"What a sweet kitty," Julie remarked, which was enough to send him skittering away just as quickly as he'd come. Nobody called him kitty and got away with it. Our guest was just lucky he wasn't in a swiping mood.

We both watched Octo-Cat settle himself in the window seat and scowl at us from across the room.

"So, you need us to find out who's taking the mail and damaging the mailboxes so that you won't keep getting blamed for it," I summarized.

Julie nodded vigorously, then frowned. "Yes, that would be fantastic. But if you don't want to help me, I'll understand."

"Why wouldn't we want to help?" My breathing hitched as I waited for her response. The case seemed pretty open and shut, so what could be the problem?

Julie hung her head and let a lone tear fall to her lap. "I can't pay anything for your help. Ever since the kiddos started college, I've had to live paycheck to paycheck, and I'm still drowning in debt. I can't afford to lose this job, but I also can't afford to pay you to help me keep it."

"She expects us to work for free?" Octo-Cat hissed in agitation. "Thank you, next! Move along, sis."

I glared at him before turning back to Julie with a grin. "We'd be happy to help. No payment required."

Julie raised her eyes to meet mine, the hint of a smile playing at the edges of her lips. "Are you sure? I know it's asking a lot. I wouldn't have even thought to ask, but Dorothy insisted and—"

I raised my hand to cut her off. "Totally sure."

"No, no, no," Octo-Cat pouted. "What kind of hobbyist works for free? I thought we were running a legitimate operation here?"

I shook my head. Sometimes it was so hard not to talk back to him in the presence of those who didn't know about our secret connection.

"Totally sure," I said again, keeping my eyes glued to the irate tabby the whole time.

And now less than fifteen minutes after it started, my meeting with Julie came to an end. "I have to go," she said, rising to her feet and offering me her hand to shake. "Thank you so much for agreeing to help. I promise I'll find a way to repay you someday soon."

"You better!" Octo-Cat spat.

"It's no problem," I said with a smile to balance out his obvious agitation. "Our P.I. practice is just that, a practice. We're happy for the opportunity to keep our skills top-notch."

Julie sighed wistfully. "It's really sweet, you and Dorothy doing this together. I hope one day when my girls are a little further away from their teen phase, they'll want to hang out with me even half as much as you do with your nan."

I laughed. "Nan's not really a part of the firm, but we do love spending time together. I'm sure your daughters will come around soon enough."

"She's not? Then what's with all the we and us talk?"

"Oh, um, it's more like the royal we. I'm the sleuth, but I do bring in outside experts as needed." I hoped she didn't notice the way I stumbled over my words and practically tripped coming down the stairs from the shock of my mishap.

I really needed to stop including Octo-Cat when speaking with others. Even the casual we could eventually expose my secret. And as someone who uncovered secrets for a living—you know, theoretically—you'd think I'd be better at hiding them.

"The royal we, indeed," my cat sneered as he followed us down the stairs.

"Dorothy has my number," Julie said, lingering near the door. "Thank you again for your help."

"Done already?" Nan appeared, wiping her hands on the edge of her frilly pink polka dot apron.

"I'm in good hands with Angie taking on my case. Thank you for putting us together."

Nan beamed with obvious pride. "Oh, I'm so glad. Please tell me you'll stay for dinner. It's nearly ready."

"I really can't, but thank you for the invite." Julie nodded toward Nan and shook my hand a second time, then excused herself from our home.

"And stay out!" Octo-Cat called as the door latched shut behind her.

CHAPTER FIVE

"That was fast," Nan remarked a second time as I followed her into the kitchen. Even I had to admit that it seemed as if Julie couldn't wait to get out of here. Was that simply because she had other plans, or could there be another less savory reason? Gosh, I hoped she hadn't hired us to clear her name for crimes she had, in fact, committed.

No, no. I shook my head and let out a deep breath. How could I even think these things about Julie? She'd always been kind to us, always been reliable and, as best I could tell, honest.

"Looks like you have lots on your mind." Nan pulled vegetables from the fridge and dropped them beside a clean cutting board. "Fill me in while you fix our salad," she said, returning to her place of honor at the stove.

I washed the lettuce, then put it in the spinner. Not to brag, but I'd gotten quite good at preparing our nightly veggies. Mostly because Nan didn't trust me with anything that required heat to prepare. Not after the burnt brisket fiasco of 2019.

"There's not much to tell," I said thoughtfully. "Someone's stealing mail and banging up mailboxes."

"Oh, I knew that." Nan moved toward the fridge and grabbed a stick of butter. "It's why I suggested you two to get together. Did she have anything else to say?"

I kept my focus fixed firmly on the salad. "Only that she's not able to pay. I told her that's fine, but Octo-Cat is pretty rankled about it."

"Well, of course he is. Such a crabby tabby." She turned and stuck her tongue out at Octo-Cat, who was sitting by his empty food bowl and scowling. I knew better than to feed him early, though. He'd be even more upset by the change in schedule than he'd become when he found out we wouldn't be getting paid for our first case.

"Well, excuse me for having standards," the cat said drolly. "And self-respect."

What a drama queen.

"Well, it's a good thing his trust fund is more than enough to cover our half of the mortgage and expenses."

"Indeed," Nan said, bobbing her head.

Octo-Cat let out a low growl but didn't add any words to further express his displeasure with me and the situation.

Nan and I worked in silence for a few minutes, each enjoying the peace that came with chopping, stirring, and plating up. That's when I remembered something from my past that may help with Julie's case.

"Hey," I said into the quiet kitchen. My voice seemed extra loud after the brief period of quiet. "Remember when Octo-Cat received his arbitration summons? That was delivered way late, almost too late for us to show up to the hearing. Do you think maybe one of Julie's colleagues at the post office could be to blame for what happened then and maybe also for what's happening now?"

"It's possible," Nan replied with a shrug. "But last time it was a case of a wrong mailing address and slow forward."

I chewed my lip as I considered this. I remembered it, too, but that still didn't mean there wasn't a connection now. "You know what? I'm going to grab that letter just in case. See if it sparks any memories or ideas. It may be nothing, but at least it gives us a place to start."

I raced up to the library where I kept my important papers stashed in a hanging file system in the bottom drawer of my desk. There wasn't too much I kept, but it did have a copy of Octo-Cat's trust fund paperwork, my various associate degree certificates, a copy of our mortgage, that kind of thing. Except…

Everything was gone.

I pulled the drawer completely off the track in case something had fallen behind, but not a single scrap of paper was to be found.

"Nan!" I called at the top of my lungs as I sank the rest of the way to the ground, needing to feel something solid beneath me as panic rushed through my veins. Even though I was sitting on the hardwood floor in front of the desk, my legs still felt weak, my knees shaky. Could all my most important documents really have vanished without a trace?

My grandmother appeared a short while later. "Yes, dear?"

I twisted around to look her in the eye. "Have you been Marie Kondo-ing my things, too?"

She lifted a hand to her chest. "Of course not. I wouldn't throw your things out without your okay first. Each person needs to go through the process herself. My joy sparklers might not match your joy sparklers. In fact, they probably don't."

I lifted up the empty drawer and bit my lip to keep from crying.

"Well, now that's a pickle." She crossed the room and took the drawer from me, giving it a good firm shake.

"Oh, dear," she said when nothing fell from inside. "I'll go call Charles."

I kept sitting there even as I heard footsteps carry down the hall. Although there wasn't really anything my boyfriend could do in this situation, it still felt good knowing he'd be here soon.

While I was the best at piecing together clues and evidence, he always had a way of knowing what to do in tough situations like this.

"What's the matter with you?" Octo-Cat asked with twitching whiskers. I hadn't even noticed him enter the room.

"All of my important papers are gone," I said with a sniff.

"What is it with you and papers going missing?" he asked with a laugh, but then sobered when he noticed I was still quite upset.

"The flyers weren't my fault," I reminded him. "And neither is this."

"No," he said with a yawn. Good to see he found my turmoil to be so relaxing. When he'd finished his enormous yawn, he added, "The first set of papers were Pringle's fault. Do you think he took these, too?"

I perked up at this suggestion. "Pringle? Hmm. But he's not allowed in the house."

Octo-Cat laughed sarcastically. "Do you really think that stops him?"

"That's it." I pushed up and onto my feet, drawing strength from my newfound anger. "I'm calling animal control."

How could one little raccoon cause so much damage to my business and personal life? And why wouldn't he just leave me and my things alone?

"Oh, goodie!" Octo-Cat trilled as he trotted down the stairs behind me. "Can I be there when they come? I can't wait to see the look on his face, when—"

He stopped abruptly when a booming knock sounded on our front door. It seemed far too soon for Charles to have arrived after Nan's call, but then who…?

Nan ran out of the kitchen, wiping her hands on a tea towel that she carried with her. "Yes," she called. "Who is it?"

"It's Julie!" the mail lady answered, her voice dripping with distress. "Can I come in?"

CHAPTER SIX

J ulie, Nan, and I stood in the foyer with Paisley at our heels and
Octo-Cat watching from what he deemed a safe distance partway up the stairs.

"What's wrong?" I asked as Julie's shoulders shook from crying.

Nan put an arm around the mail lady's shoulders and offered a
tissue she'd pulled from her front pocket.

"I was hardly here for ten minutes," Julie reminded us. "And yet
someone ransacked my truck. I didn't notice until I'd already driven
all the way home, and I still can't believe it."

"What's missing?" I asked, fearing what her answer might be.

"Some packages that I was unable to deliver since I had no one
to sign for them." Her expression grew dark, angry. "I'm already in
just about as much trouble as I can get at work. What I'm really
upset about is that my lucky angel was taken, too."

"Doesn't sound very lucky anymore," Octo-Cat quipped, then
laughed at his own joke, his striped, furry head tilting from side to side.

"Your lucky angel?" I asked, dread rising in my chest. I could
always print more flyers or order new copies of my paperwork. A
lucky angel sounded like it might be irreplaceable.

"Oh, it's not an expensive thing, but it was real special to me. It was the first Mother's Day gift my girls ever bought for me with their own money. It's mostly glass with a bit of gold-like plating along the edges. I keep it in the glove compartment since it's fragile. That way, it's always close enough to keep me company as I go about my day."

"How'd you find out it was missing?" I asked, resisting the urge to start biting at my fingernails from the mounting anxiety.

Julie got a far-off look in her eyes and she swayed slightly from side to side as if in a dream. "My youngest called to update me on college life. That's why I was in such a rush to say goodbye after our visit, because I knew she'd be calling to check in after the shift at her part-time job ended tonight. I like to hold onto the angel while I talk with either of my girls. It's the next best thing to being able to hug them in my arms."

"But when you went to get it, it wasn't there," I finished for her with a sigh.

She nodded and pointed at me. "Exactly."

"But you knew it was still in your truck before you came to visit us?" This whole thing was giving me a headache. It had to have been Pringle, which meant his kleptomania had reached alarmingly dangerous heights.

"Of course, it was!" Julie exploded. Suddenly, it didn't feel as if we were allies trying to solve this thing together. "Like I said, it's my lucky charm, and I figured I'd need a good bit of luck heading into our meeting, hoping you'd agree to help me for free and all." She dropped her voice to a husky whisper and glanced hesitantly toward Nan. "D-d-d-did you take my angel, Dorothy?"

Oh, no. It was one thing to blame me, but to even think Nan could... Impossible! Of course, I was quick to defend my grandmother. "No way! You and I both know she didn't, but I have a pretty good idea who did."

"Let me guess..." Octo-Cat descended the steps slowly and plopped himself between Julie and me. "A certain, up-to-no-good-ever raccoon?"

Paisley began to bark furiously at this. "Big, bad raccoon!" she cried. "He hurt Mommy's friend!"

Julie glanced nervously toward the upset little dog and stepped closer to the door.

"Shh, it's okay, baby," Nan said, lifting Paisley into her arms and giving her a big, wet kiss.

I kept my attention focused squarely on Julie as I explained, "There's a raccoon with sticky fingers that lives under our front porch. And, well, I wouldn't be surprised one bit if he's the one who snuck into your truck and stole your angel. The packages, too."

"Angie's also had some things go missing recently," Nan explained, and we've already caught him red-handed once.

Julie's head whipped back at this news as if she'd just received a blow right to her face. "A raccoon is taking your things? You know this for sure, and yet you haven't exterminated him yet?"

How could I explain that killing the raccoon would be akin to murdering a human in my book? No matter how much he got on my nerves, I would never hurt him to make my life run a little smoother.

"My dear Angie has a soft heart," Nan explained with a sad smile.

"Can you get it back for me?" Julie asked with another sniffle. I had no idea whether this newest round of tears were caused by sorrow or by hope—or perhaps both at the same time. "Can you get my angel back?"

"Of course, we can," I said, shooting a worrying glance Nan's way. If I was going to recover stolen property from a raccoon burrow, I'd need a bit of privacy to do it.

"Dinner's just about ready," my grandmother said right on cue. "While Angie is out dealing with the raccoon, I'll need someone to stay here and eat it with me. C'mon, dear." She guided Julie toward the dining room before anyone could argue.

I marched out the door with the animals in close pursuit. And even though I wanted to scream at the top of my lungs, I had to play it cool or risk Julie overhearing.

"I'll get him, Mommy!" Paisley volunteered, and before I could stop her she ran into the raccoon's lair beneath the porch.

"Paisley, no!" I hissed, worry beating its ugly wings within me. "Get back here!"

Pringle was about five times her size and could really hurt her if he felt threatened by her unexpected entry into his home.

"Well, this could all go terribly, terribly wrong," Octo-Cat said with a sigh. "That's dogs for you, though. Always doing. Never thinking." Yes, Paisley had become his closest friend in recent months—and, no, he hadn't waivered one bit in his prejudice toward dogs. Contradictions were okay in his book, as long as he was the one making them.

Tires crunched in the distance, and I glanced up just in time to see Charles's car pulling up our long driveway.

He parked right in front of the porch. "Nan told me you're having a little raccoon problem," he said as he moved around to the trunk of his car and popped the lid.

"More like a big raccoon problem," I mumbled.

Charles grabbed a pair of shovels and a flashlight, then slammed the trunk closed again. "Well then, let's get to work. Shall we?"

CHAPTER SEVEN

Charles and I approached the slim, jagged hole that led into Pringle's under-porch apartment, shovels in hand. Octo-Cat stayed on the porch, preferring not to get directly involved if he could avoid it. Paisley, of course, had already charged bravely ahead against my wishes.

"Pringle," I whisper-yelled at the hole, praying he was in a good enough mood to spare my poor overeager Chihuahua warrior. "Get out here!"

A little head with shining eyes poked out through the overturned grass and dirt—not Pringle's, but Paisley's. Oh, thank goodness!

"Hi, Mommy," she said with a giant, excited shiver. "The raccoon isn't home, but he sure has a lot of stuff under there!"

More than anything, I was happy to see Paisley had survived her foolish venture without so much as a scratch on her tiny head, but I was also happy about the intel she'd gotten for us.

"I guess that works in our favor," I said. "It will be easier to get in there and get what we need without raccoon interference." Glancing up at Charles, I backtracked a little and explained, "Pringle's not home."

He chuckled good-naturedly. "Yup, I got that from context. I'm getting really good at understanding your one-sided conversations, you know. I've had lots and lots of practice."

Heat rushed to my cheeks, followed closely by Charles's lips as he pressed them against my skin. Instantly, I felt better, more in control of the situation. What can I say? He just had that kind of effect on me.

I hummed a satisfied beat. "How did I get so lucky to land the best boyfriend in all of Blueberry Bay?" I asked, turning to press my mouth directly to his.

"Only Blueberry Bay?" Charles asked as he playfully twisted a strand of my hair around his index finger, then bopped my nose.

"Okay, then how about the whole state of Maine?" I suggested with a wink.

"How about eww, gross, not in front of the cat?" Octo-Cat groused, jumping off the porch and charging over to stand between us. "This is the reason I call him UpChuck. Every time he's around, the two of you make me want to vomit."

Actually, my cat had begun referring to my boyfriend as UpChuck long before we'd started dating, but now wasn't the time to argue over the timeline. We had a raccoon hideout to raid.

I raised my shovel and smiled awkwardly at my companions. "Ready?"

Charles answered by stabbing his shovel down into the ground and lifting out a giant heap of dirt. "Oh, yeah."

"This is almost as disgusting as what you two were doing before," Octo-Cat growled, returning to the porch. He loved exploring the outdoors but hated getting dirty. Sure enough, the sight of the disturbed dirt was enough to have him whipping out his sandpaper tongue and getting to work.

"How can I help, Mommy?" Paisley asked, shifting her weight back and forth between her two front paws in a merry little dance. Unlike the cat, she loved any and every chance to get dirty. On more than one occasion, I'd found her in our laundry room rolling around in the dirty clothes pile with an expression of absolutely unfettered joy.

"Stay out of the way for right now, because I don't want you to get hurt while we're digging."

Paisley's face fell for an instant. It seemed she was the only one who didn't understand how small and vulnerable she could be when danger struck—and even when it didn't. Even though I wanted to keep her safe, I knew better than to completely exclude her from our mission.

"Once we're done digging, you can help bring things out," I offered, making my voice high and hyper. "Deal?"

"Deal," she barked and ran up the porch steps. She had a hard time running in a straight line since her tail was wagging so furiously. Still, she made it to her kitty bestie's side, tail still wagging a staccato against the porch floorboards.

Turning my attention back to the matter at hand, I realized the pile of dirt beside Charles had grown by several shovelfuls now and I hadn't even broken earth yet. I raised my shovel again, ready to dig in, when Charles stopped me with a sharp command.

"Grab the flashlight and see what you can make out under there," he said, lifting yet another pile of dirt out of the way.

I searched the yard until I spotted the flashlight lying in a nearby patch of grass. Grabbing it with both hands, I switched it on. Twilight had already begun to set in. Within half an hour, the sky would be completely dark. We needed to hurry. I had no idea when Pringle would be back, but I knew he had the benefit of night vision plus knowledge of the terrain. And while Octo-Cat could see in the dark, he wasn't exactly the most hands-on when it came to tonight's task.

I approached the widened hole carefully so as not to be greeted by a shovelful of dirt to the face and dropped to my hands and knees, lowering myself all the way to my stomach. With the flashlight's help, I could now see most of the space beneath the porch for the first time ever.

"Oh my gosh," I squealed, forgetting to keep my voice low so as not to be overheard by Julie inside. "It's like a dragon's lair under there. No wonder he thinks of himself as some kind of fairytale knight."

I just could not get over how much the raccoon had managed to stash in such a confined space. Everywhere I looked, slim boxes, messy stacks of paper, bits of trash, foil, and assorted odds and ends from inside our house crowded the edges of the lair. I spotted a throw pillow that had been missing for weeks. Even one of Octo-Cat's prized teacups. Oh, he was going to be livid over that one.

"Do you see my angel?" Julie asked from behind me. I hadn't even heard her come outside, but now that she was here, I needed to be extra careful with how I proceeded.

Sweeping my light around the hidey hole a second time, I tried to focus on anything that caught and played with the light. I'd just about given up on finding it without having to physically get into the space when a little sparkle of shining gold caught my eye.

"Yes! Yes, I see it!" I cried excitedly. The sooner we could return Julie's stolen treasure, the sooner we could get her out of here and the better we could protect my secret. I reached into the hole as far as I could but came up at least a foot short.

"Paisley," I called. "Can you help Mommy get the angel?"

The Chihuahua, always eager to please, ran over with a joyous bark, then dived right back into the hole.

I continued to stretch my arm toward the angel and pointed. "Right there. Bring it to Mommy!"

Paisley darted toward the angel and clutched it in her mouth. Unlike Octo-Cat, she didn't mind when I talked to her the way humans normally talked to animals. She was just so happy to be a part of Nan's and my life, she never really questioned anything we did or how we chose to do it.

"Good dog!" I gushed as she made her way back to me. "Good dog!"

Charles helped me back to my feet, then Paisley emerged with the prized possession still held securely between her jaws.

"Oh, that's it," Julie said with yet another sniffle as she bent down to accept the trinket from Paisley. "That's my angel. Thank you. Thank you so much!"

"Sorry about that. The good news is that a little polish should have it as good as new," I said, hoping this observation would prove to be true.

"Clearly we need to do something about that raccoon," Nan added with a heavy sigh as she shook her head.

We stood in silence for a few moments, until…

A chittering yowl hurtled through the air, an angry raccoon following close behind it. "My home! What have you done to my home?" Pringle yelled, lifting both hands to his head and looking as if he were trying to push his brains back in through his ears.

"Get back!" Julie cried, keeping her eyes on Pringle as she backed slowly toward her truck. "That thing could have rabies."

"Rabies?" Pringle fell to all fours and ambled after Julie. "That's speciesist, and I don't appreciate it… Hey, wait, that's mine!"

"Stop!" I shouted just as Pringle raised himself to his hindlegs again and was making ready to swipe the angel straight out of Julie's hands.

Everyone turned toward me, waiting to see what my big plan was. Um, I didn't have one. Not yet, anyway.

"Julie, you should go. I'll call you later to check in on your case. First I need to deal with our raccoon friend here," I muttered.

I just hoped my use of the word friend might soften Pringle to what was coming next.

CHAPTER EIGHT

We all watched in silence as Julie hightailed it out of there. I couldn't really blame her for wanting to escape the disaster unfolding in my front yard. The poor thing had been framed for mail theft and property damage, had something special stolen right out of her vehicle, and then, to top it all off, she'd been chased after by an angry raccoon.

Unfortunately, what was a horror show for most people was just another day in my zany, critter-filled life—and this one wasn't even close to over yet.

Pringle turned on me, fury filling his dark eyes. "Hey, lady. You've got some serious explaining to do."

"Me?" I screeched. Finally, I could be as loud as I wanted without fearing discovery. "You're the one who stole my flyers, Julie's angel, and apparently half the neighborhood, too."

Pringle clicked his tongue and stared down his nose at me. "Haven't we moved past the flyers?"

"No, we have not moved past the flyers! Why do you keep taking everything that isn't nailed down?" A sudden shocking thought occurred to me, sending a shiver straight through my body. "Are we going to have to start nailing everything down?"

Pringle flashed a devilish grin my way. "You can try, but I know how to use a hammer."

My goodness! He knew how to read, how to use a hammer, how to break his way into a car. Was there anything this crazy creature couldn't do?

"Stop messing with my life," I said between clenched teeth.

He took a staggering step back. "Me? Mess with your life? I'll have you know that I was here first, Missy."

"Um, Angie dear?" Nan broke in at a good moment considering I had no idea how I was going to respond to his latest jab. "Do the two of you need some privacy?"

"No. Of course not," I said, shaking my head with a huff.

"Actually, yes," Pringle countered. "If we're going to have it out, it's best that there aren't any witnesses."

I gulped hard, blinking in disbelief. "Did you just threaten me?"

He shrugged nonchalantly. "Maybe I did. The question is what are you going to do about it?"

Paisley jumped into the fray, angrily kicking her feet up behind her in a move that resembled chicken scratch. "Nobody hurts my mommy!"

"Relax, half-pint. I'm not going to hurt her," he told the dog. "Although I should, considering what she's done to my beautiful home. It's in ruins!"

"Give me a break. You literally live in a hole in the ground," Octo-Cat mumbled.

Pringle sank back onto his haunches and shook his head. "That cut me deep, Octavius. Real deep."

"Um, maybe you guys should go," I told Nan, seeing as we were getting nowhere with all the intrusions to our conversation. Pringle and I needed to have this out without my cat mocking him or my dog threatening him, and I just needed to be done with this whole migraine-inducing ordeal. "Take Paisley and Octo-Cat, too."

Charles squeezed my shoulder before reaching down to scoop up the agitated Chihuahua. "Let's go, guys," he said.

"This isn't over!" Paisley shouted in her adorably squeaky and very non-scary voice. "It's not even close to over!"

"Shh, baby girl. Shh," Nan cooed.

And together the two humans and two animals marched back into the house, the animals less than enthusiastic about leaving me behind to deal with the raccoon drama on my own.

"Why are you stealing things?" I demanded with my arms crossed over my chest once Pringle and I were alone in the yard again.

"I'm not stealing." He stopped to roll his eyes as if talking to the biggest moron on the planet—I most definitely did not appreciate that implication. "Look, it's a simple case of manifest destiny. Right? I'm not stealing things. I'm claiming them in the name of Pringle."

"How is that different?" Did he really just trot out one of the terms I'd learned in middle school U.S. History and then use it to justify his crimes? This was going to be a long night, and I could feel it getting even longer.

"Look, I'm no dummy. I've read your human history books. I know all about how this country was founded. Well done, I might add. Those guys decided they wanted more land, so they took it. I decided I wanted more treasures, so I took them. So what?"

"This is not the age of exploration," I countered in disbelief. "And it's not okay to take things without permission. It wasn't really okay then, either, but hindsight and all that."

"Well, sorrrrrry. I didn't realize the rules changed depending on who they applied to."

The worst part was how Pringle absolutely nailed his argument against humanity. Any argument I made would sound unintelligent by comparison, and I didn't want to resort to being a bully.

Luckily, Pringle kept right on going. "If you're going to be such a wet blanket about it, then take all your stupid human trash back. I didn't find what I was looking for anyway."

Well, this was new information.

"What were you looking for?" I asked breathlessly, more curious than annoyed now.

The raccoon lifted both hands into the darkening sky and shook them in a bang-on display of jazz hands. "Secrets," he whispered dramatically.

That took me by surprise. "What do you mean secrets?"

"Exactly what I said. I like reading and watching TV as much as the next guy, but it's all fake, made-up stuff. The drama is far more interesting when it's real. Don't you think?"

I swallowed hard, then sputtered, "Um, what do you mean?"

"I'm talking secrets, honey." Pringle raised one eyebrow and shook his head. "Have you really forgotten already?"

I was almost afraid to ask the next question, but I couldn't keep it in. "What secrets do you have under there?"

"Most of them are pretty tame. The MacIntyres are behind on their utility bills. A kid a few blocks over has an arraignment next week on shoplifting charges. Mild stuff. Well, most of the time, anyway."

And just like that, all the remaining pieces clicked into place. "So, it was you taking the mail?"

"Of course it was me!" He threw both hands up in the air as if he couldn't even deal with my slow human brain anymore.

But I still had more questions. "Why did you vandalize the mailboxes?"

He shrugged. "Seemed like a good idea at the time. Aren't you going to ask about the big secret I have?"

I shivered. Yes, I was curious, but this had to end somewhere, and I worried that by taking too much of a visible interest, Pringle would assume his bad behavior was justified. "I don't really like gossip, so no. Thank you, though."

"That's too bad," the raccoon said, a sinister smile spreading from cheek to furry cheek. "If it were me, I'd want to know."

"Know what?" I asked, hating myself for playing right into his sticky little hands.

He dropped to all fours and closed the distance between us. Placing one hand on my shoe, he stared up at me with wide, intelligent eyes. "Know that the one person I trusted the most in this world has been lying to me my whole life."

No. No way. It couldn't be.

Why was I even listening to this? Clearly, Pringle was just trying to stir up trouble, and yet...

"Nan?" I asked, my voice shaking.

Pringle nodded, a solemn expression overtaking his dark face. "Guess it's not a secret anymore."

CHAPTER NINE

According to the raccoon that lived under my porch, my nan had some kind of deep, dark secret that would change everything. We'd already established that Pringle was a thief. Could he be a liar, too?

I should have turned away and refused to hear any more, but I just couldn't help but wonder… Might the raccoon be telling the truth?

Pringle placed a hand on my leg and gave me a short series of pats. "There, there, princess. I can see you're taking this hard. I can also see that you haven't decided whether or not you believe me, so let me do you a solid."

He turned away ruefully and slipped under the porch, emerging mere seconds later with an aged envelope gripped in his hand. He lifted it toward me in offering. "Be careful with this. I don't want you getting any dirty human fingerprints on it or otherwise contaminating the best secret I've ever collected."

My hands shook as I accepted the thin letter. It had already been covered in actual dirt from its time within the raccoon's lair, so I didn't see how my touching it could make things any worse. The envelope had been torn clear across the top, and there was a single sheet of cream-colored paper folded and placed inside.

Dorothy Loretta Lee was written in a tight, controlled script. The top corner didn't have a sender's name, only an address somewhere in Georgia. Seeing it firsthand, I had no doubt the letter was authentic.

"Read it," the raccoon urged, watching me with a shiny, probing gaze.

"Where did you get this?" I asked, still not ready, doubting I'd ever be ready.

"From your nan's things," he said with a slow nod. "It was a couple weeks ago. I noticed her going up into the attic, and then I remembered that I have a private entrance into that place, so I climbed through the hole in the roof, and—"

"Wait. There's a hole in my roof?"

"Not the point of my story." He paused, presumably to make sure I had no other questions or arguments before he continued. "Anyway, I climbed through the hole in the roof, but I couldn't find anything good. So I watched and waited. Eventually she went back, and that's when I saw she had a special hiding place tucked into the wall. There was this wooden border between the floor and the wall."

"Baseboard trim?" I suggested gently. Why was I getting caught up in the details?

"Sure. Whatever. Point is if you kick it, it falls out, and behind it, there's a hole. I found a lot of pretty green papers there, too."

"Green papers?" I gasped. Could he mean…? "Would you show them to me?"

"Sure thing, babe." Pringle went back under the porch and was gone for a little longer this time. As tempted as I was to read the letter, I still couldn't bring myself to face whatever truths it would reveal. Would I still be able to look at my beloved nan the same way once I knew?

The raccoon returned with a giant wad of bundled bills in his hands. One-hundred-dollar bills.

"Pretty, right?" he asked with a smile. "They're not exactly the right shape, but I thought they might make nice paper cranes once I get going with my origami."

"Give me that," I said at the same time I grabbed the currency from his paws. "This came from Nan's hiding place in the attic?"

"Yeah, it was with the letter and some other papers. They were boring, though." He tilted his head to the side in thought and then amended his previous statement with, "Well, all except one."

"Can I see them?" I asked, just short of begging. Anything to stall a bit longer.

Pringle shook his head and clicked his tongue. "How about you read the letter, eh? I'm going to need it back, so just get on with it already."

He was right. I couldn't stall any longer. Reaching into the envelope, I pulled out the antique letter at last and attempted to smooth the wrinkles before lifting it toward a beam of light from the porch.

"Careful with that. It's important to me," Pringle hissed, but I had already tuned him out and lost myself in the words that waited for me on that page.

D ear Dorothy,

D orothy, that was my nan. I sucked in a deep breath and forced myself to read the next couple lines.

I know what I did to you was wrong and that you'll probably never forgive me. You don't owe me anything, but I have no one left to turn to.

T hat sounded awful. What had the letter writer done? And if it was so bad, why had she kept this letter tucked away all these years? I would definitely be asking Nan, but first I had to get through this short but apparently earth-shattering missive.

D on't punish little Laura for my mistakes.

L aura was my mother's name. Could she be the "little Laura" in question? Oh my gosh. What had happened? What did this mean?

G ive her a chance at a better life, at the life we always dreamed of living together.

O h my gosh. Oh my gosh. Oh my gosh. I almost stopped right there, but it was too late. The cat was already half out of the bag. I might as well get it all the way out into the open.

I 'll be home on leave in two weeks' time and will wait for you in our place that Thursday night.

A secret meeting. Did she go? If so, what happened? What did he want? Was it a he? It seemed that way with the reference to the life they'd dreamed about living together. There was just one little line left, which I read with teary eyes.

P lease be the better person. Please come.
W. McAllister

. . .

I finished reading, even more confused than before I'd started. Who was W. McAllister and what had he wanted with my nan? Did he know my mom? Was she the Laura in the letter?

"I found this in there, too." Pringle raised another sheet of paper my way. Apparently he'd collected it while I'd been engrossed in the letter.

Of course, I recognized the official nature of the document right away. It boasted an intricate colored border and at the top of the page read Certificate of Live Birth.

The mother was named as Marilyn Jones, and the father had been listed as William McAllister, most likely the same W. McAllister that had written the letter to Nan. The place of birth was that same unknown town in Georgia, and the baby had been named Laura—my mother's name.

The date of birth matched my mom's, too. It had to be her.

Did this mean that she had never really been Nan's?

That I wasn't Nan's, either?

And what was with this all going down in Georgia? Nan had spoken fondly of her memories growing up in the south, but she'd claimed to be from one of the Carolinas.

Not Georgia. Never Georgia.

And if she'd fibbed about her home state, then what else might she have lied about over the years?

Oh my gosh, did my mom know about any of this? If not, she'd be devastated to learn now. Should I tell her? Or wait until I knew more first?

I had so many questions, and short of tracking down this William McAllister, there was only one person I could ask.

I marched into the house, letter and birth certificate in hand, to confront Nan and demand the truth.

CHAPTER TEN

N an and Charles sat in the living room, sipping on matching mugs of hot cocoa topped with giant heaps of marshmallow fluff. He wasn't a big fan of tea, so Nan kept this alternate hot drink around mostly just for him.

Paisley had cuddled into Nan's side, and Octo-Cat sat on his favorite perch looking out the window. More than likely, he'd been keeping tabs on me this whole time.

They all looked so cozy and content. I almost felt bad for disturbing that peaceful moment, but then I remembered that I was the one who'd been wronged, lied to. And for my entire life. Wow.

I stood frozen at the edge of the living room, the birth certificate and letter clutched between shaking hands. Where could I possibly begin?

"Hey! You can't just take people's things without asking!" Pringle cried from the foyer. Apparently, he'd followed me inside despite our rule that he wasn't allowed in the house. That snapped me right out of my deer-in-headlights moment.

And I turned on him so fast, he reared back in fright. "Are you really lecturing me on decorum right now?" I demanded, hand on hip. "You can't expect things from others when you're not willing to do the same for them."

Charles set his mug onto the coffee table and approached me carefully. "Angie, is everything all right, sweetie?"

"No, it's not!" I fumed, hating that I'd yelled at him now, too. None of this was his fault. Or Octo-Cat's. Or Paisley's. Or really even Pringle's.

"What's that you have, dear?" Nan asked, remaining seated firmly in her favorite chair. It was her. She'd caused the pain that threatened to rip my heart right in two. The very same woman who'd taught me the importance of honesty as a child had lied to me my entire life.

"I don't know. Why don't you tell me?" I strode over to her and dropped both pieces of paper into her lap.

My grandmother froze. It seemed as if even her heart stopped beating for a moment before she gingerly plucked the papers from her lap and set them on the coffee table. "I haven't the foggiest," she told me as she calmly delivered both mugs to the kitchen sink and then started up the stairs.

"Oh, no!" I shouted, charging after her. "You are not getting away that easily! What is this, and why didn't I know about it? Does mom know about it?"

Nan remained silent as she climbed the steps at her normal pace. It was almost as if I weren't there at all.

"Hey, why aren't you answering me?" I demanded as a new wave of tears began to sting my eyes.

Nan reached her bedroom door, then turned back to me. Her voice was quiet and almost completely devoid of emotion as she said, "I'm sorry, dear, but I'm not feeling too terribly well all of a sudden. I think I'll just excuse myself to bed for the evening."

Before I could argue, she slipped into the room and clicked the door shut behind her. Still shocked by what I'd learned, and even more so by the fact that my normally talkative grandmother refused to discuss it with me, I twisted the knob hard and pulled.

But it wouldn't budge.

Locked out by my own grandmother!

I pounded on the door instead. "You're going to have to talk about it with me eventually!" I shouted into the wooden barrier.

A warm hand brushed my arm, causing me to jump in my skin.

"C'mon," Charles said, gently guiding me back toward the grand staircase. "It seems like you both could use some space to work things out right about now."

"Did you read it?" I asked through the hot tears that flowed freely now. "Did you read the letter?"

He nodded, his mouth a tight bow.

"What do you think it means?" I asked, my voice cracking partway through that awful question.

"I hate to guess at it." His voice remained soft, comforting. "It'd be much better if we heard from Nan directly."

I let out a bitter laugh. "Well, she doesn't seem to be too keen on sharing. Do you think this means she's not my real nan?"

"Of course, she's your real nan. She raised you. She's been there your whole life. The letter—whatever it means—it doesn't change anything."

"What about my mom, though? Is she the Laura on the birth certificate? Is that what the letter is about? Did her dad give her to Nan for some reason? And does her real mom even know what happened to her?" It was all too horrible to even think about. Unfortunately, I couldn't stop doing just that.

Charles sat on the couch and opened his arms, inviting me to cuddle against him. "I know it's all so confusing and upsetting right now, but I promise you it will be okay. Whatever this is, it doesn't change who your nan is, who you are."

I laughed again. Angry. "If it's no big deal, then why would she keep it a secret all these years? Why would she refuse to talk about it now?"

"I don't know the answers to those questions, but I'll be here to help you figure them out for yourself." He pressed a warm kiss to my forehead.

"I can't," I sobbed, all my hot-headed energy ebbing away.

Charles just hugged me tighter. "What do you mean you can't? You're Angie Russo, Pet Whisperer P.I. You're the woman who solved her first official case in less than an hour. That's pretty incredible."

Oh, yeah, I guess Julie's case was solved. Pringle had admitted to taking the mail and banging up the mailboxes. All I had to do is offer him something he wanted more than whatever secrets he thought he might find, and he'd be sure to stop.

Case solved. Whoop-de-do.

I tried to smile but couldn't. Instead, Charles held me as I cried into his nicely pressed work shirt.

The one person I'd trusted most in this entire world had kept something monumental from me. If I couldn't rely on her to be honest with me, then who could I count on?

Charles stroked my hair and made soothing noises, reminding me that there was at least one person in my corner, no matter what.

Octo-Cat jumped onto the couch beside me and licked my hand tentatively. Okay, one person and one cat—and probably one dog, too. Though I had no doubt Paisley was busy comforting Nan right about now.

I ran my fingers through Octo-Cat's silky fur, appreciating his friendship more than ever in that moment.

"Angela, I can see you are quite upset," he murmured, proving just how far we'd come since fate first flung us together. "Does this mean we're out of Evian?"

Leave it to my cat to put things into stark perspective.

"No. Don't worry," I said with a chuckle, feeling lighter already. "We have plenty of Evian."

I scratched him between the ears and then pulled myself up from the couch. A nice cool glass of Evian would do us all good right about then.

CHAPTER ELEVEN

Despite the night cap of perfectly chilled Evian, I had a hard time drifting to sleep. Sometime early the next morning, I gave up on getting any meaningful shut-eye and went to see if Nan was up yet.

Oh, not only was she up…

She was already gone—and with her little dog, too. Darn, I could have used Paisley's eternal sense of optimism to help get me through what I knew was going to be a tough day.

Well, it's not like Nan and Paisley would be gone forever. Eventually, they had to come back. Eventually, the woman who was maybe not my actual grandmother would have to give me some answers. After all, Pringle had given me undeniable evidence that something wasn't quite right about our family past, and even though I was one whole generation removed from whatever scandal Nan had worked so hard to keep hidden, it still upset me deeply.

Octo-Cat sat waiting for me on the kitchen counter. Nan didn't like it when he dirtied her food prep surfaces, but I hadn't the heart or the inclination to correct him—especially not today.

"Good morning, Angela," he said, making eyes toward his empty food bowl. "You're right on time for my morning repast."

"C'mon," I mumbled as I shuffled toward the pantry and extracted a can of Fancy Feast. I also grabbed a clean Lenox teacup and matching saucer, the only dishes he was willing to eat or drink from. After setting both on the floor, I grabbed the half-empty bottle of Evian from the fridge and poured it into the delicate filigreed teacup until it was exactly three-fourths full.

During our time together, he'd learned to appreciate the nuanced flavor of chilled water, and I'd learned not to question his sometimes ridiculous standards and completely non-optional routines.

"Many thanks," he mumbled before digging in with aplomb.

I grabbed a Diet Coke from the fridge since Nan wasn't around to make coffee, and I didn't feel like dealing with my deep-rooted fear of getting electrocuted on top of everything else so early in the day.

"So what's on our schh-edule for today?" my cat asked, over-emphasizing his speech as he often liked to do when he was feeling fancy—usually in the mornings and usually post-Fancy Feast.

I considered his question for a few moments. Of course, I already knew exactly what we needed to do, but that didn't mean I liked it. He probably wouldn't, either, but there was no time like the present.

I forced a smile. "We need to talk to Pringle and see what it will take to get him to help us."

Octo-Cat groaned, refusing to even pretend he liked this plan. "Do we have to?"

"It's the quickest, most surefire way to figure out what Nan's hiding, especially since she doesn't seem to want to talk about it."

"I did find it a little strange how quickly she ran out of here this morning." His voice became deep, cold, as he cast his eyes toward the floor. "She didn't even stop to give me a pet hello."

Poor guy. There was nothing he hated more than being ignored when he wanted attention. Of course, that had never stopped him from ignoring me when it suited him to do so. Double standards were just a part of being a cat owner, and I'd accepted that a long time ago.

"Nan's always been a lot strange, but she's also always been honest and upfront. At least that's what I thought." I sighed and took another sip from my can of Diet Coke. Yes, I knew he was hurting from that morning's slight, but I was hurting, too—and if you asked me, it was for far bigger, far more painful reasons.

My cat studied me with large amber eyes. "You're really upset by this, aren't you?"

I nodded and sighed again. "I really am."

He moaned as if in terrible agony. "Well, that won't do. Let's go rouse the raccoon and get this over with." He traipsed out of the kitchen, his tail held high as he led the way to his electronic pet door and slipped outside.

Aww, he really did love me. Sometimes I still wondered about that, given his hot and cold behavior when it came to pretty much everything he ever encountered. But today his willingness to do something that mildly annoyed him in order to mend my badly broken heart gave me all kinds of warm fuzzies.

When I joined him outside on the porch, he sat and motioned with one paw toward the giant gaping hole that led into Pringle's lair. "Well, go ahead."

I approached slowly, my voice soft, beseeching. "Pringle?"

"What do you want?" the raccoon growled from somewhere under his porch. Actually, it was my porch. Must not forget that.

"I was wondering if you could help us get to the bottom of that secret you shared with me last night?" I begged.

If my cat's moods ran hot and cold, Pringle wavered between the freezing and boiling points on that same wretched thermometer. His warm was almost angry, though. In fact, did we really need his help? Was it worth dealing with his attitude and trickery?

Yes, I realized, my heart dropping to the ground. Yes, we did need him. Darn it.

He poked his head out of the hole and grimaced. "Actually, I'm not very happy with you right now." That was unexpected.

"What? Why?" I was already having a hard time coming to him hat in hands. If I had to spend half the morning groveling and begging, we'd never make any progress at all.

He rubbed his temples and squinted hard against the rising sun. Well, at least we both gave each other headaches.

"I wasn't giving you the papers," he explained with a tired yet demanding voice. "I showed them to you to see, not to keep. I refuse to help until you give back what's mine."

Octo-Cat came galloping over with impressive speed. "Excuse you? Don't those papers actually belong to Nan? Didn't you steal them away from her in the first place?"

"Not helping," I groaned, nudging Octo-Cat gently to the side with my foot, a slight I knew I'd pay for later. "I'm sorry, Pringle. That was really rude of me. I was just in such shock that I forgot. I'll go get them for you right now."

When I returned with the letter and birth certificate in hand, Pringle was waiting on the porch.

"I'll take those," he said, yanking them away even though I would've given them to him freely. He tucked both into his armpit and crossed his arms over his chest. "Now, how can I help you? Make it snappy. I'm a very busy animal, you know."

I nodded toward the papers he'd stashed within his gray fur. "Those told part of a secret, but not the whole thing. I need to know the rest. Can you help?"

He cocked his head to the side and sighed heavily. "That depends."

Octo-Cat hissed and raised the hair on his back. "Depends? Depends! Stop being a furry jerk wad and help already. You started this!"

"Madame, please control your associate." He shook his head as if this all pained him greatly.

"Octo-Cat, I've got this," I told him with an apologetic smile, then turned back to the raccoon with what I was sure had to be a very poorly concealed grimace. "Go ahead, Pringle."

The raccoon walked a few paces, then turned his face over his shoulder dramatically and sized me up. "I'm not sure how much you get around the forest these days, but I'm not just some amateur gumshoe. I'm a legitimate business animal now."

Octo-Cat exploded upon hearing this claim. "I don't believe this. Does he reall—"

As much as I hated to do it, I pushed my best feline friend through the pet door and then blocked it with my leg. "You're in business?" I asked peaceably.

He nodded animatedly; his chest puffed with pride. "Yes, indeed. You're looking at the proud owner and key talent behind Pringle Whisperer, P.I. I'll have you know that it's the very best investigation firm in the area."

I pinched the skin on the inside of my wrist to stop myself from saying something snarky. I had no idea this masked thief stole ideas and business models in addition to papers and trinkets. I also hugely resented the implication that his P.I. outfit was superior to the one I ran with Octo-Cat. But, ugh, I still needed his help.

"Congratulations," I managed, thinking it was a good thing I had pushed Octo-Cat in through the cat door, otherwise there would be a definite brawl right about now. "So can I hire you to help me out here?"

He smiled wide, revealing two rows of gleaming, pointed teeth. "Of course you can, princess. But it'll come at a price."

"You're going to charge me?" I balked, remembering the stack of pretty green bills he planned to use for origami. He didn't even know what cash was, let alone its value, considering he had a tendency to just take anything he wanted. "What do you even need money for?"

He rubbed his thumb and index finger together. "Not money. Favors."

I took a moment to soak this in. When I'd promised Octo-Cat a favor in exchange for his cooperation, I'd ended up with the giant manor house that had once belonged to his late owner. I'd grown to love our new house, but it was still a steep price to pay for getting him to agree to wear a cheap pet harness one time.

"Well," Pringle prompted me, reminding me that I still hadn't responded to his heinous offer. "Are you in or out?"

Oh, I knew I would come to regret this, but I also knew I needed him and that the longer I went without untangling Nan's secrets, the more desperate I would become.

"Fine." I squatted down and offered him my index finger, which he promptly accepted and shook in agreement.

"Excellent. Then it seems we've got ourselves a deal," Pringle said, steepling his fingers in true villain fashion.

Well, at least he was on my side this time. Um, right?

CHAPTER TWELVE

My deal with the sometimes downright devilish raccoon made, I opened the front door wide and invited him to join us inside.

"I've never been so insulted in all my life," Octo-Cat grumbled, apparently having overhead our entire conversation from the other side of the blocked pet door. "And don't you know better than to make an open-ended bargain with a crook?"

Pringle bared his teeth. "You know, I used to like you," he spat at the cat. "Idolize you, even. Pffft. Pathetic."

"Oh, and now you don't? I'm so hurt," my cat snarked right back. These two were pretty well-matched when it came to conversational gymnastics. It was a shame the only thing they wanted to do was fight each other rather than work together.

I had to do something to get everyone back on track. Perhaps asking nicely would do the trick?

"Guys, that's enough," I said with a stern look. "Like it or not, we need to work together on this one. I need you to put your differences aside and recognize that we're all the same team here."

"At least one of you has a bit of sense," Pringle said, shooting a dirty look toward Octo-Cat. Sigh.

Much to my surprise and delight, the tabby stayed quiet. His wildly flicking tail belied his true feelings, though.

I offered him an appreciative smile before moving forward with the plan. "Let's get started in the attic. Pringle, can you show me the hiding place you mentioned the other night? The one in the baseboards?"

He nodded and gave me the thumbs up sign. I swear he was becoming more human by the day. "Sure. I'll meet you up there," he said.

"Um, can't we just go up together?" I stood and pointed toward the stairs. "I mean, it's just up there."

He raised both eyebrows and shot me a goofy grin. "We could, but I prefer to use my private entrance. Remember, I'm VIP, honey. Very Important Pringle."

"Gag me on my own hairball," Octo-Cat grumbled. I wouldn't just owe Pringle after this. I was starting to think my cat would deserve a medal for his restraint in dealing with the obnoxious forest animal.

"Fine," I said even though I was already beyond irritated. I opened the front door for the raccoon so that he could sashay his way outside, then grabbed a folding chair from the storage closet and marched upstairs to the guest room where I'd found Nan Marie Kondo-ing the other day.

"Let me help you," I told the tabby in light of the nasty spill he'd taken last time we were up here.

"Don't insult me." He jumped onto the chair, wiggled his butt, and leaped through the hatch flawlessly.

I followed shortly after, also using the chair to help me gain an adequate amount of leverage before pulling myself up by my throbbing arms.

Once I was seated securely on the attic floor, I glanced around the space, surprised by the high ceilings—although I probably shouldn't have been given the general grandeur of the estate. Even in the rarely visited space, the floors were made of elegant hardwood, and the walls had been decorated in a pretty green, textured wallpaper. One hexagonal window sat within the far wall, casting a steady beam of light into the space.

Pringle was already there waiting for us. "Took you long enough."

"Show us the hiding place," I commanded, no longer worried about being courteous with the sarcastic, self-important under-porch dweller. We just needed to get on with business.

He nodded and walked around the edge of the room before stopping in the corner farthest from the window. "Here," he said, pointing.

I dropped to my knees and pulled at the edge of the wood trim, but it remained firmly wedged in place.

"It's push, champ. Not pull," Pringle explained, giving it a swift karate kick. Sure enough, the mahogany trim collapsed to reveal a dark hole.

I gulped down my nerves and reached my hand into the mysterious space.

Nothing.

"I already cleaned it out," the raccoon revealed. "Nothing left. Not in there at least."

"Then what are we even doing up here?" Octo-Cat demanded with a huff. It was only then I realized he was pacing the length of the room.

"Look." Pringle pointed toward a stack of cardboard boxes nearby. "There are some new things here since I last searched."

"Nan's Marie Kondo-ing," I whispered. "She wasn't just throwing things out. She was hiding them here, too."

Pringle rubbed his hands together in excitement. "Oooh, fun. Let's go see what new secrets we can find."

I opened each of the three boxes and set them side by side on the floor. Pringle immediately dove into the biggest one while I decided to start with the smallest.

"It's times like this I think it might be nice to have fingers, even though they look so... yuck." Octo-Cat shuddered at the thought, then stalked over to lie in the sunbeam coming from the window, leaving us to do all the snooping.

The first box I tried held a delicate collection of Christmas ornaments, all lovingly kept. Not one thing even remotely suspicious.

I moved to the next box and found Nan's favorite summer looks tucked away for safe keeping now that it was getting cold. Also nothing that helped with our search into the hidden past.

"What have you found?" I asked Pringle when I realized he still hadn't emerged from the giant box.

"Huh? What?" He popped his head over the cardboard flap with a sheepish grin. One of Nan's silk patterned scarves had been tied over his ears, and several pieces of costume jewelry lay against his furry chest. "Oh, nothing about the case. Just a small part of my P.I. fee."

Octo-Cat sighed heavily but remained blessedly quiet.

"No, no more stealing," I hissed, feeling a bit like an animal myself. The more human they became, the less like a person I felt myself. "Put it all back."

"You're no fun. You know that?" The dejected raccoon at least followed orders without arguing my instructions any further. He made sad, disparaging noises as he removed each piece of glittering finery.

"Okay, well. That didn't exactly help anything," I said once I was sure every last item had been returned to the boxes from which they came.

We each exited through the floor hatch and stood together in the guest room discussing next steps.

"What about Nan's room?" Octo-Cat suggested. "Should we search there?"

Pringle clapped and did a happy little jump. "Oh, yes, yes, yes. Let's do that!"

Normally, I'd hate to invade my nan's privacy, but desperate times and all that… and I was very, very desperate to finally learn the truth that had eluded me since long before I'd even been born. "Let's give it a try," I acquiesced.

We marched in a single-file line down the hall toward Nan's bedroom, but when I reached the door, it was still locked up tight.

"Want me to break in?" Pringle offered, making grippy-grabby gestures with his hands. I wondered, not for the first time, whether I'd be able to find a vet to prescribe my raccoon neighbor a daily dose of Ritalin for his obvious ADHD. Mmm, probably not.

"I shouldn't have any problem jimmying the lock on the window," he continued, bouncing on all four legs now.

"No," I said, feeling both guilty and disappointed in equal measures. "Nan will be back eventually. Let me try to talk to her first. Maybe she's had enough time to cool down. Maybe tonight she'll be ready to talk."

"Hey, now wait just a minute here!" Pringle cried in distress. "Even if that happens, you still owe me my payment. Remember, I'm a legitimate business animal now, and we made an unbreakable deal when you hired me earlier today."

"That's it. I've had enough," Octo-Cat said, heading upstairs toward our tower bedroom, and I had to agree with him there. So much time in the raccoon's company had me feeling like I'd just run three marathons back-to-back... but with my patience instead of my muscles.

"I'll come get you when we're ready for the next steps," I told him as I guided him back outside. As soon as he exited the house, I shut the door tight and took a deep breath.

Oh, Nan. Please put me out of my misery. All you need to do is talk to me, and we can put an end to all of this.

CHAPTER THIRTEEN

Despite many fervent prayers sent Heavenward, Nan didn't talk to me that night. In fact, she didn't even come back home. How do I know? Because I set up camp in the living room and waited all night, that's how.

Of course, now I only had more questions than before.

Was she out doing damage control or simply hiding from me to avoid a confrontation? And where had she even gone?

Desperate for answers, I called my mom the next morning.

"Angie, good morning! It's so good to hear from you!" my mom chirped in such a delighted tone that I instantly knew Nan hadn't turned up at her place.

I had a choice to make then. I could tell her everything and invite her to help, or I could stay silent.

Even though our relationship had become closer ever since I let her in on my secret ability to communicate with animals, I worried about what this new revelation would do to our relationship. Either she'd known all this time and had also chosen to keep the truth of our lineage hidden from me, or she had no idea and would be shattered by the news.

Frankly, I didn't like either option.

"Hi, Mom," I said, my mind made up. "Just calling to say hi on my way to the electronics store. Need anything while I'm out?"

"Oh, that's so nice of you to offer, but your father and I are fine." She sounded so happy. I really need to call her more, to invite her over here or swing by her place.

I smiled, hoping she'd be able to hear it in my voice. "Okay, just wanted to be sure. Love you, Mom."

"I love you, too, baby."

We hung up and I squeezed the phone in my hand, drawing strength from its warmth. I needed to learn whatever truth Nan was hiding. I owed it to not just myself, but my mom, too.

"What happens next?" Octo-Cat wanted to know then.

"Stay here and keep an eye out for Nan," I told him, even more determined than before to get to the bottom of this—and fast. "I need to pick up some equipment."

"Does this mean…?" His eyes grew large as his words trailed away.

"We're breaking into that room," I confirmed. "At least you and Pringle are."

"Well, you know what they say. Keep your friends close and your enemies closer." He crossed his paws daintily, then nodded toward the remote. "Turn the tube on for me, will you?"

I grabbed the remote as requested, but didn't turn on the TV just yet.

"Let's get on with it, please, Angela," my cat groaned.

"One thing first." I took a deep breath to steady myself, knowing he wouldn't like what I said next. "I need you to understand that I will not be buying Apple products for our mission today."

He jumped up onto all four feet, his fur puffed in distress. "What? Why?"

Yes, my cat was a major brand loyalist—Apple, Evian, Fancy Feast, Lenox—the guy had standards and stuck to them.

"Sometimes they don't have what we need," I explained gently. "But don't worry. Pringle's the one who will be using the new stuff. You don't have to."

He sighed and settled back into a comfortable position. "Then it's all for the best. That raccoon doesn't deserve i-Anything."

This made me laugh. Crisis averted. "Right!"

"Now would you, please, turn on the television?" he asked with an irritated flick of his tail.

"Sure, yeah." I clicked the TV on to the movie channel and their current broadcast of When Harry Met Sally, then blew him a quick kiss before heading toward the door. "I'll be back."

"Hasta la vista, baby." He dropped his voice so it became deep, but nowhere deep enough to deliver that famous quote properly. Luckily, I was able to keep my giggles inside until I'd slammed the car door behind me and began the trek to the big box electronics store.

Last time I'd stopped by had been to buy a GPS pet tracker for our squirrel friend Maple. I'd come one time before as well; it had been to buy an Apple Watch for Octo-Cat, although for the life of me I couldn't remember why I needed one or what ever happened to it. I knew Maple's GPS had ended up buried somewhere in the forest like one of the manic squirrel's nuts or half-eaten jars of peanut butter. And, yes, I was her supplier against my better judgement.

"Hey, I know you!" A pimply faced employee with curly hair and a brightly colored polo shirt approached while laughing. He was the same one who'd helped me the first time I came in looking to equip the animals with their own spy tech.

"How did your cat like his Apple Watch?" He made air quotes around Apple since we'd actually bought an off-brand product and stuck the preferred logo over top. Shoot. Sometimes I was way too free with information about my crazy life.

"It was great. Thanks." I'd been lucky enough not to run into him on my second visit, which meant I'd gotten in and out of there in mere minutes. It seemed today I wouldn't be quite so lucky.

"Are you here for a new MacBook Pro or an iPad Air? Maybe a matching Apple Watch for your dog?"

"No, she doesn't need a watch," I muttered, and the store clerk laughed even harder. I wasn't a violent person by nature, but I also kind of wanted to punch him in the face. Did he really think it was a good idea to tease and bully his customers? Perhaps corporate would like to hear about my experience today. Hmm.

He sobered at last, placing both hands in his pockets and turning to me with an open expression. Maybe now that he'd gotten his laughs in, he'd actually help here. "Okay. What can I get for you?"

I offered a pert smile. "I need a GoPro camera, please, and a harness to go with it."

Again, raucous laughter. "Oh, so your cat likes Apple, but your dog likes GoPro?" He could barely get the words out because he was wheezing so hard.

"Actually, it's for my raccoon, but yeah." I smiled wide just to unnerve him. He already thought I was crazy, so I might as well lean into it.

Sure enough, the next thing out of his mouth was, "You're weird, you know that?"

"And you're not very helpful, so I guess I'll just help myself. Thank you!" I called over my shoulder, already walking away.

"Hang on. GoPros are this way." He darted past me and hooked a right. "You need a key to get into the case, which means you do need my help."

"Fine, but I'm in a hurry."

"Urgent animal business?" he guessed, holding back another laugh.

"Something like that," I answered. Fine, whatever. He could make fun of me all he wanted. As long as I got the camera and harness, I'd go about my day just fine.

"Good luck!" he called after me once he'd handed over the equipment I requested. Yeah, like I needed his well wishes—or like he even meant them in the first place. Next time I'd be finding a different electronics store, even if I had to drive twice as far to get to it.

I gave the bully clerk a thumbs up as I approached the cash register, refusing to look back or say another word. I had far bigger problems to worry about today.

Nan was missing.

My mom probably had different parents than she'd been led to believe.

I owed a raccoon of questionable ethics an unspoken favor.

Oh, and also, I was about to spy on my own grandmother in a desperate attempt to learn the truth behind it all…

CHAPTER FOURTEEN

A pparently, my trip to the electronics store had gone by much more quickly than it felt. When I arrived home, Octo-Cat sat watching the final scene of his movie and sniffling mightily.

"Aww, does somebody love love?" I teased. He never reacted this way to Law & Order.

"Of course, not!" he cried, wiping at his eyes to hide the telltale signs of tears. "I'm laughing. Yeah. Still laughing. I'll have what she's having. Classic!"

"Uh-huh," I said, keeping my smile on the inside. Although I knew for a fact he had no idea what that famous scene actually referenced, I decided to let him off the hook this time. The last thing I needed was to have the birds and bees talk with my neutered cat. Nope, no thank you!

Instead, I focused on unpackaging and setting up the new GoPro while Harry danced with Sally at the New Year's Eve party and told her all the things he loved best about her. So super sweet. Okay, maybe now I was tearing up a little, too.

When the end credits finally rolled, I switched off the television and opened the front door. "C'mon, Pringle. It's time!"

The raccoon came trotting right in, ready to go, as if he'd been standing outside the door waiting this entire time. Perhaps, he had.

Spotting the new tech in my hands, he gasped and lifted both hands to his mouth, then dropped them and shouted, "Oooh, shiny!"

He then wrapped both hands around my calf and shimmied right up my body and onto my shoulder. He'd never done that before, and I didn't want him to be doing it now. Even though we were working together, I still didn't exactly trust him.

Luckily, I overcame my shock just in time to stop him from stealing the camera out of my hands and making a fast getaway with the clearly coveted device.

"Stop that," I groused and shook my arms. "Get off of me."

"I want that," Pringle informed me, refusing to be shaken off.

"Relax, will you? I bought it for you to use in today's mission."

"Give! Give! Give!" He climbed back to the floor, then jumped up and down, becoming increasingly annoying by the second.

"You need to give it a rest," Octo-Cat intervened. "Let Angela do her little speech first, then she'll give it to you."

"Oh, so now I'm predictable?" I asked with a chuckle. I'm not exactly sure why I laughed in that moment, but it probably had to do with how relieved I was to have the giant raccoon back on the floor and off my body.

"It's not just you, honey," Pringle said. "It's all humans. Such simple creatures." He made a rolling gesture with his hands and sighed. "Anyway, just get on with it."

Oh, this was rich. Mr. Must Maintain His Schedule to the Very Second and Mr. Steal Everything in Sight found me to be the predictable one.

Also, was Pringle really mocking me when I'd hired him and also agreed to pay an unnamed favor? That wasn't very good customer service. He was lucky his business wasn't on Yelp, or he'd be getting a very bad review.

"Haven't you ever heard that the customer's always right?" I asked with a snort.

"Nope. Who would say that?" Pringle chittered with unabashed glee. "The customer's often stupid, which is why they need to hire help to begin with."

Yikes. Yet another astute comment on humanity from the Peeping Tom raccoon. Thank goodness he couldn't communicate with any humans other than me.

But really, we needed to get on with our mission here, which meant it was time for me to lay down the law. "Hush up and listen already!" I yelled at them both.

When they both fell silent, I continued. "Now, Octo-Cat, you're going to like this next part."

I lifted my phone from the table and unlocked it to show the new app I'd downloaded during setup. "Pringle's going to wear the camera in a chest harness, and I'm going to stream the live feed to my iPhone so I can keep an eye on what's happening."

"Okay, but where do I fit into this plan?" my cat asked with an aggravated twitch.

"Two places." I made a peace sign and wiggled those two fingers, unsure whether either animal could count, but whatever. "First, you're going to go with Pringle to keep an eye on him and make sure he doesn't take anything that's unrelated to our case."

"Hey," the raccoon whined. "I resemble that remark."

I rolled my eyes and took a deep breath. Sometimes I really missed working at the law firm with other humans—sweet, rational humans. "Second, we're going to use your iPad to FaceTime so you can give me a running commentary to go with the video feed. I'd give you my phone, but I think the buttons would be too tiny to answer with your paws, and I don't want to take any chances, so—"

"Wait, wait, wait," Octo-Cat slurred, his eyes growing large and greedy. "Are you going to use your iPad or your iPhone to keep tabs on us?"

"Both," I said with a smile.

"It's like Christmas and my birthday and Halloween all rolled into one," he gushed in that accented tone of his.

I nodded vigorously and reached out to pat him on the head.

"Yup. Fun, right? We're all having fun? Yes? Now, Pringle, if you're ready, I can outfit you in the harness now."

The raccoon grabbed the camera and turned it over several times in his hands, then gave me an exaggerated wink. "This is some next-level spy stuff. I didn't know you had it in you."

"Yeah, well, I'm just full of surprises. And as it turns out, so is Nan. Do you both understand the mission?" I asked as I held the harness up to Pringle's upper body to get a read on how tight I'd need to make the straps.

The cat and raccoon nodded in unison.

"Octo-Cat, where's your iPad?" I asked as I finished fastening the harness around Pringle's chest, then mounted the camera on his back and tested the feed on my phone.

"Dining room table," the tabby answered and then went with me to retrieve it. "Say, why aren't you going in there with us?"

"It just feels like too big an invasion of privacy," I admitted.

"But you're still going to see everything through the feed, so how is that different?" Octo-Cat deadpanned.

I shrugged. "I don't know. It just is."

Thankfully, he dropped it without playing twenty questions as to my motive. "Fair enough."

"Thanks for understanding." I opened the door that led outside again.

"Okay, Pringle, do your thing. Get on the roof, unlock the window, and then come back down to grab the iPad. I'll leave it right here for you," I said, setting it on the edge of the porch.

"Octo-Cat, come with me." He followed me upstairs to our library office, and I opened the large bay window so he could slink onto the roof.

"I'll wait five minutes to give you two time to get into the room, then I'll call you on FaceTime," I called after him. "Make sure you answer."

"Roger that," my cat said, turning to glance at me over his shoulder and offering an agreeable smile before disappearing from sight.

This was it. Either we'd soon find some of the answers I'd been searching for... or we'd be nearly out of places we could look.

Unfortunately, if the animals didn't turn up anything in their search, I had no idea what we'd do next. It was looking more and more like I'd need to choose to let it go or force a confrontation with Nan.

Yay, me.

CHAPTER FIFTEEN

I headed outside to the front porch, both because I knew it would offer me better reception and so that I could keep an eye out for Nan just in case she finally decided to return home and face the situation head-on.

After settling myself on the steps, I took out my phone and studied the feed from our Pringle cam. I could see his focused expression reflected back in the glass as he fiddled with the window. His eyes lit up a few moments later as he raised the window high enough for Octo-Cat to squeeze through, then turned back the other way, providing me with an impressive aerial view of the forest that flanked our yard.

Fast as a shot, he appeared at my side and grabbed Octo-Cat's iPad from the stoop. "I'll be taking that now. Thank you very much."

For all his issues, the raccoon really was a great accomplice with an impressive skill set. It was also far easier on my conscience to let him do the dirty work so that I wouldn't have to.

Pringle, of course, had no trouble bending the rules of propriety or in scaling the house with the tablet tucked into his chest and held in place by one furry black hand. Hardly a minute later, he'd made it back to Nan's window, raised it a bit higher, and entered the locked bedroom without even a second's hesitation.

This was it. We were really doing it. I grabbed my iPad and placed a FaceTime call to Octo-Cat.

He answered after a few rings, his face leaning over the device and showing me the same view of kitty double chin I got any morning I dared try to sleep in past his breakfast time. "Badges. We don't need no stinking badges," he informed me needlessly.

And what was with all these movie quotes? Did he even sleep anymore or just fill his brain with anything that would fit inside?

"Good job," I told him, finding his enthusiasm adorable despite everything. "Keep an eye on Pringle, and keep me informed as you two search the room."

"Yes, Angela. I remember my role in all this," he murmured, already moving out of view.

Pringle had already made his way to Nan's dresser and was pulling open drawers willy-nilly. "Lacy underwear!" he cried with a giggle. "Oh, Nan, I had no idea!"

"Cut that out!" I shouted so loud they could probably hear me without the FaceTime connection. "You're there to look for clues, and that's it."

"Open this for me," I heard Octo-Cat say and then watched as Pringle approached the spot where my cat waited by the nightstand.

The raccoon pulled the drawer clear off the tracks and laughed as it clattered to the floor. "This is fun!" he squealed.

Well, there would be no hiding the fact we'd been in her room, even though I technically hadn't.

"Hey, look! I found a piece of paper with writing on it!" my cat cried in excitement.

Pringle bounded over and grabbed the paper, but I couldn't make out the words on the camera as the raccoon read. "It's just an old shopping list," he said, balling it up and tossing it back in the drawer. I sure hoped his assessment was right and he hadn't just discarded an important piece of the puzzle.

Maybe I should just go up there and instruct the two of them on how they could unlock the door from inside. Still, I remained frozen in place, unable to cross that invisible boundary.

"Be respectful of my nan's things!" I cried in a half-hearted attempt to exert some control over the situation.

"Why?" Pringle asked in a distracted voice as he continued to lope around the bedroom. "Think about it. Was she respectful of you when she hid such an important truth just out of reach?"

Darn him and his logical points.

"Still," I muttered. "Just, please."

"You heard the lady!" Octo-Cat growled. "Keep it professional here."

Oh, how I loved my kitty. He was definitely the next best thing to being there myself, and I was proud of him for staying on task.

The fuzzy duo searched around the room a while longer, finding nothing of consequence.

"If she's hiding anything, it wouldn't be in an obvious place," I said, trying to help from my station outside the action. "The attic hiding place was pretty cleverly tucked away. Maybe there's a similar hiding place in her room, too."

"Good thinking," Pringle said and then lumbered over to the nearest baseboard. He kicked and punched to no avail; not a single board budged.

"Hey! I think I found something!" Octo-Cat shouted from across the room. Oh my gosh. Was this it? The moment of truth?

"Coming!" Pringle called. The camera bounced unevenly as he raced toward Octo-Cat, who sat on top of the dresser—the first place they'd searched.

At that very same moment, the hum of an engine alerted me to the little red sports car pulling up our driveway.

Nan had come home.

"Mommy, I'm back!" Paisley cried from the open window, and while I was happy to see her, this meant that I had zero time to send a warning message to the guys upstairs.

"Paisley! Nan! Welcome home!" I shouted while closing the video feed and ending the FaceTime call. I hoped the animals engaged in the spy operation upstairs had heard and understood that they needed to get the heck out of there. Subtlety wasn't exactly a strong suit for either of them.

Nan pulled into the garage, and I raced after her before she could run away from me again. Maybe she was finally ready to give me some answers. At the very least, I might be able to distract her long enough to buy some time for Octo-Cat and Pringle to escape.

"I missed you!" Paisley bounded out of the car and ran over to me, begging to be picked up.

I was all too happy to oblige. "I missed you, too. Both of you."

Nan looked as if she hadn't slept the whole time she'd been gone. Perhaps she hadn't. Still, she attempted a reserved smile. Of course, the Nan I knew had never been reserved a day in her life. What had happened to her, and why was it all coming to a head now?

"Are you okay?" I asked gently.

She shook her head. "Not really. No."

"Can we talk about it?" I reached out to put a hand on her shoulder, but she shook me off.

Nan took a deep breath, then retreated into herself. I'd never seen her look so old or broken, and it worried me greatly. Tears rimmed her red eyes. "I never thought I'd have to speak of it again, especially not to you."

"I'm here, and I love you, no matter what."

She shook her head sadly. "It will change things, Angie."

"It already has," I whispered as I attempted to hold back fresh tears of my own.

Nan looked away and murmured, "I can't." Then brushed past me into the house.

Guilt surged inside my chest. Maybe this was one mystery that didn't need to be solved. Maybe I just needed to leave it alone and move on with my life the way things had been before Pringle showed me that secret letter.

I wished I could turn away, but I was already in too deep. This wasn't a simple curiosity; it was my life.

And I needed to know the truth.

CHAPTER SIXTEEN

After Nan abandoned me in the garage, I went back to sit on the porch. Lately, I'd been spending more time out here than inside the house, it seemed.

Paisley ambled after me, wagging her tail as usual, but slowly, cautiously. "What's wrong, Mommy?"

Although she couldn't communicate with Nan like she did me, I still felt uncomfortable saying anything bad about her best friend, the woman who had rescued her from the overcrowded shelter and given her a home.

Where was Nan now? Had she made it to her room? Had she spotted the mess made by the animals and known I was the one to put them up to it? Would she ever forgive me? Could I ever forgive her?

"I just feel sad," I told the sympathetic Chihuahua at last.

"Sometimes I get sad," the little dog said, snuggling onto my lap. "But then you know what I do? I decide to stop being sad and just be happy instead."

I smiled and scratched her between the ears. "That's very smart, Paisley. Hey, did you and Nan have a nice adventure?"

I was more looking for a change of topic than any additional dirt on Nan, but then it occurred to me that if I asked the right questions, Paisley might be able to crack this case wide open. She was with Nan practically every waking hour—slept in her room, too. How much did she pay attention? How much did she know?

She closed her eyes and rolled over on my lap to expose her belly for scratches. "The car ride was great, and I liked smelling the new smells, but I would have rather been home, all of us together."

"Aww, I know how you feel. Where did the two of you go?" I asked, unable to resist.

She squinted one eye open. "I'm not sure. It was a small clean room with a big bed. Nan and I cuddled and slept a lot. We also watched TV quite a bit. I know Octavius likes it, but I think it's pretty boring just watching things happen in a small glass box. I'd much rather be doing them myself."

"Yet another smart observation," I said with a sad smile. It sounded like Nan had holed up in some kind of a motel rather than talk to me. Fabulous.

I sighed and continued to stroke the happy little dog. She trusted so easily, so completely. Why couldn't I be like that? I had no doubt she was the most contented among us, and it wasn't because ignorance was bliss. Paisley was incredibly smart, yet somehow still able to push all her problems to the side and choose happiness each and every day.

We sat like that for a while until Pringle appeared from the side yard and bolted up the steps, which immediately sent Paisley barking.

She bounded off my lap and stood guard beside me, shouting, "Mommy! Mommy! The big bad raccoon is back!"

The raccoon groaned and shook his head. "Are we really going to do this every time? Every single time?" he asked me with an exhausted huff.

"It's okay, Paisley." I picked her back up and set her on my lap.

She whined but stayed in place.

Pringle came closer, something small and rectangular clutched in one hand.

"What did you find, Pringle?"

The pet door beeped, and Octo-Cat stepped out to join us. "What a thrill!" he exclaimed. "I really thought we were going to be caught there for a second."

Pringle put an arm around the tabby and smiled. "Stick with me, kid. Every day's an adventure."

Both laughed.

Crud. For the sake of this case, it was nice that they'd managed to put their differences aside, but going forward? Pringle wasn't exactly the best influence on my somewhat sweet, somewhat bitter tabby cat.

"Can I see what you have there?" I asked again, reaching out my hand.

"Certainly." The raccoon placed an old photograph in my hand. I immediately recognized a much younger Nan but didn't know the man who stood at her side with a cheesy grin and two deep dimples to match.

"We found it tucked into the corner of the mirror. Right out in the open," Octo-Cat informed me, a self-satisfied smile stretching between his whiskers.

"Go ahead. Flip it over," Pringle urged.

"Dorothy and William, summer 1968," I read aloud and gasped. "William? That's him?"

Pringle nodded and shrugged. "Seems so."

Right out in the open, just as Octo-Cat had said. I probably could have discovered this picture a dozen times if I'd ever stopped to study the collage of keepsakes she kept tucked into the edges of the mirror that hung above her dresser.

"They're holding hands," Octo-Cat pointed out. "Like you and UpChuck do all the time."

"She seems smitten," I said breathlessly as I noticed the way her eyes shone, the coy smile that played at her lips as she stared at him dreamily. "Like she loved him."

"Sad to say, doesn't look like he feels the same way," Pringle pointed out, and he was right about that, too. William stood stiff, his eyes focused in the distance rather than at my lovesick nan.

Octo-Cat traipsed over and sat down beside me. "He's right.

When you're with UpChuck, you look just like that." He touched his nose down onto the portrait of Nan. "But so does he. This guy looks happy, but not in love. Not like you and UpChuck or Baby and Johnny. Not even like Harry and Sally, and we all know what a mess their relationship was in the beginning."

"Who are Harry and Sally?" Paisley asked, giving her friend a lick hello.

Octo-Cat rolled his eyes lovingly. "Yeesh. I have a lot to catch you up on, dog," he said as if the events of his movie marathoning were an actual part of real life. Crazy cat.

I glanced back down at the photo and frowned.

Was Nan hiding a broken heart? A sad tale of unrequited love? It still didn't explain the letter or the birth certificate. Had William used his hold on her emotions to make her do something awful?

"Poor Nan," I whispered.

Paisley whined, even though I wasn't sure she knew why we were sad in that moment.

The other two said nothing.

We sat like that for a while as I considered my next move. The animals had been a huge help so far, but I needed a second opinion —a human opinion.

"I'm calling Charles," I informed them. Yes, Charles. He wasn't just the love of my life; he was also the smartest and most hard-working person I knew. He didn't become the youngest law firm partner in Blueberry Bay history by phoning it in.

I was afraid I'd reached a dead end, but maybe he'd be able to shed some new light on these old secrets from the past.

At the very least, he could give me the hug I so desperately needed to give me the strength to keep going.

CHAPTER SEVENTEEN

Charles came home from work early so we could spend the rest of the afternoon and evening going over everything I'd learned during the past couple of days.

"I've been so worried about you," he said now that we were cuddled together on his stiff, modular couch. "Has Nan opened up to you about any of this yet?"

I hadn't felt like catching him up on the phone, preferring instead to talk in person. Besides, I knew he'd be distracted until he was able to get away from the office. "Nothing. And according to Paisley, they spent that time away from home in a motel."

"A motel? But Nan has plenty of friends. Why didn't she stay with one of them?" Charles hadn't known Nan that long, but even he understood how weird this all was.

I burrowed deeper into his arms, safe there even as the rest of my world crumbled around me. "I'm worried about her. She looked so different when she came home today. So empty. Whatever this secret is, it's weighing heavily on her. I'm honestly not sure whether she'll ever be ready to talk about it."

He rubbed reassuring little circles in my shoulder. "Are you okay with that?"

I closed my eyes and thought about it for the millionth time since Pringle handed me that old letter. No matter which way I looked at the situation, my answer always remained the same. "I wish I could be, but no. I need to know."

Charles nodded. "I understand. If it were me, I'd want to know, too." Thank goodness for understanding boyfriends. It wasn't just that he understood, either. He wanted to help.

Remembering our newest puzzle piece suddenly, I pulled the picture of Nan and William from my purse and handed it to him. "The animals found this in her room today."

He held the old photograph between us, and we both stared down at the faces caught in time. "The mysterious William, I presume?"

I nodded. "Pringle and Octo-Cat found it in her room."

He chuckled softly and pressed a kiss to my temple. "Those two."

"Yeah." I smiled, but only a little.

Charles sat up straighter. "Those two," he said with more vigor this time. "They're quite the duo. Why don't you bring them here?"

I looked up at him with unblinking eyes, not quite under-standing what he wanted—or why he'd invite the trouble-making raccoon into his abode.

He stood and pulled me to my feet with both hands. "Before I bought this house, it belonged to Nan, and for more than thirty years at that. What if there are still some old secrets hidden inside?"

The last little flickering bit of hope burned brighter. "Charles, that's a great idea."

"Thank me later. Right now, let's get the rest of our search team and inform them of the plan."

We drove back to my place together and gathered the cat and raccoon for the journey. Octo-Cat was less than enthused, but Pringle whooped with joy to learn he'd be accompanying us on an off-property adventure—no stowing away required.

"This is where I grew up," I told him once we'd arrived.

He scrunched up his nose as if something smelled bad. "You

and Charles grew up in the same house together? Isn't that a little…?"

When I explained this to my boyfriend, he laughed. "I live here now, but until a couple years ago I lived in California. That's where I grew up, and it's just about as far away as you can get and stay in the same country."

Octo-Cat patrolled the room; his nose also twitched in disgust. "I wish I could say I like what he's done with the place, but that would be a lie."

"What's he saying?" Charles asked me.

A wicked smile crept across my face. "That he wants to say hi to his old friends Jacques and Jillianne," I said, referencing Charles's two hairless cats. They'd been crucial to a previous murder investigation, which meant we had spent plenty of time in their company. Octo-Cat found them creepy and tiresome, though, especially since they only spoke in rhymes and riddles.

"That was uncalled for," my cat hissed, then slinked off to hide beneath the dining room table. Although he was still in clear view, I decided to leave him alone. As he'd pointed out earlier, it was hard to search without fingers and opposable thumbs. I didn't want to force him only for him to be frustrated and mopey the rest of the night. He'd help if he wanted to.

"Well, unless we can get the cats on board, that leaves three of us for the search," I summed up for Charles. "Are you ready, Pringle?"

He rubbed his hands together and leaned forward. "Oh, yeah, baby. I'm off to find the attic. See you kids later."

We both watched him scamper away. "You do know there's a pretty good chance he'll steal from you, right?"

Charles shrugged. "Small price to pay if it helps."

"So where do we start?" I asked. Even though I'd grown up here, this was his place now and I worked hard to respect that.

"When I moved in, there were still a couple of boxes tucked away in the garage. I say we start there."

I nodded and followed him out of the house.

"How are you taking this all?" he asked once we had the boxes pulled out and opened in front of us.

"Not well," I admitted with a sigh, growing increasingly frustrated as I rummaged through the various gardening supplies that filled the boxes.

"This is hopeless," I whined and sunk to the garage floor in a crouch. "Nan kept this secret for almost fifty years. Why do I think I have any chance of solving it now?"

Charles bent over me and forced my chin up so that we could look into each other's eyes. "Because you're Angie freaking Russo, that's why. You're the smartest, the prettiest, the best, and you've got this."

My heart soared. "Charles, you're—wait!"

His eyes crinkled around the corners with curiosity as he studied me.

"Turn around and look up. Look there!" I cried and pointed toward the rafters above. There, a dusty old box sat tucked into the corner. The aged cardboard had faded to the color of the wooden planks that held it aloft, making it almost impossible to spot unless you knew what you were looking for. Well, I'd seen it, and something told me it held important information.

"I'll get the ladder," Charles said, popping to his feet. "You spot me while I climb."

With a bit of fancy maneuvering, we were able to hoist the box from its hiding place and wrestle it to the garage floor. Inside, we found the jackpot of memorabilia—an old letter jacket, school projects, a collection of homemade clay sculptures, and a photo album.

"Bingo," I said on the wings of a happy sigh, wasting no time before I began flipping through the pages. I recognized pictures of my great grandparents and of little Nan. Normally, seeing these new family memories would give me special warm fuzzies, but we were on a mission here.

"Wait, look there!" Charles cried, slamming his index finger on the page before I could turn it again. He'd pointed to a young man wearing a light-colored suit and standing before a church sign that proclaimed:

E aster Services
        This Sunday
    8 AM 10 AM 6 PM

"L ook familiar?" Charles asked, lifting his finger and pointing again in excitement.

I strained harder as I eyed the picture, finally noticing the dimples that lined either side of the man's smile. The rest fell into place shortly after that. "It's William McAllister."

"And look at the sign," he urged me.

When I read the service times aloud, he shook his head and pointed higher. "The name of the church, there." More pointing.

"Faith Baptist Church, Larkhaven, GA. Est. 1903," I read. "Do you think the church is still there? That they would have information on William or his heirs?"

Charles's smile widened. "There's only one way to find out."

CHAPTER EIGHTEEN

M y hands shook as I punched in the number Charles and I had found on the church website. Sure enough, it was still standing, still serving the small community of Larkhaven, Georgia.

But would the people who worshipped there now remember my nan and her William from all those years ago?

Part of me hoped they would, but another huge part was afraid of what they might reveal. William's letter had hinted at trouble. Did I want to know if he and Nan had been engaged in some kind of nefarious doings? Or what if Nan was innocent in all this, but William had hurt her? What if she just wanted to forget, but I was forcing all those terrible memories to the surface?

Charles sat so close to me that our legs touched from hip to knee. "You can do this. Deep breaths."

"It's the moment of truth," Octo-Cat said sagely from across the room. He'd found a sunbeam filtering in from between the slatted blinds, and now he and Charles's Sphynx cats lay sunning themselves like tiny sea lions on a thin outcropping of rocks.

"Also, you can do this," Octo-Cat added with a supportive purr.

Pringle still hadn't returned from his investigation of the attic, but I had all the support I needed to take this next step. The only thing holding me back was my own fear.

And I'd faced down murderers before and lived to tell the tale. How could this be anywhere near that bad?

Just one little phone call…

I finished entering the number and put my cell phone on speaker.

"First Baptist of Larkhaven," a woman with a perky drawl answered. She seemed nice, like she'd want to help.

"Hello?" she repeated when I didn't immediately jump to explain myself.

"Oh, hi. My name's Angie, and I'm doing some research on my family. I was wondering if you might be able to help me?" I bit my lip and waited.

"I'm here for another few hours today. Would you like to stop in for a chat?" the woman said.

Charles squeezed my knee and mouthed, "You've got this."

I kept my eyes on him as I spoke to the lady on the other end of the line. "Actually, I live out of state and—well, it's kind of a complicated situation, but I was wondering if maybe you knew a man named William McAllister? He attended your church in the late sixties, and I think he's my long-lost grandpa."

"Oh, dear." She took a deep breath, and my heart sped to a nervous gallop. "That was before my time. Sad to say I never knew a William."

Another dead end. Shoot.

"Okay, thank you for your ti—"

Apparently, she wasn't done speaking yet, though.

"But the McAllisters still attend services every Sunday," the woman continued. "Would you like a phone number for them?"

Charles gave me a thumbs up and bobbed his head enthusiastically. He smiled wide, and I couldn't help but smile, too.

"Y-y-yes." I stumbled over the short word, one that should have been easy but was impossibly difficult. "Please."

"You've got it, sugar. Just a second." The friendly secretary returned a couple minutes later and rattled off a number.

Charles typed it into a note on his phone while she read.

"That's for a Miss Linda McAllister," the church receptionist continued. "She's the oldest of the bunch so the one who's most likely to remember your grandfather. Good luck!"

"Thank you. You've been incredibly helpful," I said as new tears began to form in the corners of my eyes.

We said our goodbyes, and I sat silently holding my phone and crying huge, relieved tears while Charles placed a supportive arm around my shoulders.

"Are you going to call her?" he asked.

"I don't know," I mumbled, biting my lip again. "I'd rather Nan tell me than me having to find out from somebody else."

"Maybe. But she's not making a peep," Pringle said, returning with an overloaded armful of booty from Charles's attic. "And don't you think you deserve to know the truth about your own life?"

"What's he saying?" Charles asked, eyeing the raccoon with trepidation.

"That we should call," I said simply. Leave it to Pringle to want to learn whatever secrets he could, even if it stirred up drama.

Charles nodded and looked back toward me. "And what does Octo-Cat think?"

My cat stretched in the sun, blinking slowly. "Octo-Cat thinks Angela is smart enough to make her own decisions." It was one of the nicest things he'd ever said to me.

"He says it's my decision," I translated with a smile.

"And so it is. What about Jacques and Jillianne? What do they say?" Charles asked next. I knew exactly what he was doing, and I loved him for it. He was giving me the time to make the decision for myself, proving that there was no wrong call here.

The two Sphynx cats, however, had been strangely quiet this whole time. Even now Octo-Cat spoke for them.

"This whole thing is already a riddle, so they don't have anything to add. They're kind of nice when they shut up, aren't they? Good nap buddies." He yawned and rolled onto his back.

I laughed. "They have no opinion, "I told Charles.

He laughed, too, and squeezed my hand. "And here I always assumed they were these great intellectuals."

"What do you think?" I asked, turning into him.

"This time I agree with the cat. Your cat. Only you know the right course of action." He pressed a kiss to my lips, and for a little while, I found myself lost in loving surrender.

"I can't believe he's copying my line, using my words to do… well, that," Octo-Cat said with a shudder. "Well, J and J. It's been swell," he said to the two hairless cats on his way out of the living room. "But that's my cue to go."

"Let me guess," Charles said with a laugh. "He thinks we're disgusting and doesn't want to be around us anymore."

"Yup, but at least he didn't call you UpChuck this time. That's real progress." I sighed happily. No matter what happened next, I'd still have Charles, Octo-Cat, my mom, dad, and even Nan. Nothing had to change. I could choose what to do with the information once I had it. This was still my life, and I could live it how I wanted.

Charles kissed the part in my hair, then rested his cheek on my head. His voice rumbled through me as he said, "Well, what will it be, Angie?"

I took a deep breath, sat up straight, and placed the one call I knew I needed to make to get my life back on track.

This was my decision, and I was ready to deal with whatever consequences came with it.

Here goes nothing.

CHAPTER NINETEEN

Several hours later, I sat on my front porch with a fresh mug of tea warming my hands against the chilly night air. I leaned back against the side railing with both legs stretched out before me. Paisley sat snuggled in my lap while Octo-Cat lay snoozing at my side. Pringle had already absconded into his private apartment with the new treasures Charles had allowed him to steal from his attic, and my boyfriend had gone home so that I could have this moment to myself.

"Thanks for agreeing to talk with me," I said to the elderly woman who sat on the nearby rocking chair, holding a full cup of tea in her hands as well.

"Of course, dear," she answered with a far-off smile that seemed to take almost all the energy she had. "I should have spoken with you about this much earlier."

I turned the mug in my hands, searching for the right words to move this conversation forward. It seemed an apology was the best place to start. "I shouldn't have given you an ultimatum, but—"

"Say no more." Her voice was soft and reassuring. "I shouldn't have pushed you to that point. Thank you for giving me the chance to explain for myself first."

"Nan, you know that no matter what happened back then, it doesn't erase all the amazing years we've had together. It doesn't change the fact that you're the person I love most in this entire world. You're my best friend."

Octo-Cat stirred in his sleep, just enough to grumble a protest.

"Well, you and Octo-Cat," I amended with a chuckle.

"Show me what you found," she said without further delay. I knew this was hard for her, but I was so appreciative she was facing that discomfort to give me the answers I craved.

Instead of calling the number the church lady had given me, I'd decided to call my nan and come clean, to tell her I'd been searching for answers and may have found some but would much rather talk to her first if she was willing.

She'd asked for a few hours to gather her bearings but said we could talk that night. And now here we were.

"You've already seen the letter and birth certificate. Pringle took those back. But we also have these two pictures." I set my tea to the side and rose carefully, holding Paisley as I stood.

"Ahh, William," Nan said, memories sparkling in her light eyes. But did they spark joy? I couldn't quite tell.

"Who was he to you?" I asked, still so confused by all I knew, all I still didn't know.

She touched the photo of his face with trembling fingers. "He was my best friend growing up. We did everything together. Almost like a brother and sister, until we hit puberty, and then suddenly our relationship felt very different."

"You fell in love," I finished for her.

"I did," she admitted with a sad shake of her head. "And for a while I thought he loved me, too, but then Marilyn Jones came along."

"The name on the birth certificate." I remembered that first night standing out here by myself as I read the shocking contents of his letter, saw my mom's real birth certificate for the first time.

She nodded. "Your real nan."

"I don't understand. What happened?" I placed a comforting

hand on her shoulder, urging her on. There was still so much more that hadn't been said.

"I don't know what happened to Marilyn, only that William said she was gone, and he was going back to war. He was worried about his daughter, about Laura, your mother. And he was right to worry, because he died in battle later that year."

Tears pricked at my eyes for the friend Nan had lost, for the grandfather I'd never gotten the chance to know. "Oh, Nan, I'm so sorry."

She sniffed and smiled up at me. "By then, I'd met and fallen for your grandfather. We legally adopted your mother and raised her as our own, always fearing that Marilyn would come calling and take our daughter away. For years, we looked over our shoulders. Not hiding, since I was in the public spotlight given my choice of work, but always watching."

"And then what happened?"

She shook hard, and I knew that we'd reached the hardest part of the story. This was the part of the memory she'd tried so hard to forget.

"When your mother was eleven, Marilyn found us. She came to one of my shows and confronted me after. Said William's sister had told her what he'd done and that she wanted her baby back." Tears splashed into her tea, but she wasn't drinking it, anyway.

I wanted to comfort her, but I couldn't move. What had almost happened? How different would my mom's life be if…? And would I have even been born?

"Oh my gosh, all those years later? What did you do?" I couldn't stand another moment not knowing.

"I agreed to meet her the next day, to bring Laura." Her voice cracked here. "And then your grandfather and I packed up and left town."

"To Blueberry Bay," I whispered.

"To Blueberry Bay," she confirmed.

"What happened to Marilyn?"

Nan shook her head vigorously. Her tea sloshed over the edges of her cup, but she didn't react. "I don't know. We walked away from everything so that we could keep our family together. Your mother hadn't been born to us, but she was ours. And I didn't know why William sent his only daughter away, but I knew him and knew he must have had his reasons."

"Wow." I breathed heavily, still in shock. "Does Mom know about all this?"

"Of course not." Nan's voice faltered in a rare show of fragility. "How can I tell her that I stole her?"

And just like that my legs worked again. I pulled my nan to her feet and hugged her tight. "You didn't know. Your best friend gave her to you, and you trusted him."

"Back then, yes," she whispered into my hair. "But I made a choice when Marilyn found us in New York. A selfish one that's kept Laura from knowing her real mother and you from knowing your real nan."

"You're my real nan," I said, wrapping my arms around her even tighter. "I told you nothing can change that. Not even this."

"I appreciate that, dear." She pulled back and studied me with a small smile and bright eyes. "Sometimes I think I let myself fall even in more in love with you than I allowed myself to love your mother, because I knew no one would show up and try to take you away."

This explained so much, why she had been the main one to raise me even though my parents were here and capable. Whatever the reasons for it, I'd loved my childhood and I loved my life. I loved the woman who had risked so much to give it to me.

I kissed her on the cheek. "I've loved every single day with you, Nan. Well, every day except for the one you took Paisley to a motel and hid from me."

We smiled at each other, then laughed together for what felt like the first time in ages.

"You don't hate me?" she asked with a squeak.

"I could never hate you." I paused before saying the next part in case it hurt her. "But I do want to meet her."

Nan nodded. "I figured you might."

"Where do we start?" I needed to know more, but I also needed us to do this side by side.

"Together." She reached out her hand and grasped mine. "I've spent so many years running from the truth. Now let's walk toward it together."

CHAPTER TWENTY

A lot happened rather quickly after that.
Nan showed me all the old photos and mementos she'd kept hidden for fear of exposing her secret history growing up in Georgia and falling in unrequited love with her best friend. I still didn't know why William had decided to entrust his baby to Nan when her mother was still very much alive. I think the only person who might know the answer to that was Ms. Marilyn Jones herself, but we had no idea where to start looking for her—or even if she was still alive all these years later.

Pringle took full credit for solving the case and decided his fee should be doubled for just how fast "he" had managed to solve the mystery. He also demanded that his payment be delivered within three days or it would need to be doubled again.

That payment? A new home, since we had irreparably damaged his under-porch apartment with our shovels. And because he had decided to ask for double, he also demanded that we erect a new office headquarters for Pringle Whisperer, P.I.

Luckily, we knew the very best handyman in all of Blueberry Bay, a certain Mr. Brock "Cal" Calhoun. Not only did he do fast, quality work, but he also didn't ask too many questions—like why a single woman and her grandmother needed not one, but two, tree forts erected in their backyard or why one of those forts also needed to be outfitted with electricity and a satellite TV dish.

Once Cal had finished building the twin tree forts and Pringle was all moved in, I introduced him to reality TV, the ultimate source of juicy secrets and real human drama—at least that's what I told him.

Sure enough, he immediately got sucked in to one of the longest running reality competitions of them all, which meant there were plenty of back episodes for him to watch. He enjoyed laughing at the humans and their weak skills when it came to surviving in the wild.

"Survivor!" he quipped somewhere into his umpteenth hour of viewing. "Ha! Put a raccoon in there with them, then you'll see what a real survivor looks like!"

Pringle had already begun to spend all his time in front of his new TV, which thankfully meant he stayed out of trouble. Well, at least for now.

Brilliantly, Octo-Cat had a fairly easy time convincing the raccoon to join our investigation firm rather than continuing to compete with us.

"Think about it, Pringle," my cat crooned. "You like secrets. Now your whole job is keeping track of our secrets. In fact, that's your new job title—Pringle, MSK. Master Secret Keeper."

"Oooh, that's even better than P.I.," he crowed. "It's got more letters. Better letters!"

Really, all that happened was that we moved our filing cabinets into his rarely used work fort, but at least I knew they were safe there, given the ferocity he used to protect all his favorite treasures.

When Cal had finished building the tree forts, he also fixed the hole in our roof so that no other animals would be able to crawl into our attic. He helped us clear out the space under our porch, too, and then laid down a solid stone base—also to keep the wildlife out. I didn't mind getting up close and personal with my animal neighbors, but we needed to have at least some boundaries.

Julie, for her part, was incredibly relieved to find that all the missing mail had been accounted for. Her bosses at the post office let her off the hook but made sure to promptly deliver flyers throughout town, warning of highly intelligent and very disturbed forest animals.

Honestly, it made me laugh.

Pringle, too.

When I brought one home to show him, he grabbed it from my hands in delight and then raced around the neighborhood collecting as many as he could for his treasure trove. I had no doubt that he'd eventually turn them all into sloppily constructed origami cranes, provided he stopped watching TV long enough to get to work.

While all this was great, the most important follow-up item still remained. Nan and I needed to reunite the family.

That's why my mom was here with us now.

Nan had baked all her favorites and encouraged her to dig in while she shared pictures and explained our shared, but until now hidden, past. Pringle had even generously returned the birth certificate and William's letter to us, so we could show them to her as a way of starting the conversation.

"There's still a lot we don't know," I explained to my mom, who sat stoically, taking it all in. I guess since she was an investigative reporter, she was used to larger-than-life stories like this one. It still couldn't have made any of this easier.

"I can't believe it. I have another mother out there," Mom said with a genuine smile. "What was she like?"

"I didn't really know her," Nan explained. "But she was beautiful, just like you." She bumped my arm. "And you, dear."

"Can we find her? Can I meet her?" Mom asked with a determined glint in her eyes. She never backed away from a challenge, and that proved true now, too.

"I'm not giving up until we do," I promised, taking my mom's hand and giving it a tight squeeze. "But we have even more family out there, family we haven't gotten the chance to know yet."

Nan sucked in a shaky breath, and I offered her a reassuring smile before turning back to my mom and revealing, "I have their phone number. Should we call?"

We caught Mom up on the McAllisters of Larkhaven, Georgia, and the help I'd received from the church receptionist.

"Can we really call them?" Mom asked. "Just like that?"

"Hey, you never know," I said with a goofy smile. "Maybe they've been looking for us, too."

"There's only one way to find out," Nan said, hugging us both from behind.

"Are you really okay with this?" Mom asked. "It must be so scary for you to go back to that time, that place."

"I'm not going back," Nan said with a wistful smile. "Only forward with my two girls."

Mom nodded, and I punched in the number I'd long since memorized even though this was the first time I was actually placing a call.

It rang three times, and then…

"Hello?" a woman who sounded about Mom's age answered.

"Is this Linda McAllister?" I asked through happy tears. I already knew what the answer to my question would be. "Because I think we might be related."

Even though she hadn't expected our call, we spent over two hours chatting about our lives, growing closer and closer, until there was no doubt in any of our minds that we were, in fact, family.

"So, when are you coming down to Larkhaven to see me?" Linda asked.

"Soon," I answered with an enormous smile. "Real soon."

HIMALAYAN HAZARD

Pet Whisperer P.I.

ABOUT THIS BOOK

Ever feel like your entire world has been turned on its head? That's how I've felt ever since the gang and I found out that Nan has been keeping major family secrets stashed neatly away in the attic.

What's worse, we still don't know exactly what happened, and I have so many follow-up questions, like is she still the same woman I always assumed she was? And can I ever fully trust her again?

With Nan unable to give me a straight answer, I invite my parents to join me for a cross-country train trip so that we can all discover the truth, once and for all.

Octo-Cat hitches a ride with us, too, and it's a good thing he does, because it isn't long before a dead body joins us in the dining car. Now we have two mysteries to solve, and fast—our lives and legacy depend on it.

CHAPTER ONE

My name's Angie Russo, and lately my life has taken one dramatic turn after another. Seriously, where can I even begin?

I guess it all starts with my cat.

Think that sounds boring? Well, think again!

My cat can talk. Only to me, but still.

We met at the law firm where I used to work as a paralegal. I never really loved that job, but I did enjoy having food in my fridge and a roof over my head, so I stayed despite being treated like a glorified secretary and not the shrewd researcher I'd worked so hard to become.

We had a will reading scheduled one morning, and I was called in to make some coffee for the attendees. The machine we had was approximately a million years old and unpredictable even on its best day. This was not one of its best days. All I wanted to do was make the cruddy coffee and get back to work, but—lo and behold—I got electrocuted and knocked unconscious instead.

And when I awoke from that zap, I found a striped cat sitting on my chest and making some pretty mean jokes at my expense. Well, as soon as I realized the voice was coming from him and he realized that I could understand what he said, that cat recruited me to help solve the murder of his late owner.

That's how I and Octavius Maxwell Ricardo Edmund Frederick Fulton Russo, Esq., P.I. became an item. I've since shortened his name to Octo-Cat and have become his official owner—although he'd surely tell you that he's the one who owns me, and, well… he wouldn't exactly be wrong.

He came into my life first with a murder mystery and then with a generous trust fund and even more generous list of demands. So now here we are, living in the posh manor house that previously belonged to his late owner, drinking chilled Evian out of Lenox teacups, and operating the area's best—and only—private investigation firm.

There was a brief upset when a raccoon named Pringle set up a competing business, but we've moved past that now. Because, yeah, at first I could only talk to Octo-Cat, but with time, I also gained the ability to communicate with other animals, too.

The regular cast of mammalian characters that make up my life include an eternally optimistic rescue Chihuahua named Paisley, that infamous raccoon racketeer named Pringle—also known as the Master Secret Keeper for our firm—an easily distracted, nut-obsessed squirrel named Maple, and my crazy-daisy, live-in grandmother, Nan.

Frankly, I'd love to add a bird to our merry little gang of forest misfits, but they're all too frightened to talk to either me or Octo-Cat. Go figure.

And despite our diverse skill set, our P.I. outfit isn't exactly successful. We've only had one case to date, and we weren't even paid for it. I know it will happen for us eventually if we just stay the course and continue to believe in ourselves…

Um, right?

Well, that's what Paisley insists, anyway.

Even still, I've got this huge new thing in my life that is keeping us plenty busy, with or without work to fill our days. I just discovered that I have a whole big family in Larkhaven, Georgia, that I never even knew existed until a couple weeks ago. And what's more, they've invited me, my mom, and dad to come down for an extended visit so that we can all get to know each other.

Octo-Cat insists on coming, too. He hates long car rides and refuses to even consider getting on a plane, which means we get to take the train. Whoopee.

Sure, it won't cost very much, but it will take longer than a day of continuous travel to get there. Still, I can't exactly leave him behind when he was a big part of helping me locate the hidden branch of our family.

Yeah, Nan had kept them hidden from us for my entire life and my mom's whole life, too. But now that we've found them again, there's no keeping us apart. Nan doesn't want to join us, even though Mom and I both assured her she'd be welcome. She still feels guilty about what happened.

Maybe we can convince her to join us for the next visit. I hope we can, because even though she kept a major secret from me, she's still my best friend and my very favorite person in the whole wide world.

That's why saying goodbye to her right now is so difficult…

"Promise me you'll call every single day," I moaned, hugging my grandmother so tight I had to wonder if she could even breathe.

"Mommy, I'm going to miss you, too!" Paisley, Nan's five-pound tricolor Chihuahua, cried as she pranced on the platform from the other end of her neon pink leash.

I scooped her up and peppered her adorable little face with kisses. "I'm going to miss you, too," I cooed in a cutesy, crazy pet lady voice. Talking to the animals like this in public made people think I was weird but kept my secret ability hidden. "Mommy will be back in sixteen days. You can wait sixteen days, can't you?"

"I don't know how to count," Paisley said with a happy bark.

I handed her over to Nan and took Octo-Cat's cat carrier from my mom so she could get in goodbye hugs, too.

My cat growled during the handoff. "Hey, there's delicate cargo in here!"

Mom and Nan said a quick goodbye, and then I set Octo-Cat down to hug her again. As pathetic as it might be to admit, I'd never been away from her so long. I'd grown up under her roof and lived with her most of my adult life, too—although now she lived with me rather than the other way around.

Throngs of passengers dragging big wheeled suitcases passed us on either side, and I had to step back to avoid getting hit by a fast-walking woman who was more focused on her phone conversation than where she was going.

"Look," I told Octo-Cat. "She has a cat carrier, too."

And she did. Only it was much fancier. I wouldn't be surprised if the bling adorning the case was actual diamonds—or at least Swarovski crystals.

"Show-off," my cat muttered, even though I'm pretty sure he'd have loved a decked-out carrier like that to call his own. It didn't matter that he'd sooner surrender one of his few remaining lives than willingly get inside.

"I'm surprised there are so many people out here," my dad said, glancing around uncomfortably. "I didn't realize anyone still took trains when there are so many other options available."

"It's romantic," my mom gushed, leaning into him and possibly squeezing his butt from behind. It seriously grossed me out how in love these two were, even after thirty years of marriage. They sure acted like high schoolers, sometimes.

"I feel like I'm about to rush platform nine and three quarters at King's Cross for the first time," I said with a snort and a chuckle.

"When were you at King's Cross?" my dad asked with a furrowed brow.

Ah, jeez. Sometimes it was hard being the only avid reader in the family. Had my parents seriously not even seen the movies?

"That's it!" I cried. "We've got like thirty hours aboard that train. More than enough time for a Harry Potter movie marathon, and when we get home, I'm lending you my book collection so that we can get you all the way caught up."

"Homework?" my mom whined.

"Ugh, you're the worst ever, Mom," my dad added.

And then they kissed so long and hard that my mom's foot popped up like a fairytale princess getting her first big kiss. Only this was their six millionth big kiss at least.

This was going to be a very long trip. Very long, indeed.

"The conductor's waving you over," Nan said, pointing toward a uniformed man standing just outside of our train car. "Best get a move on."

"Are you ready?" I asked Octo-Cat.

"Just get me out of this thing," he grumbled, as if this whole method of travel hadn't been his idea.

"Relax," I murmured as we made our way over to the step up into the train. "I'll have you out in two minutes, and then it will be smooth sailing from there. After all, what's the worst thing that can happen on a train?"

Famous last words... I really should have known better.

CHAPTER TWO

After giving Nan one last squeeze, the four of us strode up to the train and climbed aboard. Well, Octo-Cat was carried in what he'd deemed his "travel prison." In the back of the car, I found a grouping of four seats that faced each other, two on each side, and placed Octo-Cat's carrier onto the aisle seat, taking the spot by the window for myself.

Nan stood exactly where we'd left her on the platform, waving furiously and hopping up and down. "Bon voyage, my dear!"

I laughed and blew her kiss.

"You're just as embarrassing as she is," my mom muttered, scooching over in her seat so that she and my dad had not a millimeter of space between them. "No wonder the two of you are always conspiring on something."

I let that one slide, despite the fact that she and Dad were way more embarrassing than Nan and I would ever be. Mom had always felt sensitive about how close me and my grandmother were, and I knew she felt left out somehow. It was even worse now that we'd recently found out Nan wasn't her real mother, that she had in fact actively kept her from her birth mom based on the request of the man both women had once loved.

Yeah, we were still untangling that one…

That's why we were headed down to Larkhaven, Georgia. My grandfather's side of the family still lived down there and had invited us to come on over for a little family reunion. Of course, we had no idea where my biological grandmother had gone, or even if she was still alive. But one thing at a time.

My dad whispered something in Mom's ear, and she giggled.

"Gag me on my own hairball," Octo-Cat drolled beside me. My sentiments exactly.

Passengers continued to pile onto the train. Dull chatter settled around me like a comforting blanket. Perhaps, this wouldn't be so bad, after all. I watched a mother with two young children settle near the front of the train, then an elderly couple settle a bit closer to us. All kinds of people chose trains over planes, it seemed.

Who'd have ever guessed that the rail travel industry would still be going strong in the twenty-first century? Not me.

A man wearing an old-fashioned fedora and argyle sweater vest slid into the seat across the aisle, then immediately withdrew a rickety looking typewriter and began to pound on the keys. His fingers moved deftly as he added word after word to the sheaf of paper hanging from the top of his old-fashioned machine.

A typewriter on a train. Two anachronisms in one.

Throw in the fedora, and that makes three.

Suddenly the man stopped typing and pushed his glasses farther up his nose as he turned toward me. "What's a good word for suspicious? Except for more subtle?" His unblinking eyes bored into me as he waited for some kind of genius revelation to spring forth from my mouth.

"Um, odd? Curious?" Kind of like you.

He rubbed his chin. "Hmm, I'm not sure those will work. Ahh, well. I'll come back to it in the second draft."

"The second draft? Are you writing a novel?"

That was kind of cool. My nan had always claimed she'd write a book, and little by little she had made progress over the past several months—although the book she was working on was a memoir, not a work of fiction. I often wondered if she planned to include the truth about my grandfather and bio-grandma.

"Oh, yes," the man said with a smile that lit up his whole face. "Not just any novel, the next great American novel. You see, it's about—"

"Angela!" Octo-Cat cried from inside his carrier, practically panting in his sudden onset of panic. "Get out! Get out now, or we will be forced to spend the entire journey listening to this guy's delusions of literary grandeur."

"It sounds wonderful," I told the aspiring novelist. "Unfortunately, my cat needs to be fed now."

The tabby yowled pitifully to help sell our story.

I still thought it might be cool to talk to a real live writer, but the fact that this one referred to his unfinished manuscript as the next great American novel was a flashing warning sign. This guy thought he was important, talented, God's gift to readers, even. I was all for credit where credit was due but believed it was better to let others sing your praises than to belt them out on your own.

"I'll be back later, okay?" I offered with a friendly smile. I didn't want to be unsupportive of his dreams, especially since my dream of becoming a full-time P.I. with my talking cat as a partner was every bit as crazy.

"And run," Octo-Cat directed.

I was not going to run away from the poor guy. At least not literally.

I stuck a Bluetooth device in my ear as we pushed through our car into the next. The thing hadn't worked in years, but it did provide a great misdirect when I felt the need to talk to Octo-Cat in a public place.

"What do you think?" I asked him as I felt the train jolt to life under my feet. My hand stretched toward the wall, catching me just in time to avoid my stumbling forward.

"Well, that was unpleasant" my cat complained with a low growl. "Can I please get out of this thing now?"

"I'll let you out as soon as we settle somewhere," I promised, pausing for a moment to glance out the window as we rolled away from the station. Nan was still out there waving like mad, but soon she became a speck on the horizon.

He sighed and thumped around in the case. "I know it was just an excuse to get away from Chatty McMyNovel, but I could use a meal or at least a spot of Evian."

"The dining car it is." I raised him higher and hugged the carrier to my chest as I pushed into the next car.

I hoped the conductor wouldn't give my parents a hard time for me being up and out of my seat already, but then again most of what I knew about trains came from old timey books and movies. Things seemed to run a bit different in our modern age of digitization.

Luckily, we only had to pass through three other passenger cars before reaching our destination. That was good news for the journey ahead. I liked knowing that snacks were nearby, should we need them.

"I should probably text Mom and Dad to let them know where we went." I unlatched the wire front door, and Octo-Cat sprang out onto the table twitching mightily.

"You do realize that in cat years that was almost a full prison sentence, right?" He shuddered, then plopped on his side and began to lick his kitty bits for all to see—and on an eating surface, no less. At least I was used to his less than courteous ways.

Shaking my head, I sent a quick text to my mom, asking if she needed anything while we were over here. As soon as I sent the message, my phone spat out a message to let me know I had a low battery. Twenty percent. Ugh, leave it to me to be so preoccupied with the upcoming journey that I forgot essentials like making sure I had a fully charged phone.

Glancing around the dining car, however, put my fears to rest. Every single table had an electrical outlet. I just needed to fine my phone charger inside my jumbled mess of a suitcase and then we'd be perfectly fine.

"I'll go see if they have any Evian," I told Octo-Cat.

He mumbled something, not bothering to pause his public ministrations to address me properly.

I sighed and shook my head again, then approached the snack station with a rumbling belly. Another basic necessity I'd ignored in my excitement over the trip.

The worker saw me approaching and forced a smile. His curly red hair fell forward into his eyes, and he reached up to brush it from his face. Perhaps I would stick to prepackaged food unless I was certain he wouldn't be the one preparing it.

I'd seen steak among the meal options, and that sounded really good right about now. Was it too early to order my dinner? I hoped not.

Before I could reach the counter to order anything, however, a woman wearing a cream skirt and matching peplum blouse intercepted me.

"Hello, there," she said with a friendly but placid grin. "Were you just talking with your cat over there?"

She glanced over my shoulder and nodded to Octo-Cat back at our table, then set her eyes back on mine with a knowing expression, aka an expression that suggested she'd already figured out my closely guarded secret.

Five minutes aboard a train, and I'd already made a major misstep.

Uh-oh.

CHAPTER THREE

I took a giant step back, but the lady reached out and grabbed my wrist, chuckling softly as she did.

"I didn't mean to insult you. After all, I talk to my Grizabella constantly. Few people understand the special bond between a woman and her cat. Wouldn't you say?" She tilted her head to the side and widened her grin.

I nodded as relief washed over me. "My name's Angie, and he's Octo-Cat."

"I'm Rhonda Lou Ella Smith." She held out her hand, which hung limp from her wrist. Did she expect a shake or a kiss? Either way, I was afraid of hurting her with my strong grip, so I settled on a fist bump… which failed miserably.

Rhonda brushed her hands off, then folded them in front of her waist. "Yes, well. Care to join us at our table? Better you than someone else, after all." She laughed again, and the sound reminded me of a bird singing at first morning light. Everything about her reminded me of a bird, actually—from the delicate bone structure to the expensive and perfectly tailored outfit and flashy jewelry all the way to her dazzling platinum hair.

"Sure, let me just order our snacks first." I turned back toward the red-headed counter attendant and he dropped his hand from his mouth sheepishly. Gross. I bit my nails, too, but not while working food service.

"Oh, don't you worry about that. I have more than enough to share," Rhonda promised, then sashayed back toward her table, moving so gracefully I had to wonder if she'd escaped from a ballet or a circus trapeze act or something.

"Okay, then. Be right over." I smiled again just in case she turned back at the sound of my voice and skulked back to my table, completely baffled by the elegant woman's interest in me. Was it really so simple as her feeling a bond to me as a cat owner?

"Whatever you agreed to, I didn't," my cat told me, sitting up straight and wrapping his striped tail around himself. "I'm staying right here."

"Then I guess you won't be getting any Evian," I whispered, turning my back to him and counting to five under my breath.

"One of these days I'm calling the animal cruelty association on you," he said from behind me, then jumped from the table onto my shoulder.

"Ouch! Claws!" He'd never hitched a ride on me before, so I wasn't sure why he wanted to do it now—other than perhaps thinking it could be a fun new way to humiliate, and thus punish, me for forcing him to make nice with the other passengers.

"What a cute trick," Rhonda chirped, clapping her hands in delight as we approached.

"Tricks? Aren't those for old dogs? I am a cat, madame," Octo-Cat said to our new friend, although I'm sure she only heard his croaky, entitled meow.

"Don't bother speaking to her," a smooth, lyrical voice rose from the bench seat. "She never understands."

My eyes darted to the gorgeous long-haired cat with dark face, tail, and paws and striking blue eyes. Must be the previously mentioned Grizabella. There were cats, and then there were cats. Grizabella belonged to the latter classification. She looked like she could have stepped out of a textbook, so perfect was her coat, her stance, basically everything about her.

Octo-Cat stiffened on my shoulder, brushing his whiskers against my cheek as he craned to see the Himalayan better. "Pray, Angela. Do you also see an angel before us?"

An angel? What?

I tried to turn to look at him, but only got a face-full of striped tabby fur. Irritated, I pried him from my shoulder and set him onto the empty bench seat across from Rhonda.

He didn't even protest. He also didn't stop staring at the other cat for even a second. As soon as I set him down, he hopped onto the table, his quest for Evian apparently a thing of the past.

"Dear beautiful feline, it is an honor and a privilege to look upon you," he said, his amber eyes growing larger the longer they beheld her. Either he'd been spending too much time around Pringle, our resident raccoon and medieval knight enthusiast, or he'd discovered one of the fantasy channels on TV. Knowing him, either was equally likely.

"I think my cat likes yours," I told Rhonda with a chuckle. I'd never seen Octo-Cat try to flirt before, and I kind of wish I hadn't seen it now.

"Careful," the woman warned. "Grizabella doesn't much like other cats, or people, or anyone, really." She reached out to stroke the Himalayan's long fur, but a quick paw batted her away.

Talk about a cat after Octavius's own heart.

"I do not appreciate your attempts to flatter me, house cat," Grizabella hissed, then cuddled up to Rhonda's side. Talk about hot and cold. Octo-Cat also had pretty intense mood swings, but normally in the space of an hour rather than mere seconds.

And, normally, such a slight would send my tabby into a mad spiral of hurling insults and lashing claws, but not this time. "You misunderstand. I am part Maine Coon, the most ancient of American-born breeds, and I am at your service, beautiful Grizabella." He dipped his head closer to the table and folded his ears out to the side in a show of respect.

"I don't need your service. My human meets my needs just fine."

"Hard to get," Octo-Cat remarked with a jaunty laugh.

"No. Impossible to get," Grizabella corrected, her tail flicking on the bench seat beside her and beating against her owner.

"Nothing is impossible." Octo-Cat winked, then licked his paw. "I will find a way. After all, solving mysteries is my job. I own half of a private investigation firm, mind you."

Grizabella did appear mildly impressed by this but said nothing.

I figured it was time for me to chat with the other human, lest we raise suspicion about our special communication link. "What brings you on board the train today?" I asked Rhonda, doing my best to focus my full attention on her.

Rhonda fingered the gold pendant that hung down from the chain of pearls around her neck. The piece was enormous and quite stunning, given the intricacy of the design carved into it. A cluster of matching pearls sat proudly in the middle of the piece, creating a real treat for the eyes. The thing must have cost an absolute fortune. On the contrary, my nicest piece of jewelry was a delicate sterling silver chain with a paw print charm that Nan had given me on my last birthday.

Rhonda glanced out the window thoughtfully. "I prefer rail travel. It's better for Grizabella."

"We're headed for Georgia," I volunteered. "Is that where you're going?"

"Not this time. We'll probably get off before then." Odd that she didn't actually name her destination, but I decided not to press. Pressing was not the point of making small talk, after all.

"I don't think I've ever been on a train before. Well, except maybe at the zoo." I laughed at my own non-joke.

Rhonda did not. "You'll like it. There's nothing quite like it."

"I can see that already."

She smiled again, then returned her attention to the window. Strange she was so insistent on having us join her when she didn't really seem to want to talk.

We fell silent. Both of us turned our attention toward the cats, who, much to Octo-Cat's chagrin, had still not made friends.

"Oh, dear Grizabella. I will do anything for you, even lay down one of my nine lives." He crept to the edge of the table and sat right in front of Rhonda, who cooed happily and stroked his fur.

"Not interested," Grizabella said, lifting her nose into the air.

Octo-Cat ignored the human and continued to beg the Himalayan for her love. "I could catch a mouse. Would you like a nice dead mouse?"

Grizabella growled and ran under the table to avoid my poor lovestruck bumpkin.

When I glanced back toward Rhonda, she was chuckling into a cloth napkin. "That's my Grizabella for you. She doesn't much approve of other cats, and they don't approve of her."

I was just about to argue that Octo-Cat approved greatly of the Himalayan, but then Rhonda said, "It's why we make such a perfect pair."

What a strange thing to say. Was this the wealthy woman's way of saying she didn't approve of me—or that she thought I didn't approve of her? Why would it even matter? And, again, why had she insisted on having us join her?

I smiled but said nothing in response. Eventually, she moved on to tell me stories of Grizabella's many mundane adventures. Honestly, I kind of wished I'd stayed with the writer guy.

CHAPTER FOUR

Although Rhonda had promised to share her cache of snacks, she never once made an offer while we were sitting together. By the time Octo-Cat and I dismissed ourselves from her table, I was too embarrassed to remind her but also worried it would be too rude to purchase snacks right in front of her. My hopes rested on my parents now and the knowledge that my sports-obsessed dad almost always had a protein bar or bag of trail mix on him.

"Are you sure you can't stay and chat a little longer?" Rhonda asked when I stood to go.

She glanced out the window again and I looked out, too. Clearly, we'd been sitting together for quite a while, because dusk had already begun to fall across the rolling landscape. No wonder I was starving!

"I'm sorry. I really need to get back to my parents," I said with a shrug, hating how childish it made me sound.

"That's wonderful that you're so close with your family. Very special, indeed," Rhonda said, stroking her cat absentmindedly as she watched me prepare to leave.

By some miracle, Octo-Cat returned to his carrier willingly and without complaint, presumably because Grizabella was watch-

ing. Man, if I'd known finding him a girlfriend would be the ultimate bargaining chip, I would have played matchmaker a long
time ago.

"So," I mumbled as I carried him back through the three cars
on the way to ours, my Bluetooth placed perfectly. "Do you always
go gaga for Himalayans, or is there something special about Grizabella in particular?"

He sighed blissfully. "I've never been in love before tonight. It's
like a whole new plane of consciousness has opened itself to me." It
seemed his first crush had turned him into Shakespeare. I didn't
blame Grizabella for finding his affections so wearisome.

I rolled my eyes. "Just remember, we're not on the train for that
long and you probably won't see her after we get off at our station.
Or actually, Rhonda said they'd be getting off first..." It took me a
moment to make sure I had recalled that detail correctly since I had
to wade through hours of cat stories to get back to the beginning of
our conversation.

Suddenly, I felt very sorry for my poor kitty. Not only did he not
stand a chance, but he'd probably never see his crush again. "Just
don't get all heartbroken over this," I warned. "I hate to see you
hurting."

"Love always finds a way, Angela," he said sagely. Although in
this particular case, I had no idea how things would work out,
considering the object of his affection actively disliked him.

Also they were cats. Could cats even fall in love? It seemed like
maybe they could. I hoped one day Octo-Cat would find a lady who
would return his romantic longings. I was also incredibly happy that
he was fixed, given his complete lack of modesty when it came to...
well, everything.

"Does this mean you'll be more accepting of me and Charles?"
I asked, hoping that my feline's own brush with love might get him
to stop referring to my boyfriend as UpChuck.

He said nothing, but a giant purr rolled up from the carrier in
what I had to assume was the kitty version of humming blissfully
while thinking of one's beloved. Wow. He really had it bad.

Speaking of having it bad, I returned to my seat only to find my parents wrapped even tighter around each other as they both stared at my mom's laptop with rapt attention.

"What are you guys watching?" I asked, noticing that they were sharing a single pair of earbuds.

"Harry Potter and the Deathly Hallows, Part Two," my mom answered without removing her eyes from the screen.

"Ugh, you guys! Why are you starting with the last one?"

"Well, we need to know it has a good ending before we invest in such a long series. Don't we?" my father asked with one raised eyebrow.

Personally, I hated spoilers. They took away at least half the fun. At least my parents were giving it a try, though. I had to give them credit for that.

The aspiring writer I'd met before stopped typing and seemed to watch us from his peripheral vision. Was he waiting for an opening to tell me about his novel again?

Looked like I had a choice to make. I could either cuddle up with my already too cozy parents and pretend to watch the movie or I could go off exploring again. After the chat with Rhonda and Grizabella, I needed some alone time to recharge, which meant I had to get out of there before the conceited writer guy launched a second attempt at conversation.

"I just needed to grab my jacket," I said, hoisting the lightweight denim from the seat and draping it over my shoulders. "Oh, and before I go, do you have something I can eat?"

"As the Boy Scouts say, always be prepared." My dad picked up his travel bag and tossed a granola bar my way, still not removing his eyes from the movie. Well, at least they really seemed to like it.

"Thanks," I called over my shoulder, already making a getaway. We'd already found the dining car, and it was probably too soon to go back if I wanted to avoid a second get-together with Rhonda. Perhaps I could find the viewing car and hang out there for a while.

We passed through the three cars between our seats and the dining car, then four more to find the empty glass-sided carriage with seats arranged down the center to face the giant walls of windows on both sides. Only the very top of the ceiling was covered in metal, providing a panoramic view as far as my eyes could see, just so long as I didn't tilt my head up or down.

I set Octo-Cat's carrier on the ground and opened the latch. He pranced right up to the giant window, his movements soft and swaying despite his hatred of that carrier. A gentle rain had begun to patter on the glass, surrounding us in a peaceful dream-like bubble.

"I wish Grizabella was here to see this," he said with a longing I'd never heard from him before, not even when he spoke of his late owner, Ethel Fulton. The poor guy had it so, so bad.

"It is romantic," I said, cuddling into my jacket and scooching around in my seat until I found the most comfortable position.

We both watched the rain for some time, and beyond that, the rolling hillside of whichever state we were steaming through now. Probably still Maine, or perhaps we'd made it to New Hampshire or even Massachusetts by now. I'd almost drifted to sleep when Octo-Cat hopped up onto the seat beside me and then climbed onto my lap, a rare move from him, indeed.

"Are you worried about meeting your family for the first time?" he asked as he padded my lap with his front paws to increase the comfiness before settling down to relax. He almost never asked how I was feeling. Normally he just told me—yes, told me how I was feeling. I decided not to point that out and just enjoy his concern. After all, I really did need someone to talk to about this.

"It's weird," I admitted, pensively stroking the fur at his neck. "I always thought I knew who I was and where I came from, and then suddenly it's all wrong. And the weirdest part is that I never would have known if Pringle wasn't such a sticky-fingered snoop."

As much as the raccoon irritated me, I would forever have him to thank for finding and revealing the truth about my mother's—and consequently, my—heritage.

Octo-Cat purred in a way that told me he could only be thinking of his new lady love. He still appeared to be paying at least some of his attention to me, too, so I asked, "What would you do if you were in my shoes?"

"Shoes?" He huffed at the suggestion. "You're such a human."

I couldn't tell whether or not this was intended as an insult, so I kept mum. I was incredibly human, after all.

He stopped purring and crossed his forelegs in front of him. "It's different for cats. It doesn't really matter where you came from. Only that you turned out right."

Such a simple thought, but a nice one. Sometimes I really liked his way of looking at things.

"Cats don't see their families again after we're taken away. I mean, I guess strays and alley cats might." He stopped to shudder at the thought. "But what happened with Nan and your mom, that's really normal for cats. We are born to our cat family but then taken away by our human family, and that's where we stay."

"So what are you saying?"

"Nan is your human, and she's a good one. Things could have been much worse."

He was right about that. Sometimes my cat was so smart, and other times he stared at the wall for no apparent reason. He was weird, all right, but luckily our weirds matched just perfectly.

And with that thought, I drifted off to the sound of his purrs.

CHAPTER FIVE

The continuous song of the rain and the unexpected bliss of kitty cuddles lulled me to sleep right where I sat. I dreamed I was Anne of Green Gables taking that first fated train ride that would deliver her to the Cuthberts. A nice dream, considering Anne was one of my all-time favorite heroines.

The lovely dream came to an abrupt end, however, when a horrible shriek rent the air and four sets of claws dug deep into my lap.

"Ouch, careful!" I cried, shooting to my feet so fast that Octo-Cat fell to the ground.

He immediately popped back to all four feet and stood with his tail drooping toward the ground and his neck stretching toward the roof. "It's my Grizabella!" he said, his ears twitching like satellite receptors. "She is in trouble. We must go to her."

The shriek shattered the night once more, and I realized then the scream was, in fact, feline and not human. That didn't make it less frightening, but it probably meant that most other passengers would choose to ignore it.

"It's this way," Octo-Cat cried, pouncing toward the door that led the opposite direction from whence we'd come. I assumed this led to the fancy sleeper cars, the ones we couldn't quite afford but that I had no doubt Rhonda Lou Ella Smith could.

My cat was too worked up now to stuff him back in his carrier, so I grabbed it and ran after him.

He stopped at the door and shouted, "I'm coming, my darling! I'm coming!"

The shriek sounded again. This time it was accompanied by the words, "Hurry!"

I had no idea what we were walking—or rather running—into, but it definitely sounded urgent. We passed through two sleeper cars, then opened the door to the third. When we entered, we found the wailing Himalayan pacing the hall.

She ran straight up to us and nuzzled Octo-Cat's face. "Thank you for coming so fast. My mistress… She—Oh, gosh. It's too horrible to even say!"

Octo-Cat appeared momentarily tongue-tied, so I took the lead.

"Can you show us?" I asked, holding my hand out to show her I meant no harm.

Grizabella took a quick sniff and then turned, her poofy tail held high while the rest of her quivered with fright.

The tabby and I followed her into one of the private rooms. The door was already cracked open, and inside our new friend Rhonda lay in a creeping puddle of blood, her flawless cream suit stained almost beyond recognition.

I brought both hands over my mouth to keep from crying aloud when I noticed one of the steak knives from the dining car sticking straight out of her stomach, where she had apparently been stabbed multiple times. But why hadn't she cried out? Surely, she would have screamed loud enough to awaken me from my dreams.

On shaky feet, I tiptoed across the soiled carpet, careful to avoid the encroaching red stain, and bent down to feel for a pulse. When I couldn't find one on Rhonda's wrist, I tried her neck, hoping beyond hope…

Her lovely pearl necklace with the gold pendant was gone. Had the murderer taken it? Did they kill this poor, kind woman just so they could rob her? The thought made me blindingly mad.

I shook my head as I turned back toward the cats. "I'm so sorry," I told the distraught Himalayan.

"Oh, why? Why?" she ground out. "Why musts humans only have one life? And why must Rhonda's have come to an end so suddenly?"

Oct-Cat pushed his face against hers, and the kindly nuzzle did appear to offer some comfort. Poor, poor Grizabella.

Even though she was still shrieking and asking various permutations of the question Why? I knew I needed to find out what she'd seen and if she had any idea who could have done this… and yes, why.

"C'mon. Let's go out into the hall," I said, not wanting to hang out around a dead body any longer than we had to. I made sure the door wasn't locked, and then shut it gently behind us. "Grizabella, did you see what happened?"

She shook her head and squeezed her blue eyes shut tight. "Only after. Not during."

"Where were you when she was attacked?" I pressed, already seeing she would be a difficult witness to question. It was to be expected for a cat, especially one in the throes of an emotional meltdown.

"I don't want to talk about it," she sniffed.

Well, that direct refusal raised more than one red flag. I'd investigated cats as possible suspects before. Would Grizabella prove to be the culprit in her owner's murder, too?

"Please," Octo-Cat chimed in, finding his voice acting the role of my partner once more. "We're here to get justice for your human, not to judge."

"Promise not to tell anyone?" Grizabella asked with a sad sniff.

"Of course we won't tell," I assured her, and not just because anyone else I talked to about this case would immediately dismiss me as a quack if I started sharing the cat's alibi.

"I was in the little kitty's room, using my box. I heard someone enter and speak with Mistress just as I was in the middle of… Well, you know. The sounds were muffled, I didn't know what she said. I waited in the other room until I heard the stranger leave, not wanting to have to play nice with any other humans for the night. No offense, but you were already more than enough for one evening." She turned toward me and crinkled her nose. Ugh, cats were so rude sometimes.

"Go on," Octo-Cat urged with a tenderness he never assumed when speaking with me. "What happened next?"

Grizabella gasped, remembering. "When I came out, Mistress was covered in blood and her skin had already started to turn cold."

I briefly wondered if I should pet the Himalayan to try to calm her down, but that didn't seem like the best idea, considering she'd barely tolerated her beloved human's touch.

"Wow, that's a lot to take in," I said instead. "If you don't mind, let me ask a few follow-up questions. First, didn't you hear Rhonda —I mean, Mistress—scream?"

"No, she did not scream or even sound upset." The set of her jaw and the firmness in her eyes told me she had no doubt about this.

"Okay. You referred to the stranger as a she. Does that mean the person who entered was a woman?"

"Oh, darling, I don't know. All humans look and sound the same to me." At least I'd been upgraded to darling, although I suspect she might use the same pet name for the help as well—well, if she could. She did seem to understand that I wanted to help and had begun to cooperate a bit better.

"That's what I always said, too," Octo-Cat said with a hum. "Until I got to know them a bit better."

"Yes, I did notice your human can talk," Grizabella said gracefully lowering herself into a sitting position. "Why is that? And don't you think it's just a tad suspicious?"

He shook his head, immediately coming to my defense. "She's here to help. We both are. Is there anything else you can tell us that might help us figure out what happened to your human?"

"Well, I know what happened. She's dead."

Great. We had a dead body that so far only I had discovered, and the only witness was a spoiled purebred who couldn't really tell us anything, anyway. This case would be almost impossible to solve before the train arrived at the next station and the proper authorities had a chance to take over. Should I still try, or should I quietly alert the staff and do my best to secure the scene until help arrived onboard?

Our train passed through a tunnel, turning the night sky even darker than before. I caught sight of heavy stone walls from the hall window and shuddered. It felt like we were passing through a tomb.

How fitting.

I pulled out my phone to check the time. Just past four in the morning. We didn't have any stops scheduled until seven thirty. Could we make it three and a half hours with a fresh corpse on board? And who should I tell given that the entire train seemed to be fast asleep?

The light flickered overhead and then blinked off with a startling pop. Oh, great, electrical problems were exactly what we needed now. Well, at least things couldn't get much worse, right?

This was always a bad question, whether or not I asked it aloud.

Because at that exact moment, the train grinded to a stop right in the middle of that dark, tomb-like tunnel. We were stuck in the countryside with a murderer—a violent murderer—on the loose, and I couldn't even see the hand in front of my face.

How very perfect.

CHAPTER SIX

I pulled out my phone to activate the flashlight. Sixteen percent battery life remained. I really needed to invest in one of those portable chargers in case I ever again found myself trapped on a dark train with a violent killer in the future.

You know, providing I survived this time…

A giant shudder racked my body as my phone chimed merrily into the silence. It's ringing!

Fumbling, I answered the call and raised the phone to my ear with shaking fingers. My mother's voice burst through the speaker.

"Angie! Where are you? Are you okay?"

"Mom," I cried. Normally, I was pretty cool under pressure, but this time I couldn't help it. Seeing Rhonda's butchered body up close and now being trapped in the dark right outside the door that led to her corpse, it was too much for me. It would be too much for anybody.

This wasn't my hometown. In fact, I didn't even know where we were on our journey from Maine to Georgia. I didn't know the other passengers and had no idea which of them might be a killer. There was no one to trust.

No one except my cat and my parents.

"What's wrong? Tell me how to get to you," my mom shouted into the phone, instantly sensing something was wrong and thankfully not forcing me to say anything more until she could first make sure I was safe.

"Past the dining car. Past the viewing car. In one of the private coaches. Hurry." I didn't have to tell her to bring Dad, because I knew she automatically would. Maybe between the three of us, we could straighten this mess out. Of course, there would be no way to save poor Rhonda Lou Ella Smith. Not anymore.

I sank to the ground against the wall and hugged my knees while waiting for my parents to make their way back to us. I'd be the calm, rational detective later. Right now, though, I needed a few minutes to feel my emotions so that I could work through them and let them go.

Something furry brushed against my arm in the darkness.

"Why are you crying?" Octo-Cat asked me curiously. "You don't cry."

"It's the dark. I think it's making everything so much worse," I sobbed while groping for him. As soon as my hand made contact with his fur, a bit of my bravery returned. We'd been through all kinds of dangerous scrapes before, but we'd always made it through. Together.

"The dark isn't so much different than light. Right?" He moved away, and I shivered from the sudden absence of his warmth.

"Maybe for a cat. Humans don't have night vision like you do." While I explained this, I was struck with an idea. The two cats were the only ones on the train who could see without the assistance of a flashlight, which meant they were the only two who could sneak around without attracting attention.

"Octavius, Grizabella," I called to them, not sure how close either was to me at the moment. "Can you two explore the train a little? See if you can find anyone suspicious?"

"What makes a human suspicious?" the Himalayan asked in her soft, melodic voice from across the dark car.

This was good. Focusing on the investigation helped to push the fear aside. Worry would only throw me off my game, and I needed all my wits about me, considering one of my senses had already been all but disabled.

"If they have blood on them for one. This person might also be sneaking around or searching for something. We still have no idea why someone would kill Rhonda, so until we figure that out, we need to look for general clues. Got it?"

"We can handle that," Octo-Cat assured me, his voice a bit deeper than normal, which I assumed was some part of his misguided flirtation efforts. "The only problem is we need a human to open the doors between cars."

Oh, right.

Just then, as if on cue, the door to our car opened, and my parents rushed in, their path illuminated by the sweeping of their twin phone lights.

"Turn one of those off," I hissed. "We need to conserve battery power. We have no idea how long we'll be stuck out here in the dark."

"Well, it's nice to see you, too," my mom scoffed.

I forced myself to my feet, keeping one hand on the wall to steady myself. "Mom, Dad. There's been a murder."

"What? When?" my dad demanded, surging forward and lowering himself to inspect me.

"Right before the lights went off and the train stopped."

My mom dropped to the floor, too, and hugged my head to her chest. "Oh, Angie. It's not safe for you to be back here on your own."

"Well, now you're here, so I'm fine. See?" I forced a smile, but Mom's light was focused elsewhere.

"I can't see much of anything at all," she grumbled.

I untangled myself from her arms and sat up higher. "Listen, Dad. Can you go find someone who works for the train company? Let them know we have a dead body back here and that it was definitely a murder. Call Mom if they need more details. My phone is almost dead."

"Sure," he answered, his voice sure, unafraid. "But what will you two do?"

"Do you even have to ask?" Mom said, and I could picture her with one hand on her hip and her eyes narrowed even though she still sat on the floor beside me.

"Solving the murder," he responded with a knowing chuckle. "Got it. Just be careful."

Mom pushed herself to her feet, leaving her light on the ground beside me. "You, too. I love you too much to lose you." After my mom said this, a sticky smacking noise filled the car. Of course.

"That goes double for you two," my dad answered before switching his phone light back on and leaving me and my mom behind to take care of business.

"Wait!" I called just before the door latched closed behind him. "Follow him," I told the cats. "Dad, take it slow at the doors. The cats are going to follow you to see if they can find anyone acting suspiciously."

"Roger that." My dad probably saluted, but I couldn't quite see due to the angle of his light. My mother had told him about my strange ability long ago, but he'd never worked with me and Octo-Cat on a case before. I liked how he agreed to my request without arguing or questioning it.

"When he comes back, you two come back, too. Okay?" I told my cat.

Octo-Cat's brown-striped body moved into my dad's spotlight, and he turned back to regard me with a frown. "Angela, please," he hissed. "I've got this. Ladies first, Grizabella."

The Himalayan walked ahead confidently, tail and nose both held high. The door whooshed shut behind them, and they were gone.

"Show me the crime scene," Mom said, not wasting even a single second. I may be the family P.I., but she was an ace reporter who loved solving mysteries, too. We'd only worked together a little before, but I sure was happy to have her on my side now.

The last of my tears having spilled, I pulled myself to my feet and directed Mom's hands—and thus her phone light—toward Rhonda's door. "In there," I whispered.

I kept my hand on hers, and we pushed the door open together. This time, I knew what we would find, which made it a bit easier to head back inside despite the pitch black that enveloped everything.

CHAPTER SEVEN

Mom led the way into our victim's private room. There lay Rhonda exactly as she'd been when I first discovered her less than half an hour ago. Poor soul.

"I'd say next time we should upgrade our travel plans," Mom said, shifting her light around the room and illuminating the cushy furnishings that I hadn't really gotten the chance to notice earlier. "But this isn't exactly a shining endorsement for first class."

"Can you shine the light on Rhonda's body?" I asked, ignoring Mom's ill-timed joke. "I want to see if there's anything I missed before." Because if I missed the entire room outside of her body, I probably missed some important clues, too.

"You knew her?" Mom asked, her voice quirking in surprise.

"We met in the dining car and talked for a little bit."

"How did that happen?" She found the light switch and flipped it back and forth, just in case. Nothing.

Having Mom here centered me. Not only was there safety in numbers, but she also might catch something that I would otherwise overlook. Together, we could do some good here—or at least keep things from getting worse.

"She asked me to sit with her and bond over our crazy cat ladiness," I admitted with a fond smile as I remembered how desperate she had been simply to make a new friend. "That Himalayan belongs to her, and Octo-Cat is quite smitten."

"He always did like the finer things," my mom said thoughtfully, then cleared her throat and focused her phone on Rhonda's body. "Did she tell you anything that might be relevant to her murder?"

I bit my lip as I studied Rhonda's face. Her features weren't distorted by terror or even anger. She simply looked at peace, which I found all the more unsettling. "We didn't say much, and I wasn't cataloging our conversation for later use, but at least one thing stood out. She either didn't know or wouldn't share her destination."

Mom flinched at this revelation, turning to face me with wide eyes. "What do you mean?"

"I told her we were going to Georgia, and she said she'd probably get off before then. Probably. Not definitely."

"So she had no clear destination in mind," she summed up.

"That's what I'm thinking. Or something happened to make her want to get off earlier than planned." She'd looked distracted and had glanced out the window an awful lot. Could that be related?

"Lot of good that did her." Mom swept the light down Rhonda's body and paused when she reached her stomach. "Stabbed multiple times. It looks like maybe five. It's hard to tell with all the blood."

I felt sick to my stomach, remembering how much I'd craved steak earlier that evening. Now I would probably never want to eat it again—or at least I'd be using a butter knife to saw off bite-sized pieces. "Someone had to have enough foresight to take the steak knife from the dining car, but the presence of multiple wounds makes me think this was a crime of passion."

"So, premeditated, but only very slightly. Hmm." Mom's carefully coifed hair didn't even move as she shook her head from side to side. Small wrinkles lined her forehead and the edges of her mouth, though, while she stared at the body pensively.

"Grizabella—that's her cat—said she heard Rhonda talking with someone after they entered the room. She was in the bathroom at the time and couldn't make out any of the words. She also couldn't tell if the visitor was male or female," I revealed, wanting to make sure she had just as much information as I did.

Mom sighed. "Meaning we don't have much to go on."

"Maybe the room has a clue. You have the light, so maybe you can search her things while I see what I can find on her phone."

She turned on me so fast, I lost my breath from the sudden fright. "Why don't you have a light?"

"My phone is almost out of battery. Trying to conserve it in case there's an emergency later."

Mom sighed. "I'd tell you to be more responsible, but I'm guessing this is already one heck of a lesson. Let's find her phone so you can get started."

She shone her tiny flashlight around the room, locating Rhonda's cell phone almost immediately. It lay on the dresser beside a small travel case that looked like it would be used for makeup or toiletries. "I'll start here," Mom said, unzipping the case and riffling through the contents.

While she did that, I picked up the phone, praying it would be easy to access. And yes! Thankfully, Rhonda had elected to use a fingerprint to unlock her phone rather than a passcode, so I returned to her body, then very carefully and very respectfully pressed her index finger to the surface. The dark lock screen gave way to a photo of Grizabella sitting on a plump pillow and staring straight into the camera.

Aww. She really had loved her cat.

While that was sweet, however, it wouldn't help me figure out who killed her or why. I needed to learn more than just the surface stuff during our search, needed to find something that could set me and my mom on the right path.

So first I checked her email.

All the unread messages made me cringe. I'd always been an inbox clearer and couldn't understand people who hoarded thousands of unread messages, especially when so much of it appeared to be spam. After scrolling through the first several dozen emails and finding nothing but cat blogs and clothing sales, I decided to move on to her social media.

Unsurprisingly, Rhonda's Instagram was actually a fan account for Grizabella. She only had a couple thousand followers, but they appeared to interact regularly with her posts. I scrolled through the recent hearts and found almost every profile picture to be either a cat or a person smiling beside a cat. Well, Rhonda clearly had one very specific use for the platform—one and nothing else.

On Twitter, she followed a handful of politicians and other celebrities but didn't appear to tweet anything herself. Also not helpful.

But what would Facebook bring? Hopefully something a bit more useful.

Here, Rhonda had very few friends and posted rather infrequently. Her most recent update was a check-in at a train station in New Brunswick, which was strange because I was pretty sure I remembered seeing her on the platform when we'd boarded in Bangor.

Rhonda's post simply read: Off on another journey!

Scrolling through her feed revealed the usual combination of baby pics, wedding pics, and humble brags from her modest friends list. Hmm.

"Angie," my mom whispered. She hadn't been whispering before, so whatever she had to say, I was guessing it would be good. "I've found something."

I swung the phone around to illuminate the room and found her sitting on the edge of the bed with her legs crossed at the ankle. In her hand, she held a small book, and on her face she wore an excited smile.

Here we go.

CHAPTER EIGHT

L ike most older people I knew, Rhonda had kept her phone
fully charged, which meant I didn't need to be careful about
preserving its battery life—and thank goodness for that. I used the
screen to illuminate my path as I moved carefully past her body and
joined my mother at the bed.

"It's her personal planner," Mom revealed, flipping through the
pages demonstratively. "You know, like the calendar app, but on
paper."

"C'mon, Mom. I know what a personal planner is." The cover
on this one was made of blue leather that I suspected matched the
exact shade of Grizabella's eyes. Gold trimmed the edges of each
page, not unlike a Bible.

Mom shook her head and continued to search through the
entries until she landed on the current week. "Here," she pointed to
the box reserved for yesterday. "She got on in New Brunswick. A bit
earlier than us."

"I found the same thing on her Facebook profile, but I could've
sworn we saw her when we were saying goodbye to Nan. She was in
a hurry, but I definitely remember that blinged out cat carrier of
hers."

Mom tucked her heavily hair sprayed hair behind her ears, but it immediately bounced back to its previous shape. "Huh. I don't remember seeing her, but maybe she just got off to stretch her legs."

"Or to a say a quick hello to someone waiting at the station," I suggested. We'd only seen her returning, though. Huh, indeed.

"So she got off, but she got back on," Mom recapped with a shrug. "Hang on. Let me see what else is in here."

While she thumbed through the planner, I returned to Rhonda's email and searched the name of the train company. Sure enough, since she never discarded anything, her travel itinerary popped right up.

"She was headed to Houston," I told Mom hardly believing anyone would want to be on a train for such a very long trip, but then again, maybe it wouldn't be so bad with a private room. Still, she had either knowingly lied to me or changed her plans quite suddenly. "She told me she'd probably get off before Georgia."

Mom stood and marched over to me, then shoved the planner in my free hand. "Her planner has a cat show in that area early next week."

So a sudden change of plans, then. "I wonder if the person she met at our stop said something that spooked her. Like maybe a threat. Maybe she reached out to me in the dining car because she felt safer with company."

Now I felt terrible. Had I been given the opportunity to save her, only to run away because I couldn't take another mundane cat story?

"That's a lot of maybes," Mom said, rubbing my shoulder like she somehow knew I was partially blaming myself for poor Rhonda's fate. "I do agree this is all very suspicious, but we don't know anything for sure."

I shook those feelings aside and focused on the facts. Whether or not I'd played a role in what had happened, the best thing I could do now was to find justice for the poor lonely woman who loved her cat more than anything else in this world.

"She was wearing a necklace when I met her, but the necklace was gone when Octo-Cat and I came in presumably just minutes after her murder," I told Mom, forcing myself to move on.

Mom frowned and set the planner down where she'd initially found it. "Missing necklace. Quick visit to the platform in Bangor. Abandoned trip to Houston. Five stab wounds. We have a lot of little bits and pieces, but not enough to know what kind of puzzle we're building."

"Don't forget the distraught feline. It was Grizabella's cries that alerted us to the trouble." Despite the Himalayan's cool demeanor when we'd first met her in the dining car, her reaction to Rhonda's death showed the cat had loved her owner just as much as she'd been loved by her.

"Now that's interesting. Could it be a jealous cat show competitor?" Mom ventured, taking the planner back from me and holding it in both her hands as we continued to talk. "They were on their way to a show, after all. Maybe someone threatened them to keep them on the sidelines this year, so another cat could take the crown."

"I don't think cat shows work the same as beauty pageants," I said with a wry laugh. Laughing was good. It kept the horror from creeping in. "But it's not a bad theory. A jealous rival killed her off and then took the necklace to make it look like a simple robbery."

Mom nodded, but her face remained grim. "There are worse reasons to take a life. Not many, mind you, but I'm sure there are at least some."

The door swung open so suddenly, it made us both jump in fright. My heart hammered a heavy tattoo against my chest.

"Helloooooo!" a young male voice bellowed. Then he gasped and his voice became higher. "Holy heck, so that guy's crazy claims are true, after all." He moved into the room and shone his lantern-style flashlight on Rhonda's body. The curly red hair immediately struck me as familiar. This was the same worker I'd spied in the snack car, the one I'd almost bought snacks from before Rhonda intercepted me.

"Hi. That crazy guy was my husband," Mom said, offering him a friendly wave.

The man—who couldn't have been much older than a teenager

—staggered back and lifted a hand to his chest. "Yeesh, don't do that! I thought the dead was rising again."

Okay, so this kid had seen one too many zombie movies in his day. He also had access to the dining car and all of its knives. Could he be the killer returning to the scene of the crime? If so, Mom and I could definitely take him. Not that I wanted to engage in a fight to the death... now or ever.

"What are you doing in here?" I asked, studying him closely. His pale, blemished skin looked ghastly in the glow of his lantern. His skinny arms didn't appear strong enough to inflict the wounds I'd seen on Rhonda, but then again, young mothers could lift entire vehicles to save trapped babies—or so the rumor went.

"My boss sent me over here to check it out, since my station was the closest. He said that—" He stopped abruptly and raised his light higher. "Ha! Nice way to distract me. What are you doing in here alone with a dead body?"

He took another big leap back into the hall, terror washing over his once accusing features. "Wait. Did you kill her? Are you going to kill me?"

"Well, that depends..." Mom said and then moved slowly toward the frightened worker.

Yikes! What was happening?

CHAPTER NINE

"Mom," I shouted, at the same time elbowing her in the stomach.

"She's kidding," I assured the young train worker. He hadn't shown up at work today knowing he'd have a dead body and a crazy small-town news anchor to deal with, and Mom's attempt at humor was definitely not helping to ease the tension this time.

Mom said nothing, so I continued chatting nervously, even going so far as to raise my hands to show we meant the young man before us no harm. "We were the ones who discovered the body. Dad went to tell your boss while we stayed here to make sure no one would disturb the scene. You work in the dining car, right? I think I saw you there earlier. What's your name?"

He stepped back into the room, his shoulders sloped forward defensively or perhaps in defeat. "Yes, that's me. My name is Dan, and I'm just trying to do my job and—you know—not get murdered."

"Aren't we all?" Mom said, and I elbowed her in the ribs again.

"I'm Angie, and I'm a private investigator back in Maine. The deceased is Rhonda Lou Ella Smith. I met her earlier today. Perhaps you saw us together in the dining car."

Dan nodded, even chanced a smile. "Yeah. Yeah, I think I did."

Good. This was good. Now that he recognized me, he relaxed enough to hold a rational conversation and to stop accusing me and mom of murder.

"I'm trying to piece together what I can, so I can hand things over to the cops when they arrive," I continued, motioning toward the planner in mom's hands and then showing him the phone in mine. "Was she there a long time before I came in or a long time after I left? Did you notice anything unusual about her?"

Dan took the phone from me but didn't do anything with it other than hold it at his side. It seemed to further relax him, though. After all, most murderers wouldn't hand over evidence that could likely convict them.

"I don't know," he said after a slight pause. "She seemed normal enough. Weird, but normal."

"Weird how?" I pressed, keeping my eye on the phone. I would need that back at some point.

"She kept talking to her cat like it was a person. I noticed people looking at her funny, but I thought it was kind of nice. Who's to say cats can't understand us, right?"

"Sure," I said dismissively, happy Mom kept quiet on that one. While she thought revealing my secret pet-whispering ability would make for a great human-interest story, she at least respected that I'd prefer not to let the world in on my strange power. "Did you notice when she arrived in the dining car or when she left?"

"She came in right when we left the Bangor station," Dan said, then nodded in confirmation. "I remember, because she was my first customer and it was just the two of us until you arrived a short while later."

"Did the two of you talk?"

"Just enough for her to place an order. It was a big one."

"Could you tell me if—?"

The door swung open again, and in marched my father. The two cats followed him inside, and then a fourth figure joined us in the private room. Dad shut off his phone—not needing it now that Dan was here with his lantern—then made his way to Mom's side.

The cats stayed quiet, watching us from near the doorway.

I couldn't quite make out who the new person was, given that the brim of his hat cast his face in creepy shadows. But then he opened his mouth to talk, leaving no doubt as to his identity.

"Wow," he said on the wings of a dramatic exhale. "You read about it. You write about it. But you never think you'll actually stumble upon a real-live murder mystery. And on a train. This is so Agatha Christie!"

"Easy, Tolstoy. There's been a murder here. Show some respect for those of us who didn't make it," my father warned, wrapping his arm around Mom's waist protectively.

"Who's this guy?" Dan asked, swinging his light closer to the writer who'd invited himself into this intimate scene.

"The name's Melvin Mann. Remember it, because one day soon you'll see it at the top of the New York Times Bestsellers list." I couldn't be sure given the current lighting situation, but I think he actually made jazz hands to punctuate his expression.

Oh, brother.

"Well, Melvin," I said slowly, trying not to gag on my words. "This is a crime scene, not Grand Central Station. I think it's time you went back to your seat."

"Oh, really? What gives you any more right to be here than I have?" He crossed his arms over his chest and stepped deeper into the room.

"Because I'm a P.I. That's why." Would I really need to establish that with each new person who arrived? Apparently.

He leaned forward, making himself several inches shorter so he could look me right in the eye. "Prove it." His words smacked of condescension. Not only did this guy think he was better than everyone else, but he also seemed to think I was worse. Infuriating.

"What? I can't prove it beyond my word."

He straightened back to full height. "Show me a business card or something." Right, because it was impossible to create cards that read anything you wanted them to.

Case in point, Melvin pulled a stack of cards out of his pocket with a flourish and handed them around. "See, Melvin Mann, novelist. Now show me yours?"

"I don't have any business cards on me. Sorry." I would have turned out my pants pockets, if I had any. He seemed the kind of guy to appreciate overwrought gestures, like purple prose in real life.

He jabbed a finger at me so hard it would probably be a bruise. "Ah-ha! See, I knew you were just pretending."

My father rushed to my side and stared at Melvin so ferociously that the other man couldn't help but take a step back.

"Look, we can stand here arguing until the killer finds us, too," my dad said, not taking his hard eyes off the writer for a second. "Or we can work together to solve this thing."

"Oooh, I like that," Melvin said, steepling his fingers in a far too sinister fashion for my liking. "This is wonderful inspiration for the mystery story arc of my novel."

I held in a sigh, an eyeroll, and a groan all at once. "Earlier you were asking me about suspicious characters, so why don't you go find some?"

"I wasn't asking about the characters. I have my characters on lock, thank you very much. I was asking about synonyms."

"Just do what she says, JD Salinger," my father growled, taking another threatening step forward.

Melvin stood in place; a smile snaked across his face. "You think calling me by classic novelists' names is an insult, but it's really quite the opposite."

Dad did not hold back the choice words he had in response to that.

I turned to Dan, ready to put this whole macho showdown—or whatever the heck it was—to rest. "Can you go check in with your bosses? See if we can get the train moving again or the police sent to our location. Something. Anything to help."

"Can do," he said, offering a thumbs up and a smile. At least he was more cooperative than Melvin Mann. The haughty writer would be a liability in this investigation, no doubt.

"Great. Thanks so much." I pushed them both toward the door.

"Oh, and one last thing. Please keep the other passengers in the dark about this. No need to start a panic."

"In the dark," my mom said with a chuckle. "Good one."

I swear, even if she and Nan weren't related by blood, sometimes it was simply impossible to ignore the similarities they shared. Mom was far more pragmatic and a lot more normal than either Nan or me, but she belonged with us all the same.

We were a family, and nothing—not even newly exposed secrets—could change that.

CHAPTER TEN

After Dan and Melvin exited, I closed the door behind them and twisted the lock to ensure those of us who remained had some privacy.

"Mom, Dad, could you continue to search the room? I'm going to catch up with the cats," I said once I could no longer hear the departing men's footfalls in the corridor.

"Oh, sure, honey," Mom answered for them both. "We'll stay out of your way, Miss Pet Whisperer P.I." She was the one who had come up with that name for Octo-Cat's and my operation and was immensely proud of it—even though I secretly hated it. Talk about parading my secret for all to see! I pretended it was just a gimmick, but I had to wonder if the unusual name was the reason our firm hadn't received a single paying case to date.

"Let's go to the bed so we aren't in the way," I told the cats, but it was my dad who moved in the direction I had dictated.

I laughed awkwardly. He hadn't gotten used to this yet. Well, he was about to become very familiar with how things went when I was working a case with animal assistance.

"Oh, you meant…" He flashed his light toward Grizabella, and the startled feline hissed.

"Well, you have fun with that, then," he finished, backing slowly away.

"Why did you hiss at him?" I asked the Himalayan, not bothering to hide my irritation as I narrowed my eyes at her.

"He shone that bright light right in my eyes. It hurt!"

Ouch. Okay.

"Sorry, he didn't mean to." Again I wondered if I should pet her as a way of offering comfort, and again I decided against it. I had a sneaking suspicion that Grizabella didn't much like me, and I'd hate to actually be proven right while our investigation was still ongoing.

We settled on the bed. Given the way the comforter lay completely smooth, I guessed she hadn't tried going to sleep before meeting with her murderer. The cats each lay on a pillow, leaving me to sit farther down the mattress.

"Okay, what did you learn while you were out there?" I had no light with me but could make out their vague shapes in the spill-off from Mom and Dad's.

"Nothing," Grizabella answered for the both of them. She sounded almost bored.

"But you followed Dad the whole way, right?"

"We did," Octo-Cat assured me. "But we found nothing that drew our attention."

Well, I hadn't expected this. I was sure my kitty reconnaissance would turn off at least something helpful. "What about anyone who looked, sounded, or smelled familiar, Grizz?"

A threatening growl rose in the dark. "Don't call me Grizz. My name is Grizabella, and no, I didn't notice anything. Just as I told you before. This is hard for me, so please pay attention the first time around."

Yeesh, she sure made it hard to want to help her.

I took a deep breath and reminded myself that she was grieving and probably even more startled by Rhonda's murder than either me or Octo-Cat. We'd investigated deaths before, but Grizabella had never had to deal with anything like this.

Why would she? Why would anyone?

"I'm sorry," I said, hoping she'd believe the sincerity in my words. I truly did feel sorry for everything she'd gone through already, everything she'd still need to go through before this case was settled. "I just have a hard time believing this was a simple robbery. Someone wanted Rhonda dead, and I want to know why."

"Look at this!" Mom called from the bathroom, appearing in the doorway. From behind her, Dad shone his light on the object in her hands. An ornately carved wooden jewelry box.

"I don't think it was a robbery," she mumbled, proving that we were on the exact same page. "Otherwise, why would they leave this behind? There's got to be thousands in diamonds and other precious stones in here."

Each necklace, bracelet, and pair or earrings she held up was more dazzling than the last. Many of the pieces boasted gigantic sapphires. And again I wondered if she chose the blue to match her cat's eyes.

"It's all silver," I pointed out. "But the necklace she wore when I met her in the dining car was gold and pearl."

Mom searched the ornate box, shaking her head. "Well, there's nothing like that in here."

Grizabella spoke from across the bed. "The necklace she wore today was her most prized possession. An important family heirloom handed down from her grandmother to her."

"So whoever took the necklace wanted the heirloom, but not the other, arguably even more valuable, pieces," I summed up for the humans who couldn't speak cat, rubbing my chin as I tried to make sense of all this.

"Or the killer struck for a completely different reason, saw an opportunity, and stole the necklace she was wearing but didn't think to search the room for other valuables," Mom ventured.

Dad nuzzled her from behind and kissed her neck. "I love seeing you in action. You're so smart."

"Not the time, guys," I spat, quickly looking away. Despite being an adult, I still hated seeing my mom and dad's flagrant and very public displays of affection.

"There is literally a dead body right there," I motioned toward

Rhonda, hoping my parents turned their light to me in enough time to read the disapproving expression on my face.

"Sorry. We'll just keep searching," Dad said as Mom turned to take the jewelry box back into the bathroom.

"Grizabella," Octo-Cat said gently. "What can you tell us about your life with Rhonda? What kinds of things did you do? What kinds of places did you go?"

Good questions, especially since asking Grizabella who would have wanted her owner dead would likely cause the Himalayan to either close right up or get overly emotional again.

The cat answered with a smile in her voice. "Rhonda was a very kind mistress. We traveled constantly, usually by train. Sometimes on a first-class jet. Mostly we went to cat shows, but sometimes we went places simply to take pictures of me amidst new scenery. I think Rhonda had a hard time staying put in one place because it reminded her of how lonely she'd let herself become."

Oh, this was good stuff. If Grizabella was willing to expand upon it, I was sure we'd learn something important.

"What do you mean?" I asked softly.

"I've been with Rhonda since I was a very small kitten. She's all I've ever known for my five human years in this world. Still, in all that time, she's never had visitors, never gone on dates, never done much of any of the things the humans do in television shows and movies."

"I love watching TV, too," Octo-Cat butted in. "Do you like Law & Order? It's my favorite."

"Heavens, no," the other cat answered in disgust. "I much prefer love stories to those with blood and gore."

Octo-Cat stumbled over his response. "Oh, yeah. Right. Have you seen When Harry Met Sally? I really like the part when she—"

"Octavius," I interrupted, assuming he preferred his fancy name in the presence of our refined acquaintance. "This really isn't the time for that. We need to hear more about Rhonda. That's what's important now."

"Thank you," Grizabella said, surprising me with her politeness and the fact she'd acknowledged I'd done something right.

"Normally I love speaking about such frivolities, but normally my human is safe and sound beside me. Oh, my poor mistress…" Her words fell away, but then she shrieked the same terrible cry that first brought us to this car.

"And oh no! What will become of me, now that she's gone?"

I wished I had an answer for her, but unfortunately I knew even less than Grizabella did—especially if Rhonda had been as big a loner as she claimed.

CHAPTER ELEVEN

G rizabella yowled again.

"What's wrong?" Mom and Dad cried in unison.

"It's okay," I assured them. "Well, I mean, it's not exactly okay. She just realized she doesn't know where she'll go now that her owner's passed."

"Oh, poor sweet thing." Mom crossed the room along the edge and then petted the mourning Himalayan. "A nice, gorgeous girl like you will find a new home in no time."

Grizabella stopped shrieking but moved away from Mom's attempts to pet her. "I don't want a new home. I want my life with Mistress."

My heart broke for the newly orphaned feline. Since discovering Rhonda's body, we'd only worked toward solving her murder. None of us had taken any time to see how Grizabella was coping.

"Anyone could see how much Rhonda loved you. Heck, she even made a fan account for you on Instagram, and it has more than two-thousand followers."

"Yes, but those are fans," the cat responded with disdain. "I don't know a single one of them personally."

"Angela will figure something out," Octo-Cat promised, purring to show her it would all be okay. "She always does."

The doorknob rattled and then someone pounded against the door, bringing the tender exchange to an immediate halt.

"Hey," Dan yelled in his squeaky, pubescent voice. "Why is this thing locked?"

The frantic pounding started again, and Dad ran over to let him in. "Sorry about that!"

"We didn't want anyone stumbling in by accident," I explained, leaving out the part about taking the extra measure to protect my secret. "What's up? What did your bosses say?"

Dan looked back toward the door as if it had personally slighted him, then turned back toward us with lantern held high. "The police are on their way, but it could be a while given our remote location. Figures, right?"

"Yeah," I said amicably as my eyes struggled to adjust to the brightness of his lantern-style flashlight again. "Anything else? Do they know what stopped the train?"

He shook his head sadly and in obvious fear. "Only that it's been tampered with somehow. Whoever it was knew what he was doing, ensuring it would be next to impossible to get moving again without an expert mechanic familiar with this kind of train."

Crud.

Dan's expression lightened and he rocked his lantern playfully. "I do have good news, though."

Octo-Cat climbed onto my lap, and I drew strength from his calming presence. Seriously, this case was so different than usual. We hadn't fought one bit. Perhaps we were evolving.

"Well, out with it already," Mom demanded. She only liked dramatic pauses when she was the one making them.

"The lights will be much easier to fix," Dan said, properly chastised. "Someone cut a few wires, but we've already found a passenger who says he knows how to fix it. He's working on it now."

"That is good news," Mom agreed, then flashed her phone at me. "And a lucky break for those who weren't responsible enough to charge up before the journey."

I groaned and pinched the bridge of my nose. A migraine wasn't exactly what I needed right now. "So at least our circumstances aren't getting worse," I reminded everyone.

"You girls stay in here," Dad instructed, moving toward the door. "Dan, bring that big light of yours and come with me."

I chased after him, refusing to be left behind. "Excuse me. None of that macho nonsense. Wherever you're going, I'm coming, too. So spill."

Dad sighed and placed his hand against the wall in defeat. "Why do you always have to assume it's something like that? I chose Dan because he has the best light and we're going to need it."

Yeah, there was no way I would be sitting out the next leg of our investigation. I turned to the young red-headed worker and held my hands out in supplication. "Dan, may I please borrow your light?"

He reluctantly handed it over, and I turned back to Dad with a giant smile of triumph. "You were saying?"

He chuckled at let out a low whistle. "You are just like your mother sometimes. C'mon, we're going to go nose around outside and see what we can find."

"Will you stay with my wife?" Dad asked Dan, and they shared a manly nod.

"I'm coming, too!" Octo-Cat called, jumping off the bed and joining us at the door.

"And I'm staying," Grizabella said, crossing her paws in front of her.

"Let's go, Dad," I said, lifting the lantern high as I followed him to the end of the car. We found an exit toward the outside there, but it appeared to be jammed up tight. In the next car over, we found the door already slightly ajar, having swung back into the car a couple inches.

"Hopefully, somebody just needed a cigarette break really, really bad," Dad told me with a shrug and then pulled the door open the rest of the way so we could exit into the tunnel.

Very little space lay to either side of the train. Dad and I could walk side by side, but not comfortably. The stone walls pressed in close as we studied the gravel beside the tracks. Add in the intense darkness and it was almost like we'd been buried alive. Creepy.

Dad stopped walking and put out an arm to stop me, too. With his other hand, he pointed a few feet ahead. "Blood."

Sure enough, dark red droplets stained the light scattering of stones and pebbles. Even creepier.

"Did you see any earlier?" Dad asked, sweeping his phone light back toward the exit we used.

I shook my head soundlessly, then continued forward to see if the blood might form a trail.

"Stay by me," Dad called out, a quiver moving through his strong voice. "We don't know how close the murderer still is. For all we know, he could be right here hiding in the tunnel just a few feet away. And I'm not risking losing you."

I gulped and returned to his side.

Dad hooked his arm over my shoulders and pulled me close. "We do this together. Understand? You have my back, and I'll have yours."

"Awww. That's great for you guys. I'll go check things out on my own, though," Octo-Cat said, trotting off in the direction I'd just abandoned.

It worried me, him going off on his own, but what reason would a murderer have to hurt a random cat? There's no way the culprit could know that Octo-Cat was investigating this crime.

Dad and I moved slowly, using my light to illuminate our path and his to search the gravel. "I'm not seeing any more blood," he said. "Are you?"

I'd never been so disappointed not to find evidence of a violent crime. At least if we had a proper trail to follow, we'd know that the killer had left the train—and we may even be able to follow the drops to find him.

"No," I answered with a racking sigh. "Someone was definitely out here, and given how close the exit and the blood are to Rhonda's room, I'm guessing it was our killer. But I don't think he was injured. It's probably a bit of Rhonda's blood that dripped off his hands or something."

"But if he had the blood on his hands, wouldn't it be on the door?" Dad pointed out, continuing to move the tiny point of light from his phone around the path. "And also, why are we assuming the killer is a he?"

"Touché," I said. "It could definitely be a woman. Good thought, though. Let's go check out that door."

We closed the rest of the distance back to our entry and exit point, and I was just about to step through into the train when an anguished cry rang out from deeper in the tunnel.

A cat's cry.

"Octo-Cat!" I shouted and took off running. There was no way I was leaving him to face whatever danger lurked nearby on his own. I just hoped Dad could keep up.

CHAPTER TWELVE

"Angie, wait!" my dad yelled, but I kept running as fast as I could toward the spot where Octo-Cat had cried out into the black night. By the time I found him lying on his side amidst the gravel, I'd practically run out of breath both from the burst of exercise and my pumping adrenaline.

Please be okay. Please be okay.

Praying hard, I scooped him into my arms and clutched him against my chest. "What happened? Are you okay? Octo-Cat, talk to me!"

"Oof, take it down a couple notches, would you," he muttered, shaking his head as if my volume had physically injured him.

"What happened? Did you see the killer?" I demanded, searching his glowing amber eyes for answers.

"The killer? Of course not. I'd tell you if I found the killer." He actually had the audacity to laugh at me.

"Then why did you scream? I thought you were hurt."

Now that I knew my cat was okay, I wanted to wring his furry little neck for striking such fear straight into my poor pet-owning heart.

"I am hurt," he said with a low growl, then shifted in my arms and shoved a paw into my face. "I got a little rock or something stuck between my toe beans. See."

"That reaction was about your toe beans?" I practically screamed but then, remembering the need not to disturb the other passengers on the train, dropped my voice to a whisper yell.

"Don't act like you don't love them." He laughed again, and it took all I had to keep listening as he spoke. "Now can you please be a good human and dislodge this thing for me?"

Quickly, I plucked the pebble from his paw and tossed it away, then set him back on the ground.

"Thank you," he said, walking back toward our exit door with an exaggerated limp that I had no doubt he was faking for my benefit.

"What happened?" Dad asked, concern still etched in his features despite my utterance of the ridiculous phrase toe beans.

"Cat drama," I explained in a growl, still beyond angry at Octo-Cat for worrying me needlessly. "C'mon, let's go back to Mom and Dan."

We marched single file back toward the open door with me leading and Dad following. Once aboard, we stopped to inspect the door handle but found no blood marring its smooth surface. We did, however, find another spot on the carpet, only a few feet from the door, but—given the fact that each car was close to a hundred feet long—quite far from Rhonda's room.

Any dripping blood fell infrequently. No gushing here.

It was fully likely we'd find more if we continued investigating outside the train, but the whole toe bean incident had spooked me thoroughly. It also made both Dad and I realize how vulnerable we were out there with no real way to protect ourselves.

"What did you find?" Mom asked, greeting us at the door to Rhonda's room and throwing her arms around Dad as if they'd been separated for days and not mere minutes. "I heard something, but Dan wouldn't let me go investigate."

"Good man," my dad said, giving the young redhead a fist bump.

"Nothing happened," I explained, then took on a cutesy voice I knew would drive my cat crazy. "The wittle kitty just got an ouchie in his wittle paw."

"Angela!" he cried, mouth gaping open in horror. "Not in front of another cat!"

Grizabella laughed, which made me laugh, too.

Dan just looked at me like I was certifiable. Maybe I was.

I returned his lantern to him, then caught everyone up on the droplets of blood Dad and I had discovered. "Did you find anything more in here?" I asked once I'd finished.

"Nope. You weren't actually gone all that long, you know," Dan answered, leaning back against the wall and crossing his arms.

Mom shrugged and offered me a weary smile. "Unfortunately, no."

We weren't going to solve anything by staying huddled together in this room. Someone had to search the train, and that someone was me.

"You guys keep searching here, and don't let anyone else inside," I said. "I'm going to see if I can find anything a bit further afield."

"Meaning you're going off by yourself," Dad summarized with a stern set to his jaw

"I'll take the cats," I said, drawing another strange look from Dan; he had the good grace not to say anything, though.

I didn't stick around to argue the point with my dad anymore. There were dozens, maybe hundreds of people aboard this train. And only one of them was a killer. That is, if the killer hadn't disembarked and run away like we now suspected.

I turned on my phone to guide our way. Twelve percent battery left. Dan said the lights would be back on soon, and I was banking on that in a huge way now.

"Why are we doing a sweep of the passenger cars again?" Octo-Cat asked, obvious irritation laced in his nasally voice. Apparently, my little trick earlier had cost me his pleasant cooperation. This didn't bother me much, given that I was already well accustomed to working with a crabby tabby. Things actually felt more natural now.

"She doesn't trust us," Grizabella answered for me.

We moved into the next car, heading in the direction of the

viewing car, dining car, and eventually our assigned seats. I paused after assuring no one had eyes on us.

"It's not that I don't trust you guys. I mean, of course I trust you guys. But sometimes things are worth a second look, right?"

"Uh-huh," Octo-Cat responded with a furious flick of his tail. "You're right. She doesn't trust us."

"Told you," Grizabella said, also flicking her fluffy tail. So glad they were bonding over this.

I sighed, then spoke while trying to keep the frustration from my voice. "Can you guys just... We're working together, not against each other. We all have the same goal here, so let's act like it."

That shut them up fast. Thank goodness for small miracles.

"Keep an eye out for any strange behavior, and keep trying to think of new ideas in case this doesn't work," I said when I was sure neither would hurl another argument at me.

"It won't work," Grizabella complained, and I had to bite my tongue to avoid flying into a full-scale lecture about what I'd only just said. Could she really not see how hard I was trying to help here?

Help for me came from an unlikely source. "She's trying her best," Octo-Cat explained softly. "Even if it's not very good."

Grizabella harrumphed but continued to follow me as I marched off toward the next car.

Oh, boy. I really hoped we'd find something on our tour of the train, because I'd love to make these cats eat crow.

CHAPTER THIRTEEN

Well, it looked like I'd be the one eating crow in the end.

Our sweep of the train turned up nothing, just as the cats had warned. Most of the passengers appeared to be sleeping. The few who had woken up seemed relaxed and unbothered, probably because they didn't know about the dead body that lay several cars back.

I corralled my feline companions into the tiny vestibule between cars to chat about what we should do next. "Before you say I told you so, listen up. We can't exactly shine lights in everyone's faces and ask them if they killed Rhonda."

"Why not?" Grizabella asked with a long, flat face as she sat back heavily on her haunches.

"Darling, please. Let the professionals talk." Octo-Cat raised a paw to the Himalayan's mouth to silence her. Wow, he had a lot to learn about women.

And, okay, perhaps I laughed a bit too hard when she bit him right on his poor injured toe bean. Served him right for condescending to her, especially after he saw what happened when I attempted to shorten her overly fancy name.

A whir sounded overhead, announcing the repaired electrical system. As the overhead lights popped backed on, muffled cheers rose from the cars on either side of us. People wanted to celebrate, but not wake their seatmates, which could definitely work to our advantage.

"Well, look at that." Octo-Cat deadpanned as I rubbed my eyes and wished for my sunglasses. "The lights are back on. Now, shall we return to plan A?"

"There wasn't a plan A," I reminded him as bright spots danced at the edges of my vision.

"Then why was there a plan B?"

"Just listen!" I yelled. Enough was enough already.

Apparently, Octo-Cat was just as fed up with me as I with him. "Well, jeez. You don't have to yell," he rasped with his signature snark.

"Octavius, please," Grizabella interjected, scooting closer to him so that their furry bodies touched at the sides.

Thankfully—and probably just as Grizabella had suspected—this rendered the chatty tabby completely silent. Finally.

She nodded for me to continue with what I had to say.

"Most of the passengers are still asleep," I explained, keeping a close eye on Octo-Cat to make sure he wouldn't derail us yet again. "If the murderer is still on board, then he or she is definitely not just sleeping it off. That narrows our pool considerably. We couldn't find any suspicious behavior when we simply walked through the cars, so I think our next step should be to add a little pressure."

"Good plan. What did you have in mind?" Grizabella asked while Octo-Cat purred beside her.

"Nobody knows Rhonda's dead except the people we've spoken with… and, well, I guess the killer knows, too. I say we pretend to have an urgent message for her and use that as an excuse to talk to the passengers who are awake."

"But Mistress is dead. How can we have a message for her?"

"I know that, and we know that. But most of the people aboard don't know that, so asking them won't freak them out, right?"

Grizabella's eyes shone bright as understanding swept over her. "Oh, yes!"

"So we're just going to go up to each person we notice who's awake and ask if they know where we can find Rhonda?" Octo-Cat asked, rejoining the conversation with a sappy grin stretched between his whiskers. Ahh, the power of love.

"Pretty much," I said. "I'll do the talking, obviously. And you guys keep all your senses peeled."

Grizabella tilted her head to the side. "What does that—?"

"Human expression," my cat translated with a giant roll of his amber eyes.

"Sorry," I said with a chuckle. "You guys can smell changes in people's hormones, right? So if someone were to get really stressed by my questions, you could tell... Yes?"

"Yeah, humans are super easy to read," Octo-Cat responded haughtily. "Such simple creatures."

I scowled at him, then turned back to the Himalayan with a smile. Finally, she was on my side, and it felt great. "Are we ready to do this?"

"Let's." She rose to her feet and waited for me to open the door into the next car for her. We'd made our way back to the very front of the train a few cars in front of the one that held my family's seats.

"Excuse me," I said to a woman who sat with a sullen looking teenager who was immersed in her phone. Probably not our killer, but I had to talk to everyone to avoid suspicion. "Do you know where I can find Rhonda Lou Ella Smith? I have an urgent message for her."

"Nope," she answered with a slight shake of her head. "I'm sorry. Good luck."

I'm going to need it.

I talked to several more people, both men and women of all ages, but not a single person showed any sign of recognizing the name. I checked with the cats between each car, just to make sure they hadn't found something.

They hadn't.

We entered the car that held our seats, and I immediately

spotted a problem that I'd forgotten we had. Our special writer friend Melvin Mann paced up and down the aisle, talking to himself and eliciting the stares of every single person as he did. No one here was sleeping. Not a single soul.

"Melvin, what are you doing?" I shouted, rushing toward him.

"Trying to figure out the murder, of course," he told me, tapping a pen against the fingers on his other hand.

Someone cleared his throat across the aisle, and I laughed nervously. "Um, Mel. This isn't the best time to plot out your next novel. These people are trying to sleep." I laughed again and shoved him toward the end of the car, hoping and praying that our culprit hadn't been sitting in that car while Melvin prattled on about all the pieces of evidence he'd either collected or overheard.

As we approached the vestibule, I rasped in his ear, "Go back to the car. Dan and my parents are there. They'll get you caught up." I was hoping they wouldn't tell our resident loose cannon anything, but I needed to offer something to get him to fall in line.

"What car?" he asked, twisting toward me. A garish smile split his face as he realized. "Oh, the scene of the murder."

I pushed him through the door. "Get out of here, and—for goodness' sake—try to keep a low profile."

"Hey, I'm a writer, not an actor." He lifted a hand overhead and shook his finger at no one in particular. Not an actor, but he sure was a character.

I stood in the vestibule, watching to make sure he kept going toward the sleeper cars without upsetting any more of the passengers.

Grizabella paced and flicked her tail impatiently. "What now?"

"We keep going and hope for the best." I thought back over the details of the night, then smiled. "He wasn't pacing and muttering to himself when we passed through the first time, so he must have just started when the lights turned back on. Just to be sure, I'll shoot my dad a text and ask him to collect Melvin and get him away from the rest of the passengers."

My fingers moved over the keyboard on my phone. Eight

percent battery now, but we had light, which made the dying phone far less of a problem that it was before.

"Now, let's get on with our search," I told the cats, pushing into the next car, more determined than ever to find the murderer before circumstances beyond my control—or more specifically, Melvin—ruined everything.

CHAPTER FOURTEEN

I'd asked so many people if they knew where we could find Rhonda that my voice stung from overuse. The corners of my mouth also hurt from all the forced smiles. The cats and I had already hit up all the cars between the front of the train and the dining car, which meant there were only a few more to cross before arriving at the sleeper cars, and only a handful of those to try before we ran out of people to question altogether.

C'mon. C'mon, please. We have to find something.

I took a few more steps down the aisle, then turned to an older woman with shoulder-length black hair and large brown eyes rimmed with thick lashes. I could tell she'd been pretty in her youth because she was still stunning even now. She wore a hooded sweatshirt that you didn't often see women her age sporting, and she definitely didn't look like the type of person who'd have associated with Rhonda Lou Ella Smith, unless she was also a cat enthusiast.

I smiled and took a deep breath, leaning closer to her as I spoke. "Excuse me. Do you know where I can find Rhonda Lou Ella Smith?" I asked pleasantly, widening my smile as I waited.

She frowned and mouthed, "Sorry" without actually making a sound. Respecting her sleeping seatmate, how thoughtful. I'd been far less considerate in my search, jostling several passengers from sleep unintentionally.

"We've got a live one here!" Octo-Cat bellowed.

"She knows something," Grizabella confirmed in her melodic voice. "I can smell it all over her."

Showtime.

"Excuse me," I said to the woman who had already returned her attention to the paperback novel in her hands. "Are you sure you don't know Rhonda? It's really quite urgent."

"No. Now please let me return to my reading," she grumbled, then raised her book higher to block me out.

"She's lying!" Grizabella shouted. "She's lying!"

I pushed the book down and forced the woman to look me in the eye. "I'm sorry, but if you don't know Rhonda, then why are you acting so nervous?"

"Nervous?" she asked, then laughed nervously. How convincing. "I'm not nerv—"

"No more lies!" Grizabella cried, jumping right onto the woman's lap and unleashing a terrible hiss.

"G-G-Grizabella?" the woman stuttered. "What are you—?"

"So you do know her!" I widened my stance to block her into her seat in case she tried to make a run for it. I might be angering a violent criminal, but at least the train car was filled to the brim with witnesses. She wouldn't be so bold as to try anything in front of them… Would she?

The woman set her book down without even bothering to adjust the bookmark. "What's the message? Perhaps I can give it to her."

"It's really quite urgent. Would you come with me? The conductor's been searching for anyone connected with Rhonda, because we need your help. Urgently." Ugh. I needed to keep repeating urgent over and over again like it was some kind of magic passcode.

"But I thought you said you had a message for her?"

"Yes, and for you. Now will you join me, or should I call security?" I didn't even know if this train had security, but the threat worked to get the woman out of her seat.

I surreptitiously texted my mom and asked her to meet me in

the viewing car so we could escort the woman back to Rhonda's room together. For all I knew, she was the killer and could try to take me out at the first opportunity.

As much as I trusted my cat partners to want to protect me, they were no match for a human with a weapon and a motive. I needed to keep her talking as I walked behind her and guided her toward the sleeper cars. Maybe she hadn't figured out that I suspected her —or at least not yet.

"I'm Angie," I explained. "The conductor asked me to keep an eye on Grizabella since I have a cat of my own with me on the train," I yammered on. I needed to stop going on about the conductor every few minutes, but I didn't know what the other train people were called and I wanted to sound official.

"Is Rhonda okay?" the woman asked, trying to look back at me over her shoulder as we continued to stumble forward.

"Oh, yes," I lied, needing to get her somewhere private—and with backup—before sharing the truth. "Thank goodness we found you just in time. Say, how do you know her?"

"Oh, um, well, she's my sister. Half-sister, actually," she corrected herself immediately, then added, "We weren't close."

"I know how that goes," I said with a smile in case she looked back again. I was an only child, but I would do anything I could to keep her talking and moving, anything to build up some kind of rapport, seeing as it could just save my life. "What's your name?"

"Sariah Smith," she mumbled. "Will this take long?"

"Almost there," I promised as we finally headed into the viewing car. My mom was already there waiting.

"I know you," Sariah said, stopping in her tracks and raising a hand to point at my mother. "You're—"

Mom's hand shot out in greeting. "Laura Lee, Channel Seven News, serving Blueberry Bay, the great state of Maine, and now the full Northeastern Seaboard."

"I watch you on the news," Sariah stuttered. "What are you doing here? Investigating a story?" She glanced back toward the rear exit, but Mom placed a firm hand on her shoulder.

I moved toward the other end of the car, but Sariah didn't follow.

Mom jumped in to help out. "Yes, I'm investigating a story. And I need to speak with you, if you'll just come with me."

"Um, don't I need to sign a waiver or something?"

"Nope. This one's off the record. C'mon." Mom shoved her perhaps a bit too forcibly into the next car.

"Almost there," I assured her again, practically pulling her as Mom pushed from behind now.

"I don't think I can—" Sariah grunted. I'd have felt bad had I suspected she was innocent in all of this, but as the cats had said, she reeked of guilt. Even I could practically smell it with my weak human olfactory sense.

"And we're here," Mom announced before Dad swung open the door to Rhonda's room.

Sariah screamed the moment her eyes fell on Rhonda's dead body. She tried to run, but Mom and I formed a barrier in the doorway, blocking her misguided attempt at escape.

Sariah sobbed, choked, and screamed again. "Oh my gosh, what happened to Rhonda? Help, help, help! Somebody get me out of here!"

"We need to shut her up," Dad cried as Sariah continued to shout and shove at me and Mom. "What should we do?"

Melvin darted forward, a weapon held at waist height but disguised by his jacket. All I could see was an ominous bulge along with the manic rage splashed across his face, but from the way he postured, I was sure it had to be a gun under there. "Quiet, or I'll give you a reason to be quiet."

Oh my gosh, this was wrong on so many levels. A very big part of me wanted to tie Melvin up and stash him somewhere so he couldn't cause any more problems.

But then Sariah stopped crying and started confessing everything.

CHAPTER FIFTEEN

"Everyone calm down," Dad said in a patient, measured voice that must have been so hard to keep, given the current circumstances. He bravely stepped forward and inserted himself between Melvin and Sariah, daring either of them to continue acting out. "There's no need for things to turn violent."

Melvin stepped around dad and narrowed his gaze on Sariah. "There is, if she doesn't start talking and fast."

"That's not ne—"

"He wasn't supposed to hurt her!" Fat tears rolled down Sariah's cheeks and onto her sweatshirt. "You have to believe me. I didn't know he was going to hurt her."

"Who?" I asked from the doorway, anxiety ripping the words from my throat. If Melvin shot at Sariah, the bullet would likely tear into me, too. I so did not feel like dying today.

"Who wasn't supposed to hurt her?" I asked again when she failed to answer.

Our witness cried so hard she staggered forward, barely able to keep herself on her feet.

Mom draped Sariah's arm over her shoulder and guided her over to the bed. "C'mon, sweetie. It's okay. You're safe with us."

Melvin followed, his weapon still threatening from beneath his jacket. "That's right. As long as you keep talking, then you have nothing to worry about." I wanted to bonk him on the head. Couldn't he see that he was terrifying everyone around him?

Dan twisted the lock on the door, then looked to my father for guidance, who crossed his arms over his chest and took up sentinel at the room's one exit point.

It was like we were billiard balls. All of us suddenly rearranging, bouncing into new positions, staying near the edges of the room. I moved close to where Rhonda still lay splayed across the floor. That way, every time Sariah spoke to me, she'd be forced to glance upon her dead half-sister. It wasn't to be cruel, but rather to keep her honest and remind her how much was at stake here.

Not just for her, either. For all of us.

"Who wasn't supposed to hurt her?" I pressed again, keeping my voice kind and hopefully free of judgment.

Sariah sniffled and shook her head. Perhaps we needed a more indirect approach to ease her into talking.

"You know, I met her," I said with a far-off smile, even though the past I was remembering had only happened several hours prior. "We sat together for a while in the dining car and talked cats."

Mom handed Sariah a tissue from her purse, and she blew her nose into it. "That sounds like Rhonda all right."

"I thought you weren't close," I pointed out, again trying my best not to sound accusing even though Sariah had for sure played some part in the crimes that had happened aboard this train tonight.

She shook her head and balled the tissue in her first. "We weren't, but I follow her online. That's how I recognized Grizabella."

The cats. I hadn't noticed where they'd gone.

"Over here," my tabby called from near the bathroom, either reading my mind or sensing the worry that crept up on me when I realized I'd lost sight of him.

I turned toward him and smiled upon spotting him unharmed and unafraid.

Grizabella, however, stared at Sariah with fierce, unblinking eyes. She needed the answers, needed to know why this horrible thing had happened to her mistress.

"You said he wasn't supposed to hurt her," I reminded Sariah again, approaching my follow-up differently this time. "What was he supposed to do instead?"

Sariah shook her head and peered at me through red-rimmed eyes. Apparently, my sudden change in questioning had thrown her. "He was only supposed to take what's ours. That's it."

"And what was that?"

"The necklace."

The image of that beautiful piece of jewelry flashed in my mind's eye. Pearls, gold, amazing craftsmanship, but worth killing for? Not to me.

"The family heirloom?" I asked.

"Yes, she was wearing it tonight. I saw her when she came off the train to speak with us at the Bangor station."

That's right. I knew I'd seen her on the platform. With Sariah here, all the pieces were finally starting to feel like they belonged to the same puzzle. Soon we may even be able to discern the picture. I suspected I knew what happened next but asked anyway. "What did you talk about?"

"We asked for the necklace back. She never should have gotten it." Sariah balled both of her hands into fists, then let them go, looking at me with equal parts anger and sorrow.

"I'm guessing she said no."

"He barely even got two words out before she turned away and ran back for the train."

"Then what happened?" I asked.

All the others in the room remained quiet as Sariah and I continued our conversation. They all needed to hear this, too.

She turned to Mom and addressed her answer there. "He said that one way or another the necklace would be ours, and then we followed her onto the train. He knew she would say no, so we were already ready with the tickets."

"And what was the next part of your plan? What were you supposed to do after she said no?"

"Not my plan. His. I was supposed to find a way to stop the train in the middle of the night so that he could pay her a visit and take the necklace back. Then we were going to meet in the viewing car and exit together from there."

"But you're still here," I pointed out with raised eyebrows.

Sariah faced me once more. "Yes. He never showed up."

Desperation clawed at the edges of my brain. I so badly wanted to know who the he in Sariah's story was, but there were other details I needed to find out first—rather than risk her breaking down again.

"Why did you both want the necklace so badly?"

"It rightfully belonged to us. It had been passed down for generations, long before our ancestors ever settled in America. Not only is it worth a fortune, it has sentimental value, too."

"So it's a family thing, but you said yourself that Rhonda was family." I crossed my arms over my chest and waited, hoping my words had the incendiary effect I wanted. If so, they could blow this whole thing open and finally get Sariah to reveal the identity of her mysterious partner, the he.

"No." She closed her eyes and her cheeks turned red, but still she spoke. "Her family took everything from us. And it was a cold, hard slap to the face when Father gave the necklace to her instead of one of us."

I didn't say anything, hoping Sariah would volunteer more on her own. When she didn't, someone else stepped in.

"How did her family hurt yours, sweetie?" Mom asked from her spot beside the sobbing witness. Most of her tears had dried up now, however, anger taking their place.

"When I was five, my father left to start a new family. He said he had fallen in love and the lady was pregnant, so he had no choice. But he did have a choice! He just didn't choose us. He left and he took everything from us. All of the money and privilege that should have been our birthright went to the new family, went to Rhonda.

So, when he told me his plan to get our necklace back, of course, I wanted to help. Wouldn't you?"

"I understand where you're coming from," I said, nodding along. "I also believe that even though you hated Rhonda, you hadn't planned for her to die."

She straightened and sat taller on the bed. Some of the tension drained from her fists and tightly set jaw.

There, I'd given her something important. Now she had to help by providing that final piece we so desperately needed. "Can you do me one last favor and tell me whose plan it was? We need to know who hurt Rhonda so that we can make sure you and everyone else on this train stays safe."

"He's not going to lay a finger on me. I'll kill him first," Sariah said between clenched teeth, and I believed her.

"But who is he? Who's he, Sariah?" I practically begged now.

"He is our brother. Jamison."

CHAPTER SIXTEEN

A ll eyes were on Sariah, including mine.

"There," she growled at Melvin, who still held his weapon at the ready. "I've told you everything I know, so how about you stop threatening me with that gun or knife or whatever you have in there?"

Melvin snickered and pulled the weapon from his jacket, causing us all to flinch as he tossed it onto the bed beside Sariah. "As they say, the pen is mightier than the sword." The smug grin on his face showed just how clever he felt he'd been.

Sure enough, a gold-tipped fountain pen lay on the comforter, shining in the light cast down from overhead. A pen!

Crazy Melvin had proven useful, after all.

"Gotcha!" he cried, and I half-expected him to break out into an endzone-style victory dance.

A collective groan rose throughout the room.

Sariah sneered at the false weapon, then picked it up and threw it back toward Melvin. "Figures."

"How did you stop the train?" Dad asked, pointedly ignoring Melvin.

The writer withered when he realized we wouldn't spend the

rest of the night applauding his clever ruse. But our investigation was far from over. We still hadn't caught the killer.

"That's easy for a mechanical engineer," Sariah answered with a casual shrug.

"No one has been able to get the engine going again, but they were able to get power back," Dan added from his place beside Dad.

Our witness chuckled wearily. "Lights, that's electrical engineering. Not my area."

Clearly, this woman was very educated. Being abandoned by a parent definitely sucked, but did she really end up having such a bad life? Were things truly bad enough for Jamison to murder Rhonda as a way of paying for their father's sins? Everything in me screamed no.

My own family had a twisted backstory, one Mom and I had only recently discovered and still didn't quite understand. But I would never in a million years hurt someone for answers—or for revenge.

I guess that's why I was the P.I. and not the murderer. And thank goodness for that!

"Have you seen Jamison since the train stopped?" I asked, remembering my role.

"No. Like I said, he never turned up at our meeting spot. The jerk probably made a run for it without me."

"He was probably trying to frame you for it," Melvin pointed out. "That's what I would do if I had to write a character like that. As a novelist, I mean."

When still no one gave him the attention he craved, Melvin cleared his throat, then quieted again.

"We did find a bit of blood outside the train," Dad offered, bringing all eyes to him.

Sariah sighed and fell back on the bed, making us all tense. "Well, then, there you go. Betrayed by both my siblings in one night. Yay me."

"Sariah," Mom said gently. "I don't think Rhonda ever meant to hurt you. It's not her fault, what happened with your family. Things were probably hard for her growing up, too."

"She was lonely all the time," Grizabella said softly from her spot by the bathroom. "My poor, poor mistress."

Since Sariah couldn't understand Grizabella's words, she spoke over them. "Well, whatever the case, I'm sure the cops are on their way to arrest me, and meanwhile Jamison gets away with the whole thing."

"He's not going to get away with it," I promised. "We know it was him, and I'm sure the police will agree." We'd solved the murder. Catching the bad guy should be the easy part, right?

Sariah sat up and shook her head bitterly. "Yeah, but he's gone. He got away."

"Not necessarily," Octo-Cat piped up as he crossed the room to stand at my side. "Remember how cats are superior to humans in pretty much every way?"

I wanted to respond to that—if only to set the record straight, lest he later claim I had agreed with him—but we had a room full of people who didn't know my secret. Instead of asking him to explain himself, I widened my eyes at him, willing him to explain.

Thankfully, he understood. "Yeah, yeah, you don't want to talk in front of the others. Anyway, cats are awesome. Cats are the best, and this cat can find that killer who's on the loose."

"Yes!" Grizabella cried in delight. "Yes, we can sniff him out. Brilliant idea, my darling."

Octo-Cat became stock still, turning only at his neck to stare at the Himalayan with bright, beseeching eyes. "Your darling?"

She nuzzled him and purred. Everything about her softened. "And my hero."

Octo-Cat melted like a giant slab of butter. "Oh, Grizabella. I'm so glad you love me back! I will devote all my lives to you. At least all the ones I have left. I will never let you down. I—"

"Will you help avenge my mistress?" Grizabella asked pointedly.

"Oh, yeah, baby."

The cat soap opera playing out before me would have been cute under any other circumstances, but right now, we had a bad guy to catch.

"Sariah, I have an idea," I said, eager to get on with it.

"Sure, it was your idea," Octo-Cat scoffed, then immediately went back to cuddling and licking his new girlfriend.

"What I told you before about watching Grizabella because I have a cat, too, that was true. But I didn't tell you that my cat is also a highly trained stunt cat. We were, uh, on our way down to Georgia to do some work on an upcoming film before all this happened. Anyway, Octavius here is extremely well trained, and I think if we give him something of Jamison's, he could use it to track the scent and find our guy."

Sariah studied Octo-Cat as if trying to decide whether he was up to the task. In the end she frowned and said, "Great thought, but Jamison's probably made it pretty far by now. What's the point?"

"Probably. But, then again, do you know how fast a cat can run?"

"I'm not really familiar with—"

"Up to thirty miles per hour," Melvin interjected, waving his phone to show us he'd found the answer in record time.

Sariah quirked an eyebrow and glanced at Octo-Cat again. "Okay, that's pretty fast, but how are you sure your cat will even stay on his trail? And aren't you a little worried about sending him out there on his own? It sounds like he's really valuable if he's a celebrity and all that."

"Well…" I pretended to hesitate, seeing as Sariah seemed to need a few more moments to get on board with the idea. "Let's just say I trust him, and I know he can do this for us."

"I've seen him in action before," Mom said from her perch on the bed. "And she's right, that cat is pretty incredible."

"Thank you, thank you," Octo-Cat said, waving his paw at his subjects.

Grizabella cooed and cuddled closer to his side.

Dad asked what we all needed to know. "So do you have something of Jamison's or not?"

CHAPTER SEVENTEEN

Sariah took off the hooded sweatshirt she wore, revealing a beautiful fitted blouse beneath. "This is his," she said, tossing the sweatshirt to me, then reaching her arms up to hug herself and replace the lost warmth.

"Thanks. I'll get him started on the scent outside. Everyone else stay here. He doesn't work as well with a crowd."

"Why not?" Grizabella asked, intertwining her tail with Octo-Cat's in what had to be the feline version of footsie. "I love an adoring audience."

He lifted his head and sniffed the air for no obvious reason. "She says things like that sometimes so the other humans don't figure out she can talk to us."

"Octavius!" I called, moving toward the door and making a clicking noise. "Here kitty!"

He groaned as he trotted after me. "Enough with the kitty already. You know I don't like that."

Grizabella followed us outside into the dark tunnel. Luckily, the now illuminated train cars cast enough light to save me from having to use my remaining battery on the flashlight function.

I set Jamison's sweatshirt on the ground. "Can you get anything from this?" I asked my cat.

He took a big whiff of the fabric, then sneezed. "Whoo, boy. It's got that lady's stench all over it. There is a thing as too much perfume, honey."

"A lady can never make too many efforts with her presentation," Grizabella purred. Leave it to a D-list Instagram celebrity to side with vanity.

I bit my lip and said a silent prayer for patience. The thing about working with cats was that it would always be on their timetable.

"Can you smell him, too? Or is she too overpowering?" If this didn't work, I had no idea what else we could do, especially since Sariah seemed to believe that her brother would have no trouble evading the authorities.

"Yeah, I got him, too." Octo-Cat yawned and stretched each of his four legs, one by one—showing off for his lady friend, no doubt. "Let's do this!"

She appeared to swoon at his heroic catliness. Whoo, boy, indeed.

"Wait." I crouched down, so that I was closer to his height. "I don't have a way to track you. We didn't bring your pet GPS and my phone is going to die any minute. It's dangerous, and you're going it alone. Can you promise me—?"

"He's not going alone." Grizabella stood, fierce determination swirling in her blue eyes. "I'm going, too."

"My love, I couldn't possibly ask this of you. As Angela said, it's dangerous. I've already injured one toe bean in pursuit of this investigation. I could never risk your lovely toe beans like that." Octo-Cat nuzzled Grizabella, but she stepped away before he could make contact.

"Rhonda was my human. I owe this to her." The Himalayan took a deep breath and then took off in an impossibly fast run. The only time I'd ever seen Octo-Cat move anywhere near that fast was on the rare occasion when he had the zoomies—and we weren't allowed to talk about that.

"What a woman!" he said, taking one glance back at me before sprinting after her.

"But I don't know how I'll find you!" I called into the lonely tunnel, but it was too late. Both cats had already disappeared from view.

Please, please, be safe.

I turned back toward the train and found Dad waiting in the doorway.

"I wanted to give you some privacy in case you needed it," he said, stepping down to join me on the gravel. "Is everything okay?"

I looked back down the tunnel longingly. "Yeah. I just worry about the dangerous things he gets himself into sometimes."

Dad laughed. "Believe me, I know how that goes. Both you and your mom are going to put me in an early grave."

I shivered, not wanting to think about my dad or anyone else dying. I'd already seen more than enough to last a lifetime. Some occupational hazards were harder to accept than others.

"We'll do anything to take care of our kids. That's what being a parent is about." Dad's voice was soft, kind. "And before you say anything, yes. A pet parent is still a parent."

Octo-Cat would hate hearing himself referred to as my child, but sometimes it really felt as if he were. I knew Mom and Nan would move mountains to protect me, too. I'd always been loved, protected, valued…

And suddenly I knew that Dad's words referred to so much more than their surface meaning. "Nan and my real grandparents," I stated simply.

Dad nodded. "Just because you're not blood, that doesn't mean she isn't your real family," he said, echoing my thoughts from earlier. "She gave up so much to keep your mom safe, even though she didn't know why at the time."

"We still don't know why." I wanted to know so badly for myself, for my mom, but more than anything, for Nan who had lived her whole life having no idea why this strange, scary, and even wonderful thing had happened to her.

Dad chuckled again. "Between you and your mom? You'll figure it out in no time. If there's one thing I've learned in life, it's to always bet on my girls."

I wrapped my arms tight around him. Even though we'd never been very close, I'd never had to doubt his love for me.

"This whole trip has been a lot," I told him once we released our embrace. "I just don't know if I have the energy for two weeks meeting the family now."

"Then we'll go home. Just as soon as we can get off this danged train, anyway." He glanced around, then chuckled again. The tension lessened with each sound of my dad's laugh. It was one of my safe places. "Well, you know what I mean. As soon as we're out of this tunnel and allowed to officially disembark."

"Won't they be mad, though? The family in Georgia?" As much as this entire situation wrung my heart out like a soapy dishrag, I was still excited to meet them, to see our family grow despite the unusual circumstances. Could I really risk ruining that?

Dad shook his head and smiled reassuringly. "We've waited this long to meet them. Heck, we didn't even know they existed until a few weeks ago. It can wait—they can wait—until you're rested and ready."

"That's good. Because I really need to get home and be with Nan," I said, desperate to be reunited with my favorite person. Nan had raised me. She'd become my very best friend, and I just didn't feel normal without knowing she was nearby.

"I know you do," Dad said, and we hugged again. "I know you do."

CHAPTER EIGHTEEN

J ust over half an hour later, the police arrived and swept through the train. They kicked us out of Rhonda's room to secure the scene. While two officers investigated the body, another officer took Mom, Dad, me, Sariah, Dan, and Melvin to the viewing car to keep an eye on us while a detective questioned us one by one outside.

"I hadn't met Rhonda before the train, no," I assured the detective, but I could sense the suspicion lingering in her eyes.

She looked down and referenced her notebook. I had to wonder how well she could actually see in the dim light of the tunnel.

"Then why did you spend nearly two hours with her in the dining car?" she asked.

And I answered with a shrug. "Just being friendly."

"Angela! Angela!" Octo-Cat bellowed in the distance.

"Did you hear that?" the detective asked me, tilting her head to listen.

"Angela! Angela!" he cried again. To the detective, his words probably sounded like a horrible caterwauling.

"Yes, I think it's my cat," I said, equally excited and afraid of what news he would bring.

"Strange noise for a cat to make," the detective observed.

"Angela! Angela!" my cat cried again, growing closer and closer to where we stood. A few moments later his fuzzy body hurtled into mine, and he screamed again. "Angela! Angela!"

"Stand back, that animal could be dangerous!"

"He's just my cat. See." I scooped Octo-Cat up and cuddled him to my chest to show her he meant no harm.

He panted heavily, which he never did. The poor guy must have been running for a very long time—or be very, very stressed. I was hoping for the former.

"Can we get him some water?" I asked her as his panting continued unchecked.

"No... time," he wheezed, then hacked, then tried to speak again. "Griz... abella. We... have to... go to her!"

The detective studied me carefully. "Ma'am, is everything okay?"

Ma'am? I was younger than she was. Okay, not important right now. I needed to figure out my next step, and I needed to do it in a way that didn't raise suspicion.

Earlier that night I'd told Dan, Sariah, and Melvin that I was a celebrity pet trainer as an excuse for setting Octo-Cat on the trail. And now it was time to take on another false persona with the detective. I just hoped she would buy it.

I swallowed hard and then raised my eyes to meet her questioning gaze head on. "I know this may seem a bit unorthodox, but I'm a psychic, you see, and I believe the victim's ghost is telling me where to find her killer."

She placed a hand on her hip. "Her ghost?"

"Yes." Sorry, Rhonda, but this is the best way to catch him. "Rhonda says he's moved quite a way from the train. We'll need a vehicle to get to him."

"Yes, good!" Octo-Cat cheered. His words seemed to be coming more easily now. "I can take you... to her. To them."

The detective tipped her chin and quirked an eyebrow. "So you need a police escort?" she asked slowly, either to mock me or to make sure she understood.

"I know it's crazy, but——"

"Let's go," the detective said, surprising me with her sudden agreeableness. "Our department has been known to work with psychics from time to time, and right now you're the best lead we've got. The cruiser's about half a mile that way." She pointed down the tunnel, then turned back to me. "Try anything funny, though, and I won't hesitate to make an arrest."

When I nodded my consent, she took off in the direction she'd pointed earlier. It was the opposite way from the path Octo-Cat had taken to return to us.

I followed, keeping Octo-Cat in my arms because I could tell he needed the rest. While I grew more tired, he regained some of his strength.

"We found him," he explained as my feet scrambled for purchase on the uneven terrain. "And Grizabella was marvelous. She scratched him up real good. He threw her, and I think she may have gotten hurt. But she wouldn't leave his side. She sent me back to get help while she continued to track the bad guy."

Well how about that? Grizabella had proven to be the hero, after all.

I just hoped she was okay from the injury she sustained during her fight with Jamison. I hated not being able to comfort Octo-Cat while we were in the presence of the detective, but I had to believe he understood that I would do everything I could for both Grizabella and Rhonda.

At last we reached the end of the tunnel and broke out into the open sky. The sun had just begun to rise, infusing the clouds with celestial fire—beautiful and eerie at the same time. The cruiser sat facing the tunnel, and the detective and I both bolted for it.

I climbed in the back, just in case I was still a suspect. We'd already lost so much time, and I couldn't cost us anymore until I knew that Grizabella was safe, and Jamison had been apprehended.

"You can sit up front, you know," the detective said, studying me in the rear-view mirror. A smile crept across her face as she spoke. So maybe I wasn't a suspect, after all.

"I can't smell anything from in here," Octo-Cat informed me

from the footwell. Either the detective hadn't noticed I'd brought him along or didn't really mind.

"I'm fine back here," I assured her, buckling in for what was sure to be a wild ride. "But could you please roll down the windows? My, uh, powers work better when I'm one with nature."

She nodded and lowered both of the front windows.

"Ahh, that's better. They're this way." Octo-Cat moved his body to the car's left.

"Let's start by going left," I told the detective.

The engine roared to life, and we were off.

"How fast should I be going?" she asked, and I had no idea what to tell her.

Octo-Cat moved to the right of the footwell. "This way, but not too much this way."

"Make a right, but not a full right," I instructed, ignoring her earlier question, focusing on what I did know instead of what I didn't.

She guided the cruiser in the direction I'd indicated.

"Too far. Too far!" Octo-Cat cried and moved back toward the left.

"Um, less right than that," I said. "Bring it back to the center a little."

Man, it was hard to give driving directions when there were no roads and I had no idea where we were actually going. Still, I trusted my cat, and I knew he'd get us there one way or another.

"Perfect," he said after the detective had finished her course correction. He hopped onto the bench seat beside me and then climbed onto my lap. "Now straight on to my Grizabella."

CHAPTER NINETEEN

W e drove for a good twenty minutes before I finally spotted movement on the horizon.

Octo-Cat noticed her at the exact same time as me. He screeched and dug his claws into my lap. "She's there! My beautiful Grizabella! We've found her!"

Sure enough, the Himalayan trotted across the landscape ahead. Her beautiful fur appeared almost ghastly in the soft morning light and her once perfect gait now fell unevenly, but she was alive and still moving forward. I had to admire her determination to see this through.

Even though she'd seemed more than a bit spoiled when I first met her, she was a good cat. A really good cat.

"Suspect sighted." The detective jolted her cruiser forward even faster than before, then veered to a stop.

"Tell Rhonda's ghost she did a good job," she told me before racing outside to chase the man hobbling down the hill.

Octo-Cat sprinted through the open door after her, but rather than following the detective, he turned back the way we'd come. "My darling! My darling!" he cried.

As much as I wanted to help, I stayed put in the back of that cop car and sent a quick text to my parents in a group chat: We found Jamison. Detective is apprehending him right now. All is good.

And with that, my battery finally gave out, rendering my phone useless.

Less than five minutes later, the detective returned, dragging a handcuffed man along with her. "Get to the front, psychic," she barked at me.

As soon as I got out, she shoved Jamison in. For a moment, my eyes met his and I was surprised to see that they weren't cold or calculating. Instead, they appeared soft, kind, not so unlike my father's. A smattering of freckles on his cheeks and nose gave him a boyish appearance. Bloody scratches covered his arms, and his shirt had even been slashed through, thanks, no doubt, to Grizabella's attack.

This guy didn't look like a killer at all, and yet I had no doubt he'd done the deed.

"Meet me outside the tunnel," the detective murmured into her radio as she brought the police cruiser back to life.

"Wait!" I shouted, panic rising in my chest. "My cat!"

"I'm bringing the witness back, then taking the suspect in," the detective continued on, ignoring me completely.

The cruiser hadn't picked up much speed yet, so I swung open the door, unbuckled my seatbelt, and prepared to jump. Seeing what I was up to, she hit the brakes hard, jerking me clear out of the car.

I fell to the cold ground, landing on my back in such a way that all the air whooshed out of my lungs. Ouch.

Despite the nagging pain, there was no time to waste. I was okay, and I had to make sure the cats were, too. I sat up in a hurry, wincing from the pain of making such a sudden movement.

"Oh, Angela," Octo-Cat said with a light-hearted chuckle as he and Grizabella approached from nearby. Despite her limp and obvious fatigue, they fell into perfect step beside each other. "I may be a stunt cat, but you are definitely not a stunt human."

I couldn't tell whether he was just giving me a hard time or if he actually believed the lie I'd said about him earlier. Knowing him, I'm sure he believed every word of it.

"You were very brave," the Himalayan told me. with an approving nod.

"But not as brave as you, darling," Octo-Cat cooed in that special lovestruck voice he reserved expressly for his new girlfriend. "You were marvelous. Miraculous, even."

She giggled, and I pushed myself back to my feet with more difficulty than I would have liked. Ouchie ouch ouch. "C'mon, guys. Let's get back to our ride."

I let myself back in through the passenger side and both cats leaped up to join me.

The detective did not look happy. "That stays between us," she said in a low growl. "I'm already going to get a hard time for consulting a psychic on this case. The last thing I need is for the guys at the station to hear about you hurling yourself from the car before we even hit ten miles per hour."

"But you said—"

"I know what I said. Turns out you're not the only one who can bend the truth a little to get the job done." She glanced at Octo-Cat, then back toward me and winked.

My jaw hit my chest. Not really, but whoa.

What? How could she possibly…?

No, it didn't matter. Even though I had no idea how she'd figured it out, I knew my secret would be safe with the detective.

By the time we made it back to the tunnel—and thus the train—the sun hung high in the sky and the day was alive with energy. The detective's partner waited with Mom and Dad outside the tunnel.

When they saw me get out of the cop car, they ran forward. Mom hugged me from the left, and Dad hugged me from the right.

"Why are you all dirty?" Mom swatted at my pants, trying to brush the mud and dirt away. I glanced down and saw just how messy I'd gotten as a result of my fall from the cruiser.

Oh, well. Clothes could be cleaned or, if needed, replaced. What we'd all just been through together was worth so much more.

"It's a long story," I hedged. "What time is it, anyway?" I asked, suddenly feeling the weight of fatigue washing over me. I'd only gotten a few hours of sleep sitting in the viewing car before this latest murder mystery had consumed the rest of the night and early morning hours.

"Why don't you check your phone?" Dad asked with a smirk.

"I can't because it—" I stopped and laughed sarcastically when I realized his joke. My parents were never going to let me live my low phone battery down.

"It's about seven thirty," Mom said, stifling a yawn of her own. "Dad told me you were thinking about heading home instead of finishing our trip down to Larkhaven."

Guilt washed over me. Mom had really been looking forward to this trip, and now I'd ruined it for her. No, this was important. I could summon strength and mental fortitude from somewhere. "Yeah, but we don't have to if—"

Mom shook her head and smiled. "I think it's a great idea. I'll call the family in a couple of hours and let them know. Hopefully, by then the techs will have us moving again. We heard they were bringing in a new engine to take us back to the nearest station."

I met my mom's smile with one of my own. "Smart. Even if they continue, I bet nobody's going to want to keep traveling aboard that murder train. At least I wouldn't want to."

We stood together, watching the police work, saving up our energy for the half-mile walk back through the tunnel. I watched as Octo-Cat tended to his girlfriend's wounds in a nearby patch of grass.

Sure, their love story was still on its first chapter, but already he was a changed cat. My heart ached, knowing that we may never get the chance to see her again, to even know where she'd ended up.

"You're worried about her. Aren't you?" Dad asked, motioning toward the Himalayan with his chin.

"She loved Rhonda, and now she has no idea what's going to happen to her next." An idea struck me, allowing a brief burst of hope to fill me up. "Do you think Sariah will take her?"

"I think Sariah will go to prison as an accessory to murder," Mom said with a sigh. "Or at least for tampering with the train. Such a shame."

"Then what about Grizabella?" I asked, trying not to cry before we knew for sure what would happen. She'd literally lost everything when Rhonda died, and like Octo-Cat, she was accustomed to having only the best things in life. Would a new owner know how to care for her properly?

"I don't know, sweetie," Mom said, kissing the side of my head. "We can only hope for the best."

She was right. Grizabella's fate was out of our hands for now, but I would definitely be following up with the police every single day until they could tell me what had happened to her.

I owed it to Octo-Cat. I owed it to Grizabella, and I owed it to that sweet lady on the train who had only wanted a friend to keep her company for a couple hours.

CHAPTER TWENTY

THREE WEEKS LATER

After a quiet Thanksgiving at home, life returned to its usual insanity. Nan crafted a custom advent calendar, which guided us through a series of over-the-top holiday festivities. A simple trip to get the pets' photos taken with Santa Claus had somehow managed to turn into a fresh murder investigation, and it was honestly even crazier than the one we'd looked into on the train.

Despite that little hiccough, Nan kept Octo-Cat, Paisley, and me busy practically every second of every day, and for that, I was incredibly appreciative. She was my nan, my favorite person in the whole wide world, and whatever the circumstances that had brought us together, I would always be grateful to have her in my life.

Yes, my little corner of the world had grown by leaps and bounds, but Nan would always be my original number one. That was one thing I knew could never change.

"Quick, quick!" Octo-Cat, a close number two, cried as he scratched at the door to my personal library, begging to be let in. "We won't have much time before she makes us celebrate again."

I laughed when he shuddered at the word celebrate as if it were the filthiest curse word he could possibly imagine.

Once inside the library, I booted up my laptop and logged into my Instagram account. Octo-Cat had begged for his own account, but as his parent and someone who wanted to protect our secret, I had insisted he use mine instead.

"My love!" he cried when a brand-new photo of Grizabella popped into our feed. She wore a Santa hat and an enormous scowl on her flat feline face. Peak cat.

Octo-Cat purred and rubbed his side against my computer screen, which is precisely the reason we no longer used his iPad to access Instagram. He couldn't help but snuggle her image, but always threw a fit when doing so accidentally booted him from the app.

I clicked heart on the photo and sat back in my seat. I knew this could take a while based on past experience. "Well, what would you like us to comment on this one?" I pressed when he did little more than purr and rub up against the screen for a solid five minutes.

"Tell her she's beautiful and I love her and miss her and cannot wait until fate brings us together again," he gushed, pausing briefly to actually look at the photo before he resumed all the rubbing.

I groaned at the melodrama but complied—very thankful I'd made my profile private. I was also thankful that I knew for a fact Grizabella's new owner read all the comments to her. Otherwise I would never agree to be these two lovebirds' go-between.

Still, no matter how embarrassing this all was for me, I loved how happy it made them both to keep up their long-distance relationship. Sometimes they even video-chatted and took naps together. It was super sweet, actually.

As for that new owner?

She was a friend of Rhonda's from the show cat circle. Christine. And even though they hadn't been close outside of the competitions, they'd always made sure to grab a meal together whenever they wound up in the same town—and that was as good as any friend poor, lonely Rhonda ever had.

Christine was a good one, though. She loved cats every bit as much as Rhonda had, which meant that Grizabella now had a host of new sisters, also award-winning show Himalayans.

Unfortunately, the injury Grizabella had sustained when Jamison threw her in their fight meant that her show days were over, but even though I knew she'd never admit it, I suspected Grizabella was happy to retire and live out the rest of her days as a well-loved pet and a very minor Instagram influencer.

I typed the comment: Octavius says, "She's beautiful and he loves her and misses her and cannot wait until fate brings them together again."

Christine and everyone else thought I was just being an overly dramatic pet owner with these comments, and I was happy to let them believe that. After all, I really did love my cat bunches.

Right after I pushed enter, the doorbell chimed to the tune of "Memories" from the Broadway show Cats. I hadn't realized Grizabella was named for the play, but Nan made the connection immediately and made sure we mixed in plenty of Andrew Lloyd Weber scores to complement our constant string of Christmas carols.

"I'll be right back," I told the swoony tabby.

He didn't even acknowledge me as I dismissed myself, such was the enormity of a new photo from his lady love—even though we got at least one of them every single day. Young love, adorable.

"Coming!" I called as I bounded down the stairs. The stained-glass windows that hung on either side of the entryway cast rainbow shapes against the hardwood floor but did not reveal the identity of the person waiting on the porch.

When I flung the door open, an unfamiliar young woman stood waiting with a suitcase at her side.

"Cousin!" she cried and reached out to hug me.

I awkwardly accepted her embrace, and upon pulling away, I realized that I did recognize her.

Mostly because her face was almost an exact replica of mine. We were also both tall and curvy. The most noticeable differences between us were the fact that her hair was so blonde it was almost white while mine took on more of a sandy brown hue. Also, I wore an awesome 80s inspired outfit while she sported a prim cardigan buttoned up to the neck and a flowing peasant skirt that reached down to her ankles. A giant gold filigree locket hung halfway down her chest, reminding me of Rhonda's heirloom necklace.

She bit her lip as she studied me, then started to panic, her skin turning bright red as she did. "Oh, no. You are Angie, aren't you? Oh my gosh. If you're not, I'm so embarrassed right now."

"I am Angie," I said with a friendly smile. "I just didn't realize anyone was coming."

"My aunt told your nan and… Let me guess, she didn't relay the message?"

"Sounds like your aunt and my nan have a lot in common," I said with a laugh. "Please, please come in."

I took her suitcase and set it by the stairs, then guided her to the kitchen in search of snacks. Snacks made everything better, especially Nan's homemade baked goods.

My cousin accepted a bottle of Evian and twisted the cap off at once. "You must have gotten quite the shock. I'm sorry nobody told you I'd be coming for the rest of the year."

This made me pause in my search. "The rest of the year?"

"Well, I mean it's just a couple more weeks, right? Sixteen days total, actually, just like you were supposed to have for your trip to Larkhaven. I couldn't wait to meet you, so Aunt Linda suggested I come to you instead. Only I flew instead of taking the train. I mean, who would want to take a train when there are so many faster ways to travel these days?" She giggled and made a funny face. If I hadn't already decided I liked her, that would have definitely done the trick.

I laughed again as I handed my guest one of the chocolate chip banana muffins that Nan had baked just yesterday. "Well, I may not have known you were coming, but I'm really happy you're here. This may be a teensy bit awkward, but… Um, what's your name?"

"Oh, gosh! Sorry! Mags McAllister here," she said, hugging me tight again and speaking around a mouth full of muffin. "Your long-lost cousin from Larkhaven, Georgia, and I can already tell that we're going to get along just great!"

Warmth spread through me as I relaxed into her embrace.

I'd never had a sister, brother, or cousin with Mom being an only child—a fact I constantly bemoaned growing up. But now with Mags here, I sensed how important this new cousin would become to me.

And even though I didn't quite know it yet, the next couple weeks would show just how important, indeed.

HOPPY HOLIDAY HOMICIDE

Pet Whisperer P.I.

ABOUT THIS BOOK

Nobody does the holidays like small-town Maine, and my particular small town just so happens to be the very best at decking the halls and rocking around the big Christmas tree downtown.

Yes, every year, Glendale puts on a Holiday Spectacular that's grander and greater than the one that came before. Unfortunately, the only thing everyone's going to remember this year is the two dead bodies that show up in the center of the ice sculpture garden.

With the whole town having come out to play, everyone's in close proximity to the crime scene—and everyone's a suspect. A great many fingers are pointed my way, too, since it was me and my cat that discovered the deathly duo. With only my whacky Nan, recently discovered cousin, overly optimistic Chihuahua, and snarky feline to help me, can I clear my name and save Christmas all in one perfectly executed investigation?

Hold on to your jingle bells, because it's going to be a wild ride.

CHAPTER ONE

Hi. I'm Angie Russo, and while you may not immediately recognize it, I'm probably one of the most unusual people you'll ever meet.

Why?

Well, how many other people do you know who can communicate with animals? And, no, I'm not talking meows, woofs, and chirps. We have actual conversations, and we even solve crimes together—but I'm getting ahead of myself here.

Before I say any more—*shhh!*—my strange ability is a secret that must be protected at all costs. Not because I'm in danger or anything, just because I'd rather people not know.

Okay?

And, no, I'm not a witch, werewolf, or other kind of fictional supernatural creature. I'm just a normal girl in her late twenties who got electrocuted by an old coffee maker and woke up with the power to communicate with animals.

First, it was just the one cat, Octo-Cat as I call him. He was in the room when I got zapped. We were both there for a will reading, me as the lowly paralegal and him as the primary beneficiary.

When he realized I could understand him, he revealed that his late owner had been murdered even though everyone thought the rich old lady had died of natural causes. Turns out that wasn't what had happened at all.

She'd been murdered, and now he needed me to help him prove it.

Well, we got justice for Ethel Fulton and eventually wound up living in her stately manor home. Since none of the relatives wanted Octo-Cat and I really, really wanted him, we ended up together, too.

We live with my eccentric grandmother, who's known around these parts simply as Nan. A few months ago, we also adopted a rescue Chihuahua named Paisley. She's the sugar to Octo-Cat's spice, and the cute little thing can never say a bad word about anyone...

Well, except the naughty raccoon named Pringle who lives in our backyard. He used to live under the porch, but then he kind of blackmailed us into building him a custom treehouse—two tree-houses, actually. Oh, boy, is that a long story.

Speaking of long stories, I've got several of those. Just you wait.

You see, a lot has changed in the months since Octo-Cat and I officially opened our P.I. business together. We haven't had a single paying client yet, but we're still getting tons of experience by acci-dentally stumbling into one mystery after the next.

Hey, whatever works. Right?

Oh, also, I'm in love with my boyfriend and former boss, Charles Longfellow, III—although I haven't exactly told him that yet. Octo-Cat is also in a long-distance relationship with a former show cat and minor Instagram influencer named Grizabella. And he never stops telling her—or anyone who will listen—just how much he loves her. He's even started giving me guff about how slow Charles and I are moving by comparison.

Then there's the fact that we've discovered Nan isn't actually biologically related to me or my mom, but we're still working on digging up the full story there. Yes, this entire time, she hasn't understood the reason we were shoved together, either.

On the positive side of that crazy bit of news, we have connected with long-lost family in Larkhaven, Georgia. I was supposed to visit them last month, but a murder derailed our travel plans just a bit. So, instead, my cousin Mags showed up here and is staying through the end of the month.

Mags is a hoot, and we all love her. She and I have so much in common and look so much alike that I sometimes wonder if we're not actually twins instead of just cousins.

She's a couple years older than me, though, and as far as I can tell, she's completely normal. Her family owns a candle shop in her town's historic district, and she's promised to teach Nan and me how to make our own candles before she heads back home.

We have lots to do before that happens, though.

For one thing, it's almost Christmas. Nan keeps all of us busy with the custom advent calendar she made at one of her community art classes, and today we're also scheduled to head into town for the twelfth annual Holiday Spectacular!

The Holiday Spectacular is a time-honored tradition for our small town of Glendale. People come from all over Blueberry Bay to gather around the big tree downtown, compete in the ice sculpture competition, and celebrate Christmas with the staggering variety of small businesses downtown.

We get everything from hot cocoa stations to learning Christmas carols from around the world to meeting local authors and getting signed books from them to...

Well, each year is completely different, and that's what makes it so much fun. I can't wait to show Mags my hometown at its best. I hope she'll love it every bit as much as I do.

Hey, look at that, it's time to go find out!

I smacked my lips together after dragging my new cranberry red lip stain across them. Perfect for the holidays. Normally, I wore very little makeup, since my clothes made enough of a statement without any outside help. Lately, though, Nan had begun insisting I put a little more effort into my appearance. She claimed it was for all the holiday festivities, but I suspected she secretly hoped that my glamorous new efforts might rub off on my cousin, Mags.

It's not that Mags was plain, but she did prefer a simple, non-fussy wardrobe. While working in her family's candle shop in the historic district, she sometimes wore old-fashioned clothing with big skirts and a bonnet—and I suspected that was all the fuss she could handle. I didn't blame her for wanting to keep it easy during her leisure time.

Mags's signature knock sounded at my bedroom door—three short, one long, two short again.

"Come in!" I called, turning away from the mirror and toward the door.

Mags wore a white button-down shirt and white skirt with white flats. Her white-blonde hair fell midway down her waist, and her fair skin had not a stitch of makeup on it. She looked like a snow angel... or a ghost.

"Can I borrow an outfit from you today?" she asked with a frown. "I think I'm letting Nan down with my color choices."

I laughed. "Don't worry about Nan. I let her down constantly. She still loves us both, though."

"She offered to let me wear something from her wardrobe, but Angie—" Mags dropped her voice to a whisper and motioned for me to lean closer. "Everything's hot pink!"

We broke apart in giggles.

"Seriously, though, please help a cousin out," she begged, joining her hands in front of her and shaking them at me.

I skipped toward the closet, loving every minute of having my long-lost cousin here. I couldn't believe we had little more than a week left together. I was going to miss her so much when she went back home.

"How's this?" I asked, tossing a Santa-print party dress at her. It was the same one I'd worn when we took the pets to get their pictures done with Santa at the pet shop in Dewdrop Springs. While it was one of my favorites, I had tons of holiday wear that hadn't made it out of the closet yet this year.

That was the thing about doing most of my shopping at Good

Will: everything was so cheap and went toward a good cause, so I had zero issue indulging my addiction. Today I wore a pair of jeans with the ugliest Christmas sweater I owned—it had giant pom-poms stuck in a huge ring to form a three-dimensional Christmas wreath, complete with jingle bells and a giant satin ribbon.

It was wretched, and I adored it.

"This is perfect," Mags said after a quick appraisal of the dress.

"Goes good with pigtails," I said.

She turned crimson. "I think that's perhaps a little too much for today."

Octo-Cat trotted in with Paisley following close behind.

"Mommy, you look gorgeous!" the Chihuahua cried.

"One day that sweater will be mine," my tabby swore. "You can't tell me that's not meant to be a cat toy. Look at all those mischievous floofs!"

Well, he had me there.

"Mommy, can I come, too?" Paisley asked, her tail wagging so fast that it was little more than a black blur.

"She can't talk to us in front of Mags, genius," Octo-Cat said, looking bored with the whole thing.

Mags smiled at me, probably wondering why I had suddenly stopped talking when the animals entered. Let's just say it was incredibly hard to keep my secret from her, especially considering she was family. Still, the fewer people who knew, the better. And I didn't know if she would even believe me. I didn't want to send her screaming back to Georgia and ruin our relationship with the rest of the family before we even got the chance to meet them.

Just one more week to go. I could keep my secret for that long…

Um, right?

CHAPTER TWO

M ags looked absolutely adorable wearing my Santa-print dress. She complemented the look with a fuzzy white beret and then asked for my help applying that new cranberry stain to her lips and a bit of blush to her cheeks.

"Selfie time!" she cried, maneuvering her phone to capture a photo of us from several angles.

"Wow, we really do look alike," I said when she showed me the resulting pictures. Despite her fairer coloring, we both had the same brown eyes, perky nose, and heart-shaped face. She had the perfect poise of a supermodel while I had somehow managed to give myself a triple chin and the viewer a front-row view straight up my nostrils.

This right here was why I didn't find myself addicted to social media the way so many others in my age bracket tended to be. I'd much rather be behind the camera than in front of it, but if given the choice, I'd go for no cameras at all. I could thank being raised by two newscasters for that.

"You're way more photogenic than me," I mumbled as Mags texted our selfie to a few family members back in Georgia. I hadn't met any of them yet and wasn't super thrilled with the awful photo being one of their first introductions to me.

"It comes with lots and lots of practice," Mags revealed with a coy smile. Unlike me, she seemed much more comfortable interacting with people online as opposed to in person. "I'm on screen a lot for my candle-making videos, so I've learned my angles."

"Girls!" Nan called from the bottom of the stairs that led to my bedroom tower. "Ready to paint the town red? And green?" She chuckled at her own joke as she moved down the grand staircase and into the foyer.

Mags looked to me for confirmation as she stuck her phone into her small handbag and pulled at the hem on her borrowed dress.

A huge smile crossed my face as I yelled, "Coming!"

Mags, the animals, and I pounded down the two flights of stairs to the foyer where Nan had relocated to bundle up in an eclectic assortment of bright pink winter wear.

Nan pulled out a tiny brown jacket and knelt to the ground. "Paisley, come here, you sweet dog!"

The Chihuahua ran, her whole back half wiggling with joy. "Yes, Nan. Coming, Nan. I love you, Nan."

While she called me "Mommy," her greatest loyalty definitely lay with Nan. I'd asked her about that once, and she said that she couldn't remember what it felt like to have a mother since she'd lost hers when she was still too young to remember. Since Nan insisted on being called *Nan* by everyone who knew her—and because she couldn't communicate with Paisley the way I could—the little dog had taken to referring to me as *Mommy*.

She stood mostly still now as Nan worked her legs and head through the little brown jacket, which upon closer inspection was actually a reindeer costume. The hood had two tall, erect antlers that put Paisley off balance somewhat as she hopped away from Nan and attempted to prance about the house.

"Mags, you look lovely," Nan said as she straightened back into a standing position. "And you're well-matched to Paisley in that Santa dress, which is good because I'll need you to keep an eye on her while we're out."

"Oh, are you not coming?"

Nan shrugged into her hot pink coat lined with black faux fur around the collar and cuffs. "Of course I'm coming. But I need both arms for hugging all my old friends who only journey home for the holidays. Paisley will have a much better time with you."

I stepped forward and grabbed Octo-Cat's neon green leash and harness from the back of our coat closet. He hated having to wear it, especially since he'd gotten better about being off leash during our outdoor adventures. Unfortunately for him, I'd be with Mags the whole time today, which meant I couldn't use our ability to converse to keep him in line.

At the end of the day, safety won every time, which meant the harness was non-negotiable. Of course, that didn't stop my cat from trying.

"I'm not wearing that," he said, glaring at me as he spoke. "Last time you put it on me, Santa Claus got murdered. And before that, you granted me a favor in exchange for my compliance. That was a long time ago, so as far as I'm concerned, you owe me a whole new favor if you expect me to wear that thing today."

I shook my head and bit my tongue to keep from talking. The favor he'd tricked me into granting was the purchase of this giant manor home, since he didn't like my previous rental. As much as I liked the luxe estate now, I didn't think him wearing the harness a handful of times over the past year and a half was anywhere near equivalent of an ask.

I reached for Octo-Cat with both hands and he swatted at me.

"No, Angela. No!"

"I don't think he wants to wear that," Mags said with a nervous laugh. "Why are we bringing him, anyway? It seems to me that an outdoor festival wouldn't be very fun for a cat."

"Trust me, I'll never hear the end of it if I leave him behind," I said, then quickly added, "He'll be yowling for days to punish me, and mostly at night, because he's got an evil streak a mile wide."

"Smart cat."

"You have no idea." I chuckled with relief. You'd think I'd be better at minding my secret after so much time, but you'd be very, very wrong.

"Well, here." Mags grabbed Octo-Cat so quickly neither he nor I saw it coming. "Let me help."

He struggled and spun in her arms, but Mags held on tight while I worked the harness onto his furry little body. "You will live to regret this, Angela, and it might not be all that long."

I set him on the ground and stifled a laugh as he took a couple steps, twitched, and then frantically began to lick his fur where it touched the neon green straps.

"Are we all ready to go?" Nan asked cheerfully, completely unbothered by the angry kitty standing near her feet. While Octo-Cat generally held me to a higher standard of behavior and let Nan's foibles pass by unmentioned, one of these days, he'd get her, and he'd get her good. Hopefully, he'd at least wait until after the holidays.

A minute later we'd all piled into my sedan, and less than fifteen minutes later we'd arrived downtown for Glendale's Holiday Spectacular.

Even though it was early, we had to park several blocks away in order to get a spot.

"Wow," Mags said when downtown finally came into view. "It's like we're inside a snow globe."

We had half a foot of snow at best, but Mags never got white Christmases at home in Georgia, so I let her enjoy the moment without explaining the snowfall was actually light for this time of year.

"Welcome! Welcome to the Holiday Spectacular!" Mr. Gable, the owner of our only local jewelry store and the head of the planning committee, greeted us with his pet rabbit in one hand and an old-fashioned camera in the other. He wore a Santa costume without the classic fur-trimmed coat, revealing black suspenders on top of his thick wooly undershirt. "Have a seat on the sleigh. Let Santa and E.B. take your picture."

"E.B.?" Mags asked as she and I slid into the rear seat of the sleigh and Nan jumped up front with both animals.

"It's short for Easter Bunny," I explained, having just met the bunny for the first time myself earlier that month when we went to the pet store for photos with Santa and ended up solving a murder mystery instead. "Apparently, she was an Easter gift for the grand-kids gone wrong. He was quick to rescue the bunny and give her a better life, and the two have been together ever since."

Mr. Gable set E.B. in the nearby nativity scene which had been lined with hay and outfitted with food and water for the little rabbit, then he stepped forward to take our picture.

"Do you see that?" Octo-Cat demanded just as Mr. Gable instructed us all to say cheese. "That ridiculous rabbit has the exact same harness as me. I've never been so humiliated in all my life. Oh, you will pay mightily for this, dear Angela."

Sure enough, E.B. also wore a neon green harness, although she didn't seem to mind nearly as much as Octo-Cat did. In fact, she'd already fallen asleep cuddled up sweetly in baby Jesus's manger.

CHAPTER THREE

After getting our photo snapped at Santa's sleigh, we made our way over to the extreme cocoa station. Here, festivalgoers could order crazy custom concoctions with more flavor and mix-in varieties than even made sense for a cup of hot chocolate.

Seeing as we'd arrived at the very start of the festival, the crowds were still sparse, and that came with the added bonus of no lines. Mags and I stepped right up to the outdoor counter and ordered the unicorn drink made with white chocolate and swirled with raspberry, rainbow marshmallows, pink drizzle, sprinkles, and a gold-and-white candy cane horn. We watched in awe as the barista whipped up our order.

Nan took this opportunity to shout a quick goodbye and then disappear on the arm of a comely silver-haired gentleman I don't think I recognized. Nan knew everyone both in town and outside of it, but she hadn't dated a single soul since my grandpa's death more than a decade earlier. Judging by her coquettish laughter and sparkling eyes, I'd definitely have to learn more about this mysterious new friend of hers.

For now, however, I'd simply focus on this special time spent with my cousin and our two favorite animal companions as down-town Glendale did what it does best—celebrate the season.

"There you are," my mother crooned, rushing over to saddle both me and Mags with giant warm hugs. "Merry Christmas! Happy Holiday Spectacular!"

"Merry Christmas Eve, Mom," I said, grabbing my freshly delivered unicorn cocoa from the pop-up table and dropping a tip in the barista's gift-wrapped jar. It felt a bit odd to be wishing her a happy eve when it was hardly even ten o'clock in the morning.

The Spectacular ran from ten in the morning to ten at night, giving people all day to drop by and enjoy the festivities. Most favored the night hours because of the majesty and wonder added by the light displays, but I knew the committee was working hard under Mr. Gable to get more folks coming out early and spreading a steady stream of business out over the entire day.

"Where's Dad?" I asked, then took that first decadent sip of my sugary drink. *Mmm.*

Mom studied her reflection using her camera's selfie mode and fluffed up her hair as she answered. "The first reindeer game is about to begin, so naturally he's covering it for the station. It's the three-hooved race, sure to be a lot of fun."

Dad did the sports report for the local news while Mom was an anchor. She covered a lot of human-interest pieces around Maine, especially now that their broadcasts were viewed regionally, thanks to her role in solving the beloved Senator Harlow's murder.

And, naturally, the Holiday Spectacular had been big news since it first started. Tourists now came from out of state to celebrate the season with us, and each year, the festival became bigger and bigger, thanks in part to Mom's ace coverage of the event and to the expert leadership under Mr. Gable.

"I need to get back," Mom said, glancing back over her shoulder toward the games field. "But I saw the two of you from across the way and figured I'd dash over to ask a quick favor."

"We'd be happy to help," Mags said as she held Paisley tucked under one arm and the steaming souvenir mug filled with cocoa in her other hand. "Just tell us how."

"Great. It shouldn't take too much of your time, but it is really important. I'm afraid the judges for the ice sculpture competition are no-shows. Would the two of you mind filling in?"

"Not at all," Mags said, shaking her head so hard, some of her cocoa splashed onto the freshly shoveled street below. "Oops! Sorry about that. It sounds like a lot of fun judging, though. I'd be happy to help, if Angie is up for it."

"Wonderful. We have over thirty entries, if you can believe that, but you don't need to write up score cards or anything. Just pick first, second, and third place, and text me with what you decide. The ice sculpture garden is at the far end of our setup near the bridge and the little park. Think you can find it?"

"I know we can," I answered, taking a step toward Mom but being unable to go any farther without yanking my stubborn cat who refused to move from the spot. "Now go get back to Dad before you miss out on that race."

"Will do," Mom said, already jogging back in the direction from which she'd come. "Thanks again, girls."

"What do you say? Should we go now?" Mags asked, then took that first tentative sip from her half-emptied unicorn cocoa. Her eyes grew wide and her head shot back. "Wow, that's a lot of sugar."

I took another swig of mine and moaned in pleasure. "If you ask me, it's exactly right. Then again, you probably don't eat Nan's homemade baked goods every day of the week."

"I wish I did, though!" Mags enthused as we wound our way through the fancifully adorned streets.

We strolled past a number of local craftsmen and women peddling their wares, and I spied a particularly eye-catching necklace that I wanted to make sure we came back for once our judging duties were behind us.

Mags stopped dead in her tracks and gasped with glee. "Whoa, are those live reindeer?"

I laughed at the look of wonder that overtook my cousin. I'd been coming to the Holiday Spectacular since it was first founded twelve years ago, but I was sure seeing it all for the first time would make anyone drop their jaws to their chests like Mag was now.

"Yup, eight of them. There are also sheep, goats, pigs, and even a camel. It's a full petting zoo. Part Santa's workshop and part little town of Bethlehem."

"We've gotta come back." Mags grabbed my hands and gave one last longing look toward the animals. "I'm petting every single thing they've got in there."

"I promise we will," I said, squeezing both of her hands then letting go.

"I'd rather not spend my precious time around stinky, sweating cattle," Octo-Cat groused.

Well, too bad for him. He'd complain about whatever we did, and Mags was truly excited to come back and spend time among the reindeer.

We strode past more pop-up restaurants, merchants, and local groups manning their booths, progressing nearly a full block in our trek before Mags ground to a halt once again. "Candles!" she cried. "Oh my heart!"

I nodded toward the pair of women sitting outside the tent. Mags had already disappeared inside where it was dark, save for the glow of tealight candles set up carefully around the inside.

"She makes candles for a living," I explained to the ladies sitting outside the tent. I felt odd standing here with them while Mags was inside but knew better than to take my cat and dog into a space with open flames. "Yours are beautiful. How much are they?"

"We're not selling the candles," the younger of the two women explained with a kind smile. "We make and sell menorahs. Other members of our synagogue are also set up selling potato latkes a few booths down."

"Oh, for Hanukkah. I've never celebrated myself but have always loved the story about the Maccabees and the miracle of the oil."

"It's not just a story," the older woman said. "It's God working miracles. He still does that to this day, you know."

"How much is this?" Mags asked, rejoining us with a small silver menorah in her hands.

The women told her the amount, and she handed over a couple twenties. "Thank you. I will cherish it always. Happy Hanukkah."

"Happy Hanukkah," the women called after us as we continued toward the ice sculpture garden.

"They have a bit of everything here. Don't they?" Mags asked.

"You have no idea," I said with a giggle. "Just wait until we check out some of the reindeer games."

"I'm glad we got here nice and early. There's so much to do, I'm afraid we won't have time for it all."

"Well, here's the ice sculpture garden. Let's make sure we give each contestant fair consideration, then pick our winners and get back to the streets."

We crossed the road and entered the park where rows of enormous and intricately carved ice statues stood in a spiral configuration. A sign at the beginning of the path read: "Start here and follow the path until you reach the center. Once there, follow the red ribbon for a shortcut back to the start. Enjoy!"

"It's like the Guggenheim," I said, thinking of the fantastic museum I'd studied during my humanities coursework. "You never have to turn or think about where to go next, freeing you up to enjoy art for art's sake."

"Look at this one!" Mags cried, already a few sculptures down the path and admiring the carving of a swan splashing into water with wings spread wide. "Isn't it lovely?"

"How about this one?" I said pointing to a giant, elaborate snowflake. "It must have taken so much time to get all the details exactly right."

"It's sad that this gorgeous art is all going to melt away." Mags stood in front of the statue of a woman wearing a gorgeous flowing gown now. "And it's going to be very hard to pick just three to win."

"Let's start by just looking. Then when we reach the center, instead of taking the shortcut out, we can walk through again and try to make a short list of our favorites."

Mags nodded. "So far, everything is my favorite."

"It may take a few back and forths," I agreed. "So let's get started."

We walked through the spiral, admiring sculptures of animals, people, nature, and even abstract creations. Hardly any time had passed at all before we wound up in the center, and a swatch of bright red caught the corner of my eye. I turned toward it, expecting to see the promised ribbon that would guide festivalgoers out of the garden and prevent traffic jams.

Instead I saw deep pools of crimson marring the otherwise pristine snow. *Blood.*

CHAPTER FOUR

M y eyes darted to Mags, who stood trembling like a leaf in the wind.

"Is that b-b-blood?" she stammered, allowing Paisley to leap from her arms to the ground below. I hated it when the small dog took these bold leaps, but somehow she never seemed to get hurt when she collided with the ground.

Octo-Cat yanked on his leash. "Of course it's blood, genius. What else would it be?"

I glowered at him, sorely wishing I could reprimand him for being so insensitive in this delicate situation. "Yes," I whispered carefully to Mags. "And where there's blood, there may be a body. At least that's been my experience. Wait here while I take a look around."

Mags trembled even more violently and refused to meet my eyes. She kept her gaze fixed on the deep red as it crept through the snow, feeling more dangerous with each new inch it gained. Her hands shook harder and harder, sloshing the remaining cocoa from her mug.

Wow. Maybe Mags and I weren't quite as similar as I had once thought. While I didn't exactly enjoy finding myself in these situations, I'd learned to mostly control my emotions so that I could focus on the mystery rather than the horror. Mags, on the other hand, had already become a terrified, blubbering wreck—as most normal people would, I supposed.

I ran forward and took the cup from her, then set it on the ground with mine. Both of us had most definitely lost our appetite for the sweet stuff, anyway.

Paisley nuzzled my leg with her snout. "Mommy, is there a bad guy nearby? Is he going to hurt us?"

Without thinking, I scooped the little dog up, placing her under one arm, and grabbed Octo-Cat with my other.

"Angela, unhand me. I am not your cuddle toy. That's what this one's for," he said, jerking his head toward Paisley.

I remained quiet as we crept between the ice sculptures, searching for the source of the blood. It didn't take long for me to spot a large hand lying palm up beside a sculpture of a Christmas tree. I swallowed hard and stepped in for a closer look. There I found not one but two fresh corpses—one facing the sky with unseeing eyes and the other face down in the cold snow. From above, a light sprinkling of snowflakes danced through the air and landed on the bodies, giving them an impromptu beginning to their burials.

"Are these the missing judges?" I whispered.

"That would be the obvious conclusion," my tabby said, squirming beneath my arm.

My own blood ran cold as I wondered why someone would resort to murder and whether Mags and I were now at risk, having been the ones to take their places.

That's when I saw a thick glistening spear of ice rising from the smaller corpse's back. She'd been impaled by an icicle, and it was already beginning to melt. Fat water droplets ran down the spear and drenched her already blood-soaked jacket.

I turned back toward the man expecting to find a similar weapon emerging from his chest, but there was no murder weapon to be found. I briefly searched for any signs of strangulation, stabbing, gunshot wounds, or any other method of murder I'd come across in my year and a half as an investigator.

Nothing.

Paisley, dressed in her elaborate reindeer costume, leapt from my arms and crept over to the victims and licked at their cheeks. "Mommy, Mommy, are they going to be okay? Will they wake up soon?" This made me realize that Paisley hadn't seen nearly as many dead bodies as Octo-Cat and I had in our day. Poor thing was probably every bit as terrified as Mags.

Octo-Cat curled his upper lip, content now to remain in my arms. "Surely even you can't be that dense, dog." He loved his Chihuahua sister and only took to calling her *dog* when he was feeling particularly superior, which, I guess, was still quite a lot of the time.

"Quiet," I muttered almost absent-mindedly. "Let me think."

"A-A-A-Angie," Mags stuttered, her voice rising above the tall sculptures and crashing back down on me. "What's going on? Is everything okay?" From the tone of her voice, she clearly already knew the answer. Still, I'd need to tell her what I'd found, then we'd have to tell the authorities together.

With one last lingering glance toward the poor people who had come to enjoy the Holiday Spectacular but had ended up as dead as grandma after she got ran over by the reindeer, I took a deep centering breath and returned to my cousin. "We need to find Officer Bouchard and let him know there's been a murder."

Mags cried out as if in physical pain. "Really? A murder? Here? But, but... everyone seems so nice."

I frowned as I tried to remember a time when I had been so innocently optimistic. *Never,* I thought. I'd always been too bookish not to be at least somewhat suspicious of the world around me. I used to consider myself paranoid, but that was before bodies started piling up whenever I was near.

Mags stared at me with wide eyes as she waited for an answer that wouldn't come. She wanted me to take it back, to make everything okay again, but I simply couldn't.

Instead, I nodded. "Yes, unfortunately. Actually, there's been two. And we have to get the police. Now."

I dropped Octo-Cat into the snow and grabbed Mags by the hand, yanking her along as I wound my way back through the spiral garden.

Octo-Cat followed behind on his leash, yelling the most profane kitty curses that had ever spilled off his sandpaper tongue. He could be angry for all I cared. Some things were more important than following the many elaborate and contradictory rules he'd established to govern our lives.

Besides, unlike Paisley, he always landed on his feet.

I wasn't quite so sure Mags and I would be as lucky, especially when a dark figure swept across the quiet garden moving quickly and coming straight for us.

CHAPTER FIVE

The dark figure drew closer, but still not close enough for me to make out his features or intent.

Mags yanked out of my hold and stopped cold, seemingly unsure of whether to run, hide, or do some strange combination of both. Instead of doing either, she stood a couple paces before me, frozen like a shocked deer on a lonely country road.

I braced myself for the worst and turned around to get a good look at the new arrival. His silver badge flashed brilliantly in the sunlight, set against a dark blue uniform shirt. He continued to close the distance between us quickly, concern pinching at his features. *Not a threat. Not a threat at all.*

"Officer Bouchard," I cried, elated that he had found us and realizing that maybe I was still a bit paranoid, after all.

Mags visibly relaxed and took a tentative step toward us.

"I heard screams," he said, moving his hand to the gun at his hip. "Is everything okay here?"

Mags's face reddened as she tried to push an entire dictionary's worth of words from her mouth at once. "Oh, it's horrible. There's blood. Lots of blood. Angie saw bodies. She said there's two. People died. And I don't know who they were or who killed them.

But it's so scary. Things like this never happen back home in Larkhaven. Aunt Linda says trouble won't find you unless you go looking for it yourself. But I swear, we just wanted to enjoy the festival. And now Angie is acting like it's up to us to figure out what happened here. I don't know who the victims are. I don't know who the killer is. I don't know anything other than I think I need to go home." Finally finished, her voice cracked, and Mags drew back into herself.

Officer Bouchard stayed on high alert. "Whoa there, slow down. Start by telling me who you are and how you discovered the bodies."

I placed a hand on Mags's shoulder to let her know that I could handle things from here. "Go get some latkes or more cocoa or gingerbread cookies, or something. I'll catch Officer Bouchard up on what we discovered."

"Should I go with her, Mommy?" Paisley asked from somewhere near my ankle.

"Mags," I called after her. "Take Paisley with you."

The little dog took off running and also barking, though for no apparent reason.

I watched until Mags scooped her into a cuddle, then I turned back to the waiting policeman. "Let me show you what we found."

As we walked the short distance to the hulking Christmas tree sculpture and the bodies that lay behind it, I informed Officer Bouchard of the no-show judges and the last-minute change up that required Mags and me to take their places. I also explained that Mags was my cousin visiting from Georgia.

"I didn't know you had family in Georgia," he said, tilting his head to study me as we walked.

"Neither did we. At least not until a couple months ago. Anyway, here's the crime scene." I motioned toward the bodies, even though he couldn't have missed them if he'd been blind in one eye and couldn't see out the other.

"Are we done now?" Octo-Cat groused. "I know your imagination's already running wild with a hundred thousand ideas of who done it and why. But I heard that the Little Dog Diner has a booth set up somewhere around here, and Octavius needs himself a lobster roll."

It took all the strength not to roll my eyes at this expression of my cat's misplaced priorities. Thankfully, I think I managed to pull it off. Studying the melting ice weapon, I asked the officer, "Do you know who they are?"

Officer Bouchard hooked his thumbs through his beltloops and rocked on his heels. "Can't see the woman's face, but the man I recognize as Fred Hapley. He sells health insurance all across the state, and I'm pretty sure he's one of the missing judges you mentioned. If memory serves, he was also a last-minute addition."

My breaths rose in icy little puffs as I thought about where we should take things from here. "My mom should be able to confirm it and let us know who the other judge was supposed to be and whether this is her. She's not technically on the planning committee, but she'll have memorized the setup before coming out as part of planning her news piece. Should I call her over?"

Officer Bouchard sucked air through his teeth. "Not just yet, if you don't mind. Your mother's a good woman and an ace reporter, but I need some time to investigate and call in backup before the press gets involved. You understand, don't you?"

I nodded vigorously. No one understood my mother's drive to get the story at any cost better than I did. "What are you going to do when festivalgoers start coming through the sculpture garden?" I asked, worried we'd end up creating a scene whether or not we wanted one.

He quirked one eyebrow. "You said you and your cousin are the new judges, right?"

"Yep."

"Then why don't you get her back here? And you two can guard the entrance so that nobody wanders inside."

"There's an exit, too," I pointed out, searching for that red ribbon the sign had mentioned.

"Well, that's perfect then," he said with a grin. "There are two ways in, and there are two of you. I shouldn't need long, but I sure do appreciate your help in keeping this under wraps."

"Okay, let me go find Mags," I said, hating to leave before we'd figured out much of anything.

"*Finally,*" Octo-Cat grumbled. "I'm starving. I may have even lost a life because of it. I can't believe you've made me wait so long for my lobster roll."

Little did he know his lobster roll was not even close to next on our agenda. I had to find Mags, and then I had to find out what had happened to the slain judge and the as-of-yet unidentified body.

CHAPTER SIX

I found Mags at the latke stall, pushing potato pancakes dipped in applesauce into her mouth almost faster than she could chew them.

"Oh, I didn't know you'd be coming back so soon," she mumbled with one hand covering her mouth politely. "Otherwise, I would have saved you some." Her face turned red with embarrassment. "I'm a nervous eater, you see. These things didn't stand a chance."

I laughed and shook my head, happy to see her at least a little more relaxed than she'd been a few minutes back. "No judgment here. We have to get back to help Officer Bouchard, anyway."

Mags tossed her trash into a nearby canister and wiped her mouth with the side of her hand. "Are you sure we have to go back there? I don't know if this kind of thing happens often here, but I'm not used to dead bodies turning up back home in Georgia." She said this with more of a Southern twang than usual, no doubt longing for the safety of good ol' reliable Larkhaven.

"Well, it's kind of my job as a P.I.," I explained with a shrug. "Although it's not always murder. Sometimes I deal with other kinds of crooks, too."

"But can't we just enjoy the Holiday Spectacular? You've told me so much about it, and I've been looking forward to this part of our visit. Plus, you might not be scared that there's a murderer on the loose, but I sure am. Maybe we can make a quick circuit and then get the heck out of here."

I looped my arm through my cousin's and marched back with her toward the ice sculpture garden. "We just need to do this one quick thing to help out Officer Bouchard, and then we'll get back to the festivities, I promise."

"Where's my lobster roll?" Octo-Cat whined, then growled, then sighed in defeat. "Unhook me from this hideous torture device, and I'll go grab one for myself, seeing as you're proving to be rather useless today."

Paisley growled from deep within her throat. "Don't talk to Mommy that way. She's busy being a superhero, and it's our job to be her sidekicks."

Octo-Cat tensed on the end of his leash. He definitely thought of himself as the Sherlock to my Watson, so Paisley's suggestion that I was the one in charge was sure to rankle.

"In case you haven't noticed," he said with a sneer, "she's pretending we're not even here. So, why do we owe her anything when there's really no way to help?"

Now it was Paisley who whined as her prick ears fell back against her neck while her tail went between her legs. "Just because it's not easy doesn't mean it's not the right thing to do."

"Oh, dear sweet dogling, you have so much to learn. For starters, the best life should always be easy and also filled with sunspots and Evian and my long overdue lobster roll."

Hard as it was to not jump into that particular conversation, I kept my eyes glued straight ahead and my feet focused on returning to the crime scene as quickly as possible.

Mags seemed to wilt more and more the closer we drew to the garden.

"Sorry for dragging you into this," I offered with an apologetic smile. "But it will be over soon. He just needs the area secured until backup can arrive."

We reached the sculpture of a crystalline rose that marked the start of the spiral viewing trail. I left Mags there and headed toward the exit.

"Wait! Where are you going?" she called after me, trembling uncertainty returning to her voice.

"I'll just be over there, keeping an eye on the exit. If you take a few steps out onto the street, you'll even be able to see me," I explained calmly. "Text if you need anything, even if it's just to chat and pass the time. We'll be finished up here before you know it, and then we can let the police handle the rest. Okay?"

Mags nodded, but a row of worry lines stretched across her normally smooth forehead. "Great. But now that I've had time to think about it, I'd really rather just find Nan and go home as soon as we're able. I don't feel so safe anymore."

As much as I loved the Holiday Spectacular, I loved my cousin so much more and wanted her to leave Blueberry Bay with happy memories instead of horrible ones. I'd do whatever it took to salvage our holiday.

"That's okay," I said with what I hoped was a reassuring smile. "We'll make our own fun. How do fresh-baked cookies and a Hallmark Channel Christmas movie sound for tonight?"

Mags smiled bravely and bobbed her head. "Sounds like a plan, Ms. Pet Whisperer P.I."

I chuckled as I walked away to take my place at the garden exit. First, though, I dipped into the center to let Officer Bouchard know Mags and I were on duty. Once I'd returned to the end of that red ribbon trail, I pulled out my phone and opened a group text with my mom and dad.

There's been a murder in the ice sculpture garden.

Officer Bouchard is securing the scene while Mags and I make sure no one wanders in.

After that, we're going to head home.

Mags is feeling a bit scared by everything.

Can you guys see that Nan gets home okay?

I asked in a series of fast texts.

Both my parents texted back immediately.

"Are you serious?" Mom's read.

"Are you safe?" Dad asked.

"I'm fine," I replied, "but I also don't think we'll be able to finish our judging duties before heading home."

"Poor Mags," Mom lamented with a frowny face emoji. "This is not the best introduction to our quiet corner of the world."

Although I didn't say it, I actually thought it was the perfect way to show my new cousin how life had been for us lately. Ever since I first met that snarky talking tabby a year and half ago, my entire life had been one danger, one investigation after the next.

Thanks to us, crime didn't pay around these parts, but apparently it also didn't rest. Not even for the holidays.

An incoming call lit up my screen. This one was from Nan. "What's this I hear about you and Mags leaving early?" she demanded, though her voice remained cheerful.

"Well, the murders kind of cramp the style of our Holiday Spectacular," I explained in a whisper, making sure none of the people further down the block heard.

"Well, that's really too bad. Could you do me a quick favor and ask Mags if I can get her anything from the artist's corner? I'm sure she'd at least like a souvenir or two. Right?"

I heard a deep voice speaking faintly on the other end but couldn't make out the words. "Who's there with you, Nan?"

"Just my friend, Mr. Milton," she answered dismissively. "Now, can you ask Mags about those souvenirs for me, please?"

"Sure, I'll check with her in a little bit. Right now, we're guarding the crime scene, and there are two different entrances. It's not a very good time to—"

"You're at the ice sculpture garden. Aren't you? That place isn't very big. Just run over and ask her so that I know."

I sighed but still followed her instructions. There was little point in arguing with Nan when she wanted something—especially something quick and relatively easy like this.

Clutching my phone tightly in one hand and Octo-Cat beneath my other arm, I power walked over to the front entrance of the garden with Paisley following close at my heels. I was just rounding the corner when I caught sight of Mags.

Her eyes were wide, and her fair features looked even paler than usual as a hooded figure dragged her into the back of a cargo van, slammed the door, and sped away...

CHAPTER SEVEN

I dropped everything I'd been holding into the fresh snowbank at the side of the road and took off running after the van.

"Even though I land on my feet, it still hurts to be dropped, you know," Octo-Cat shouted after me.

But I had no time to respond. I put everything I had into following that van even though I knew I'd never be able to catch it on foot. Perhaps I would still be able to make out the license plate or catch a glimpse of the driver, something, anything to keep me connected with Mags.

I squinted hard at the departing vehicle, trying so hard. I didn't wear glasses, but I'd always been a bit nearsighted due to my obsession with reading. And unfortunately for Mags now, I couldn't make out a single digit beneath the dried mud that coated the plate.

I stopped running and bent over with my hands on my knees, gasping for breath while Paisley continued to run and bark up a storm drawing the curious stares of all who were near.

"Get back here, you bad guy!" the Chihuahua shouted. "It's not nice to take people when they don't want to be taken. Bad human, bad, bad."

Once I caught my breath a little, I scanned the downtown area for Octo-Cat but came up short. Maybe he'd gone to get that lobster roll after all, or maybe he was off somewhere nursing his wounded pride—both at having been dropped so unceremoniously into the snow and at having been forced to wear the harness he so loathed.

A burst of bright pink flashed onto the scene. Nan had arrived, and unlike me, she didn't appear winded in the slightest.

"You dropped this," she said, pushing my fallen phone into my hand. "And you worried me silly. What happened?"

I couldn't help the tears that splashed onto my cheeks. It was one thing to find the bodies of people I'd never know and quite another to witness my cousin's kidnapping firsthand. It had been my job to look after her, to take care of her. And I'd really messed it up.

"They took Mags," I said, my voice trembling in the same way hers had upon the discovery of the bodies in the ice sculpture garden. "They took her, and they're gone." Fresh tears welled, and I choked back a sob as Nan wrapped her arms around me and made a soft shushing sound.

"Oh, dear. Dear. Dear. Dear," she repeated like a chant.

Her gentleman friend moved closer and placed a hand on Nan's shoulder. I hadn't even noticed his arrival earlier, but now here he was, pushing his way into this family moment.

"Who took her?" he asked in a deep rumble.

"I don't know." I kept my eyes on Nan instead of looking toward Mr. Milton. "I couldn't see the face, but they put her into the back of a white van and drove away. I didn't even get the license plate number."

"Well, that's a rotten thing to do and not with keeping the spirit of the season either," Nan mumbled into my hair. "But we'll get her back, I promise."

I fell apart in my grandmother's arms, asking her the many frantic questions that swirled through my mind. "What if it was the same people who killed the judges? What if they're going to kill her, too? It's all my fault. She doesn't even know anyone here. I don't understand. Why would they take her? I mean, why would anyone want to take Mags, especially someone who doesn't even know her?"

A small paw patted the back of my calf. I turned around and bent down, expecting to find Paisley, but instead, it was Octo-Cat who sat there looking rather pleased with himself.

"Now that I've finally filled my stomach, I can think a little clearer," he explained, then stopped to lick his paw and drag it across his forehead. I waited impatiently as he licked and dragged—licked and dragged half a dozen times—without providing further commentary.

Finally I blurted out, "Do you know something? Do you know who took Mags?"

He dropped his paw back to the ground and stared up at me with large amber eyes.

"I don't know anything," Mr. Milton answered, assuming I'd been talking to him. How could I have forgotten he was here? I needed to be more careful with my secret, no matter how much I was worried about my cousin in that moment.

"Of course I don't know *that*," Octo-Cat answered with an exasperated groan. "But I think I know something else that might help." He paused again for emphasis, the way he so often liked to do when he was building the drama of the scene.

My cat's love of theatrics would be the end of me one day. Quite literally. I'd probably have a heart attack while waiting out one of his dramatic pauses.

"Well?" I demanded, unable to take it anymore as I moved my hands to my hips. I shifted my eyes from the cat to Nan, pretending she was the target of my ire so that I'd at least have a cover in front of Mr. Milton.

Ugh. Why had she brought him along?

"*Yeesh.* So impatient." My cat stopped again and stared at me, challenging me to push him again.

I bit my tongue and waited him out while Nan filled the silence to keep up our charade.

After several moments, Octo-Cat seemed appeased and blinked his eyes slowly before continuing. "Even though you're being a bit rude, I'll tell you what I know. You know how all humans look the same? You and Mags look even more the same than most."

Even though I was pretty sure I knew what he was getting at, I asked for clarification, anyway. "What do you mean?"

Nan gave an answer, but my ears were focused firmly on Octo-Cat.

He shook his head, flicked his tail, and sighed yet again. "*I mean* whoever took Mags probably meant to take you instead. Think about it, and you'll see that I'm right. As usual."

CHAPTER EIGHT

The moment Octo-Cat spoke those words, I knew they .were true. Mags didn't know anyone in Blueberry Bay besides my family and me.

No one had any reason to take her.

True, she had no friends here, but also no enemies.

Me, on the other hand… Well, let's just say I'd ruffled more than a few feathers during the course of my investigations. But was that enough for someone to want to kidnap me?

Rather than continue to puzzle over this myself, I decided to ask Nan. Even though I already knew I believed in Octo-Cat's theory, I still had a hard time wrapping my head around the fact that someone had meant me harm.

"Do you think the people who took Mags meant to take me instead? Everyone is always saying how similar we look, and well, maybe…" I let my voice trail off.

She bit her lip and nodded. "It would seem that way, wouldn't it?" she asked, shaking her head now.

Mr. Milton wrapped an arm around Nan's shoulders and pulled her tight into his side. The familiarity of this gesture made my stomach turn over.

"Who would want to take her—or you—so badly that they'd risk doing it in the middle of a crowded festival?" he asked, his eyes boring into mine.

Although that was an appropriate question, it still rankled me. I wished Nan would ask Mr. Milton to go away and leave the investigation to us.

He was also wrong. The streets had begun to fill out a bit more as the morning wore on, but we still didn't have anything near a crowd, especially in the mostly empty area that housed the ice sculpture garden outside of the main action.

Scanning the streets, I did a quick count and noticed four people in the nearby vicinity. If they'd seen what happened with the van, they certainly weren't letting on. Those who had witnessed my frantic run had already departed, more than likely not realizing how serious matters had become.

Nan remained cuddled up against Mr. Milton, although the lovey-dovey look she'd had in her eyes earlier had long since flown the coop.

"It wouldn't be that hard to sneak in and out with a plan," she pointed out. "People will be coming and going all day, there's parking in at least half a dozen different places, and many vendors are bringing their vans and SUVs in to load and unload. So, you see, it would be relatively easy to take her. Easier than it normally would be, at least."

"We're going with my theory, then. Right?" Octo-Cat asked impatiently. "Because I'm right about this, just like I'm right about most things. Really, you need to start listening a bit quicker."

I nodded in response. While I also hated to waste time discussing already established points, I also couldn't trust everything he said at face value. Not only was he often crabby and sarcastic, but some of his ideas were a bit too influenced by the melodramatic TV shows he liked watching before and after his morning and afternoon naps.

Octo-Cat sniffed the cold air above his head. "Are you answering me or simply humoring me? It's so much harder when you're not talking to me. Are we proceeding with the assumption that you were the target instead of Mags?"

"Yes," I hissed partially under my breath. It's like he didn't care about keeping my secret at all.

"What was that?" Mr. Milton asked with a furrowed brow and a quizzical expression.

"Oh, *uh*, just talking to myself," I stuttered as heat flushed my cheeks. "What I meant was *yes, Nan's absolutely right.* Anyone could have taken her, and the longer we wait to go after her, the harder it will be to find her. We need to do something, and we need to do it now."

Nan wriggled free of his arm. "Yes, yes, we need to go after her."

"But she could be anywhere," Mr. Milton said with a sigh. "Someone dangerous could have her. We could be walking into a situation that we might not walk out of."

I glowered at him, hating that he had any say in this at all.

"It's what family does," I said. "It's what good people do. They show up. They help each other."

"Especially at Christmastime," Nan added, making a tsking noise as she shook her head dolefully. "It's what we're going to do."

"Yeah, and if you're not up for it, we can handle this ourselves," I added, hoping that he would take the bait and make a run for it.

He cleared his throat and fixed his eyes on me with a bit of a grimace. "Well, I can't leave you two lovely ladies on your own, especially when the situation could be dangerous."

I shrugged. "Suit yourself."

Then I turned toward Nan, intentionally facing away from Mr. Milton. "The first thing we need to do is call Mom and Dad and make sure they know what's going on. We'll need everybody working hard to find Mags—and let's not forget, the ice sculpture murderer."

"What a Holiday Spectacular this is turning out to be," Nan pointed out grimly.

She turned to the side and faced Mr. Milton. "Would you please give us a moment, dear?" she asked with a slight smile.

"Oh yes. Oh yes, of course. I'll just go get us some latkes. They looked good, and perhaps a hot snack is just what we all need now."

He stumbled away, clearly sore about Nan's dismissal, but I was happy she'd done it and hoped she planned to avoid him during the rest of our search as well.

Her eyes flashed as she turned them on me, speaking quietly and quickly. "I'll take care of the call to your folks," she said. "You see what the animals know."

"Already on it," I said, nodding just once before scooping both animals up in my arms to Paisley's delight and Octo-Cat's disdain.

"Listen up, guys," I said. "There are people down the block, so I can't be too loud, and if anyone comes close, I might have to quiet up mid-sentence. Okay? Let's chat. Did you hear anything? Or see anything? Or smell anything that can help us find out what happened to Mags?"

Octo-Cat shifted into a more comfortable position but still seemed put off by being clutched to my chest beside the wagging ball of Paisley. "They do this to cats all the time, you know. Come in vans, take us away, put us in the pound. I've never had to deal with such indignities, obviously, but nobody calls for reinforcements when it happens to us."

Paisley whined and dipped her head. "It happened to me. That's how I got to the shelter in the first place. After my first mom died, me and my brothers and sister were living in the street and so hungry we didn't know what we were going to do. But then a big van came and took us to the shelter. It wasn't quite as bad there, but then Nan came and found me, and everything was perfect, and it's been perfect ever since."

Octo-Cat rolled his eyes at her. "If you're suggesting that Mags is better off because some random hooded guy in a van took her, then you would be very, very wrong. It doesn't work the same way for humans as it does for us."

Paisley whimpered again. "But you said if it were a cat…"

"I know what I said. Sometimes I just need to give Angela a hard time, so she knows I'm paying attention."

Now I rolled my eyes.

"Paisley, sweetie," I said softly, "thank you for telling me your story, but in this case, Octo-Cat is right. Whoever took Mags doesn't want to help her."

"Are they going to hurt her?" the little dog asked, shaking violently at the prospect

"I hope not," I said in a strained whisper.

At the same time, Octo-Cat answered, "Yeah, probably."

I choked back a sob.

If something happened to Mags, I'd never forgive myself. Not just because she'd come to Glendale on my account, but because the kidnapper had most likely meant to take me instead.

Would he be angry when he realized Mags was the wrong person?

Would he come for me, too?

Would he dispose of her?

Let her go?

Oh, how I wished I knew.

CHAPTER NINE

Mr. Milton returned with two orders of latkes about fifteen minutes after he first departed.

Nan accepted hers by giving him a quick peck on the cheek.

I shook my head and said, "No thanks," still clutching Octo-Cat tight.

Paisley had already jumped down to dance at Nan's feet.

Honestly, there was so much fear in my stomach already that I didn't have much room for anything else.

They made quick work of their snack while I racked my brain trying to figure out how best to proceed. "I'm going to go find Mr. Gable," I announced before heading decisively to the right, leaving them both behind.

"Mommy! Mommy! I'm coming, too!" Paisley cried, frolicking after Octo-Cat and me in her silly reindeer costume.

We found Mr. Gable in the same place I left him earlier that morning—at the main entry to the festival dressed up as a jacketless Santa while guiding visitors into his sleigh for the perfect photo op.

His bunny sidekick E.B. sat nearby in the nativity scene half covered in hay and looking hilariously out of place as a life-size bunny nestled among miniature plastic shepherds, wisemen, cows, camels, and angels.

Mr. Gable finished with the family of four he was photographing, wished them a Merry Christmas, and then turned toward me, concern furrowing his brow.

"Why, Angie… Why do you look so out of breath? Are you coming from the latest reindeer game?" He chuckled in that soft, happy way that old men had, but not quite vibrant or boisterous enough to match his role as Santa.

Once again I was reminded that I needed to make some effort to get into better shape, especially since my seventy-year-old Nan could run circles around me—and often did.

"Mr. Gable, have the police been in touch with you?" I drew out my phone and looked at the time displayed on its screen. Surprisingly, little more than half an hour had passed since I'd told officer Bouchard about my discovery of the two corpses in the ice sculpture garden and even less time than that since Mags was taken.

Mr. Gable's cheeks turned red to match mine. Now he looked more like Santa, which made me happy somehow. "Why would the police have been in touch? What happened?"

As much as I didn't want to be the one to tell him, it looked like I had no choice. I caught him up on the discovery of the bodies and that we already knew at least one was a judge his committee had hired. I also told him how Mags had been kidnapped shortly after and hauled away in a speeding cargo van.

He stared at me for a moment, eyes wide and unblinking. "All that happened this morning? Right here at our Holiday Spectacular?" His voice cracked on that last syllable.

"Afraid so," I answered with a frown. "Officer Bouchard is taking care of things at the crime scene. He's already called for backup and I'm trying to figure out who took Mags and how I can get her back."

That was one problem with living in a small town. We didn't really have enough cops to handle the double homicide, let alone a kidnapping on top of that. That's why my work as a private investigator was so important. Officer Bouchard had let me partner with him on investigations more than once for this very reason.

"What should we do?" Mr. Gable asked, his face turning from red to white to red again, a flashing display of his anxiety.

"We've been planning the Spectacular all year. Vendors have come from all over Blueberry Bay. Folks travel from out of town to be here. Hundreds more are on their way right now. Do we close everything down and call it a loss, or do we try to keep going despite the crimes that were committed here this morning?"

I shook my head, wishing I had an answer. "Seems like a lose-lose, no matter what you do. I wouldn't want to be in your position."

He sighed heavily and ran both hands through his thick white hair. "Ugh. This was not a responsibility I thought I'd ever have as chairman of the committee. But even if I'm the head, we are a team. I think I need to let the others weigh in before I make a definitive decision. Wouldn't you say?"

I set Octo-Cat down on the front seat of the sleigh and then joined him on the bench.

Paisley pranced below, too short to hop up for herself. So I bent over and gave her a lift. She immediately licked my face, happy to be reunited after our fifteen-second separation.

"That sounds like a good plan to me," I said, largely because I had no other ideas to offer. "I'll stay here to greet people and take their pictures while you go talk with the others."

"Oh, wonderful, wonderful," he said, pushing the sleek digital camera into my hands. "Would you mind watching E.B. too? She'll probably just sleep through everything. I have her leash tied to that back camel's leg there, so she shouldn't give you any trouble."

"Of course we'll keep an eye on her. No problem at all," I assured him.

"Bunny-sitting duty? Gag me," Octo-Cat moaned beside me.

Mr. Gable smiled quickly, but the slight look of happiness disappeared from his face in an instant, and he rushed off muttering something to himself.

I glanced toward the nearest parking lot but couldn't see any new festivalgoers arriving. That meant I had a small bit of privacy and could talk to the animals again.

"I thought we were going to find Mags," Paisley whined.

"That is what she said we were going to do," Octo-Cat added. "But you know how fickle humans can be. Angela, how long are we going to be stationed here, away from the action?"

I wished I knew. There were a lot of things I wished I knew right about then, and only one new creature I could ask for information.

I slipped down from the sleigh's bench seat and tiptoed toward the nativity display, careful not to disturb the rabbit. From last I remembered meeting her, she was a very nervous sort and I needed to see if she knew anything that could help me. If I frightened her, though, chances were she wouldn't talk to me at all.

I needed to play this exactly right.

For Mags.

CHAPTER TEN

O nce I reached the nativity display, I sat down gently beside
the manger. An icy dampness immediately saturated my
bottom, but I didn't care.

"E.B.," I said softly. "E.B., it's me, Angie. We met at the pet shop
when we were there for pictures with Santa. I don't know if you
remember me, but—"

The hay beside me twitched, and a little gray nose poked its way
out, followed by two dark eyes. "Oh my gosh, oh my gosh. Who are
you? What are you doing here? Where's Mr. Gable? Are you going
to eat me? Am I going to die? Is everything okay? Oh Merry Christmas, what a Christmas…"

Octo-Cat appeared at my side with a snarky grin stretched
between his whiskers. I couldn't tell whether he was here to help me
or to have some fun at E.B.'s expense.

"Relax, rabbit," he snarled. "She's not going to eat you. But if
you don't cooperate, maybe I will."

He laughed devilishly in the same way he did when he threw up
outside my bedroom door, enjoying the means much more than the
end. So he'd be helping me and making things more difficult at the
exact same time. *Great.*

"Oh, Merry Christmas, Merry Christmas!" E.B. sputtered, using the holiday greeting as a curse word. "I do not want to be eaten. I do *not*. I knew I shouldn't have left home today. Mr. Gable made me, but I didn't want to go. I just wanted to sleep at home and eat carrots, and oh!"

With a wildly flicking tail, my cat shouted, "If you know what's good for you, you'll listen to what the lady has to say. No more of this 'Merry Christmas' business. You got me?"

The bunny nodded slowly, her long ears flopping in the hay. "I'm sorry," she sputtered in fear. "I didn't mean to make you angry, Mr. Cat. It's just... I always have to be on alert or bad things can happen. Life isn't so easy when you're prey, you know? Anybody here could hurt me. Lots of bunnies don't get the chance to live as long as I've lived already, and I want to keep on living. I love my human."

Paisley joined us now. I had no idea where she'd been the last couple minutes, but we still seemed to be free of any newly arriving visitors, so I pressed on.

"Do you——" I began, but Paisley interrupted me, which was very uncharacteristic of her.

She let out a sad howl. Now her normally erect ears fell forward as she tilted her head and studied the bunny with an expression of sorrow. "Oh, you poor bunny. I can't imagine what life is like for you. Do you want to talk about it? I'm a very good listener."

I was just about to say something to get us back on topic when an increasingly perturbed Octo-Cat came to my rescue.

"Once again, this isn't the Dr. Phil show, and we're not here to talk about the bunny's feelings. We need information. We need to find Mags. Keep your eye on the prize. Keep your head in the game. Yada yada. And all those other favorite human clichés, too. Now," he said, turning back to E.B. with flashing yellow eyes. "One of our humans has been kidnapped by dangerous men."

The bunny gasped.

"*Yes*," said Octo-Cat dramatically, nodding as he did. "*Dangerous*. And we need to get her back before it's too late."

He took two quick steps forward and unsheathed the claws on one paw demonstratively. "Now tell us what you know, rabbit."

The bunny's nose never stopped wiggling even as the rest of her body grew still with fright. "I don't know what you expected of me," she said weakly. "I'm sorry something happened to your human, but I don't know anything about it. Now, please, can I get back to my nap?"

Octo-Cat licked his exposed claws while narrowing his eyes on the rabbit. I hadn't realized my cat was such a mafioso when it came to the pets of Glendale. I'd have to monitor his television-viewing habits a bit more carefully, it seemed.

He began to speak, but I cut him off by placing a hand on his back. "More flies with honey than vinegar," I mumbled.

"Who would want flies?" the tabby asked. "Disgusting and completely off topic."

I rolled my eyes and focused them on E.B. "You've been here all morning watching as everyone comes and goes. Did you see anyone acting suspicious?"

"I see everything," E.B. said with a nod before freezing up again. "That's the difference between staying alive and becoming a snack."

"Okay…" I said slowly, given that she hadn't actually deigned to answer my question. "Did you see anyone suspicious?"

One of her ears twitched, then the other. "I find every predator suspicious," she said. "Including you. And especially that cat."

Octo-Cat laughed gaily as if this was the best thing he'd ever heard as well as all he'd ever wanted for Christmas.

"I understand," I said slowly, once again hoping Mr. Gable wouldn't get back soon so we could pursue more productive means of inquiry. "Was anyone more suspicious than the others? Or suspicious in a different way?"

E.B. thought about this. "Well," she said at last. "Now that you mention it, yes. I did see some suspicious humans come through."

Now we were getting somewhere.

CHAPTER ELEVEN

"Do you know who took Mags?" Paisley asked, wagging her tail hopefully as we all stared at E.B. waiting to find out what she knew.

"Who's Mags?" the bunny asked distractedly. "Your human just asked me if I saw anyone suspicious."

"Yes, that's right," I jumped in to steer the conversation back to the right path. "Tell me about those suspicious people."

E.B. tentatively lifted one ear, then set it back down. "Lots of people have come through, and almost everyone stopped to say hello to Mr. Gable and get their picture taken, but a couple people seemed in too much of a hurry."

"So you're saying they refused to have their picture taken?" I asked to make sure I understood.

"They didn't even let him ask. It was very strange to see a predator behave in that way. One of them was looking all around, back and forth, like I do when I'm trying to figure out if danger is nearby. The other moved very quickly and raced right past us without so much as a hello."

"That is strange," I agreed thoughtfully. "Can you tell me

anything more about those two people? Did they come together? What did they look like? Did you recognize them?"

E.B. blinked slowly and wiggled her nose. "Everyone else got their picture taken, but not those two. They didn't come at the same time, either. First one came, then some time passed, and then the other. I don't know who they were."

"Do you know, if they were male or female? Old or young? Can you describe how they looked?"

E.B. turned her head slightly, eyeing Octo-Cat for a moment before returning her attention to me. "I don't know. All humans look the same, really. You don't even have any special markings on your coats to help show the difference. It makes it hard to tell you apart."

"Exactly," Octo-Cat said, nodding. "Isn't that what I've always said?"

E.B. flinched. "That's all I know. I don't know anything else. Please will you go away now?"

"Thank you for your help," I told her, rising to my feet and dusting a light smattering of hay from my bottom, which by now was soaked completely through from the melting snow on the ground. So much for the hay creating a drying buffer. "We told Mr. Gable we'd watch you, but we can do that from a little bit farther away."

"Thank you," she murmured, watching us warily as we left the nativity scene.

"Well that was pointless," Octo-Cat hissed. If I'd taken the moment to look over to him, I'm sure I'd have seen him rolling his eyes. "I'm so glad we took time to ask the bunny."

"There's a lot of things she did help us with," I pointed out, raising the camera in one hand. "E.B. mentioned that there were two suspicious people and that neither had their photo taken."

"So what do you suggest we do?" Octo-Cat asked with a flick of his tail. "Look through all the photos on that thing and cross reference it with everyone who's attended the festival so far?"

"For a start," I said, impressed he had understood with no explanation on my part. Then again, he was becoming quite savvy with photography given his long-distance Instagram relationship with Grizabella.

"There's more than one entrance into this place," I continued on. "People can start from anywhere. There are, no doubt, many people who didn't stop for a photo who perhaps never even made their way over here."

"*And*," Octo-Cat added, his amber gaze fixed on me knowingly,

"what's suspicious to the rabbit might not be suspicious at all. So there were two people she thought were acting funny, but it's possible that neither of them had anything to do with the murders or the kidnapping."

"I know," I said with a sigh, "but at least it's a place to start."

I powered the camera back on and flipped through the last few photos on display. Before I could make it very far, however, several people converged on us at once.

Nan and her gentleman friend, Mr. Milton, came from one direction while Mr. Gable returned from another. Lastly, my boyfriend, Charles, approached as well, immediately slinging an arm over my shoulder and giving me a kiss on my forehead.

"I finished up my work early at the firm and thought I'd surprise you," he said with a giant grin. "So tell me, what did I miss?"

Mr. Gable groaned, Nan winced, and Mr. Milton looked pointedly at the ground.

Octo-Cat had an answer for him, but it was one he couldn't decipher without my help. Also it wasn't very nice.

Paisley barked and stood on her hindlegs, doing her sit pretty dance to get Charles's attention.

"Hey," he said, lifting her into his arms and giving her a kiss on the forehead, too.

"Why is everyone so quiet?" he asked, his eyes darting around our impromptu circle. "I really did miss something, didn't I?"

I put a hand on his shoulder and gently informed him both of the murders and the kidnapping as well as the fact that we were pretty convinced the kidnappers meant to nap me instead of Mags.

"All that in one morning?" he asked with an empty expression.

I nodded sadly. "I don't know what to do," I moaned. "Do you have any ideas?"

Mr. Gable cleared his throat. "I've spoken with the other committee members, and we all think it would be best to shut down the festival. We're circulating word to the vendors now and giving them the option of setting up at the local park. We'll man the exits and send anyone who comes by over there instead while the police are doing their thing."

Mr. Milton nodded and raised a thumb and finger to his chin. "Lots to lose, canceling the biggest event of the year. Vendors aren't going to be too happy about that."

"They'll lose money," Nan agreed, "but at least they won't lose their lives."

"That's the goal," Mr. Gable agreed.

"Come on," Charles said. "Let's go find Mags."

And even though I didn't need my boyfriend to save the day, I was very glad he was now here at my side.

We would find Mags. We would.

I wouldn't accept any other outcome.

CHAPTER TWELVE

"Do you think the crimes are linked?" Charles asked me matter-of-factly as I led him toward the spot where Mags had been abducted. He carried Paisley while I carried Octo-Cat, who had the good grace not to complain this time.

"I just don't know," I answered, keeping my eyes on the ground as if it held some answer we had yet to discover. "I don't think they are, but I also don't want to overlook anything. Just in case."

"Good thinking," Charles said, squeezing my elbow since I required both of my hands to carry Octo-Cat comfortably, lest I wanted his complaining to pick up again. "I'm sorry I wasn't here earlier," Charles said.

"That's okay. You didn't know. How could *anyone* know these terrible things would happen? And on Christmas Eve, too…"

Charles remained quiet for the next half block, becoming lost in thought as he so often did. "Do you think it's possible they happened not despite it being Christmas Eve but *because* it's Christmas Eve?"

"What you mean?" I asked, risking a glance at him even though I needed to keep both eyes on the street in order to avoid bumping into one of the many departing vendors.

"Well, maybe the Holiday Spectacular gave our murderer and/or kidnapper an opportunity he wouldn't have otherwise had. Or maybe the murderer is somehow related to the festival itself. You said the victims were meant to judge the ice sculpture contest. Right?"

"Well, at least one of them," I answered. Thinking back, Officer Bouchard didn't recognize the woman, and I hadn't been back to chat with him because of what had happened to Mags.

"I know every second counts right now," Charles told me as we neared the ice sculpture garden, "but let's take a quick moment to check in with the police. They may have information that could help point us in the right direction for Mags, too."

Less than two minutes later, we found Officer Bouchard standing with a couple other police personnel near the giant Christmas tree sculpture. "Angie," he said. "I'm surprised you weren't back before now."

"Didn't you hear? I asked, my voice dry and itchy. "Somebody took Mags. Kidnapped her right off the street."

"Mags? Your nice cousin? But why?" His eyebrows pressed together. "And why wasn't I informed before now?"

That was right. We hadn't even stopped to inform the authorities of Mags's abduction. Nan had probably assumed I would do it while I assumed she would. At least I could tell my favorite police officer now.

"It's all been a blur," I admitted "I can't believe I forgot to come to you, but I know you've been busy over here."

He sighed and rolled a kink from his neck. "Busy is an understatement."

"Learn anything new?" Charles asked, shaking the officer's hand hello. "Anything that might help us find Mags while you hunt the killer?"

"*Hunt*'s not exactly an appropriate word. Sounds like somebody's been reading too many Stephen King novels," the officer quipped. "But yes, we were able to confirm that the female victim was our second judge. A Miss Zelda Benedict. She taught art at the university in Portland and drove up special to serve as our judge."

I sucked air in through my teeth. This just kept getting worse and worse. "What a way for us to make a good impression on outsiders. *Come to Glendale's Holiday Spectacular where you just might get murdered.*"

"It is unfortunate," Officer Bouchard agreed. "She was very well respected in her field. Her colleagues will no doubt ride us hard until we find out who the culprit is."

"Did she have any connection to Fred Hapley?"

"As far as I know, the two of them never met a day in their life. At least not until they wound up dead side-by-side in the snow here. By the way, the murder weapon for old Fred was a gun. It must've had a silencer since no one reported hearing anything. But Zelda? She was stabbed straight through with an icicle."

"Why not kill them both the same way?" Charles asked, wrapping an arm protectively around my waist and eyeing the nearby ice sculptures warily.

"That's what we wondered, too," Officer Bouchard said with a nod. "Seems to me that somebody had come prepared to commit one murder but then had to commit a second when Fred here walked in on the scene."

"So we're looking for someone who knew the festival well enough to plan a private moment with Zelda Benedict in the ice sculpture garden before most of the tourists arrived and the scene got busy. But also someone who didn't know the agenda well enough to anticipate Fred Hapley's arrival," Charles summarized.

"That's what we're thinking." Officer Bouchard bobbed his head and reached over to give Paisley a quick pat. "But now you tell me someone took your cousin, too. She didn't arrive on the scene until after both judges were slain and the murderer had disappeared. So why would someone take her?"

"The murderer disappeared from view, but maybe he stayed close to keep an eye on things," I ventured, hugging Octo-Cat tight to my chest for strength. "Maybe he watched us the entire time as we discovered the bodies, talked with you, and then got ready to guard. But then why wouldn't he take me too?"

"Unfortunately, we've got a lot of questions and very few

answers so far." Officer Bouchard hung his head and sighed. "I'll call Mags's kidnapping in to the station. Even though our men are occupied with the homicide scene here, the neighboring police forces are all on standby given the size of our event, and the folks in Dewdrop Springs have dealt with their fair share of kidnappings over the years. They really are the experts on that kind of thing while murders are becoming far too common in our little town."

"Thank you for your help," I mumbled, hating everything about how this day was turning out.

"I wish there was more I could do. But if I know you, you're already halfway to finding her yourself."

We said goodbye, then Charles, the animals, and I headed toward the spot where I'd last seen Mags before she was hauled away and this whole nightmare had gone from bad to worse.

Hopefully we would find a definitive clue soon. I still didn't know where to go in the search for my lost cousin, and as time ticked steadily on, my heart sunk lower and lower.

"Please, God," I mumbled in a nearly silent prayer, looking toward the sky as fat snowflakes fell to the earth. "Please let her be okay."

CHAPTER THIRTEEN

Even though the snowfall had remained light that morning, it had also been consistent. That meant the footprints I'd left when I chased after the van that took Mags had already mostly filled in with fresh fall. Nearly a dozen other pairs of prints wove through the street and around the block, too, adding a new layer of difficulty to retracing my steps.

More and more people had begun to arrive for the festival, only to be turned right back around and sent on their way. Could this be the end of their town's most favorite tradition?

No, that doesn't matter now.

"This is where they took her," I told Charles, motioning toward an alley that cut between the shops. "He pulled through there, and then I lost track of him."

"I chased them, too!" Paisley interjected proudly. "But my little legs were no match for that big, bad van."

Sometimes I wondered whether my Chihuahua thought other humans could understand her, too. Either that or she just felt it was polite to talk to everyone, whether or not they had any idea what she was saying.

"The snow has filled in most of the tire tracks, but I still see some slight grooves." Charles stooped down and touched the ground. "Let's follow them as far as we can and see where that gets us."

"The kidnappers weren't the only ones to have a car," Octo-Cat grumbled within my arms. "We're in the middle of downtown. Practically everyone has a car. That's how we got here. UpChuck, too."

"Thanks for that observation," I told my cat, thankful for the relative privacy of the alley.

"What's he saying?" Charles asked, both eyebrows raised.

He definitely knew that Octo-Cat talked bad about him. After all, I was the one who had revealed my cat's nickname for the guy was *UpChuck*. Still, I hated translating all the sarcastic barbs that came from my naughty kitty's mouth.

"Uh… nothing," I said slowly, glancing down the alley and hoping to spot something that would help change the subject— preferably something that would also help lead us to Mags.

"I can tell when he's being mean, you know," Charles said with a self-effacing chuckle.

"What?" I stopped to study him for any signs that he was joking at my expense, but his expression remained serious as he met my gaze. "How could you possibly know something like that?"

Charles shrugged and put an arm around my waist.

Paisley now skittered before us, leaving his arms free while Octo-Cat preferred to stay in mine and avoid the damp snow.

"I don't know. I can just tell. Maybe it's all the time I spend with Jacques and Jillianne, now that I've become a cat owner myself, or maybe I'm just getting to know him and his ways."

"You don't think you can…" My voice trailed off. This question was almost too crazy to ask, but if Charles really could understand Octo-Cat's tone when he was being facetious, maybe he could…

"Do you understand him?" I asked, placing eerie emphasis on each word in that sentence.

"No," he responded, chuckling again. "I wouldn't want to, either. It's one thing to know he says bad things about me and it's quite another to hear them for myself. Especially when we're all trying to work together to solve the case. And especially when it's Mags."

Charles had come to hang out with us a couple times since Mags's arrival and the two had hit it off splendidly—the way Charles did with everyone.

Beyond that, I knew he just wanted me to be happy and to make sure nothing bad happened to the people I loved. He was a good guy, Charles Longfellow, III. He never wanted anyone to get hurt. That's what made him such an expert lawyer. He went the extra mile for his clients every single day.

"Mommy! Mommy!" Paisley woofed, running back toward me so fast she looked like a tiny reindeer blur on the horizon.

I'd been so preoccupied with Charles's revelation I hadn't even realized she'd pulled ahead.

"Mommmmmmmyyyyyyyyy!" she shouted again, drawing out the word for a couple extra beats. "I smell it! I smell her!"

"What do you smell, sweetie?" I asked, trying not to get my hopes up. Paisley always tried her best to help in whatever way she could, but her natural lack of suspiciousness made her a poor sleuth.

The dog had now reached us and was wagging her tail so hard I thought she might fall over. Even though I knew Nan preferred to keep her Chihuahua companion dressed while she was out on the town, I decided to free Paisley of her over-the-top costume.

She'd be much more of a help to all of us if she wasn't in constant danger of toppling over. Just like the Grinch's dog when he, too, had been dressed unceremoniously as a reindeer.

"Thank you, Mommy," she said with a happy sigh, shaking out her fur in the same way she did right after a bath. Hopefully, she wouldn't start zipping around like a maniac and rolling around in a frantic blur, which were the next two steps in her post-bath celebration.

"That feels much better," she said, then shook again but thankfully resisted taking her happy dance any farther. "Do you want to know what I smell?"

"I can tell you what she smells," Octo-Cat said from within my arms, a slight purr rising from his striped form. "It's those fried potato things."

"*Hey,*" the little dog whined. "I wanted to be the one to say. I wanted to help Mommy, so she would tell me I'm a good dog."

"You are the very best dog, Paisley, and don't worry, you can still tell me. Go ahead."

Octo-Cat had discovered this clue and chosen to keep it to himself. As far as I was concerned, Paisley was the one who deserved all the praise here.

She rolled on the ground once and then popped back up and sang, "It's the la-la-lokis. Or the latlatkes? I forget, but Mags ate a lot of them. She gave me a little piece, but I didn't like it. I think I would've rather had a lobster roll like Octo-Cat."

This piqued the cat's interest. "They do make a mighty fine lobster roll at the Little Dog Diner. Mighty fine. Shall we have another before heading home?"

"Not the time," I scolded him. "So you smell the food that Mags was eating just before she was taken?"

Paisley nodded and then stumbled slightly to the side, apparently needing to get used to being out of the costume just as she'd needed to get used to being in it. "Yeah, I smell it and it's going this way." She spun in a full circle and then ran down the alley and turned.

"Let's go," I said, shoving Octo-Cat into Charles's arms because I knew he could run faster and easier with the extra burden than I could. I also didn't want to take the chance my cat would disappear if left unsupervised.

Nothing mattered other than getting to my cousin.

Well, at least not to three of the four members of our little search committee.

We all jogged.

The Chihuahua kept moving fast but occasionally lapped us while yelling high-pitched words of encouragement. "Mommy, you can do it! You're a good runner! Yes, you are! You're a good girl! Come on, Mommy!"

While I found her cheerleading cute, it wasn't entirely helpful. At last, when my legs had begun to feel a bit prickly from all the unplanned movement in my tight jeans, Paisley stopped, let out a low growl, and stood with her head angled slightly toward the ground.

Charles and I slowed.

"Well, that was terrible," Octo-Cat complained. "Let's not do that again. Shall we?"

I ignored him and followed Paisley's line of sight with both my eyes and my feet.

"Do you see, Mommy?" the Chihuahua asked, impossibly keeping perfectly still despite the obvious desire to wag her tail hard. "This spot smells a lot like cousin Mags."

Charles and I both bent down to examine the fallen items that were partially covered in snow.

"That's because these are Mags's things," I revealed with a little gasp. I lifted her fuzzy white beret, discarded cell phone, and the shiny silver menorah she'd only just purchased that morning with shaky hands.

"Why did she leave them here?" Paisley asked with a little whine.

"I don't think she wanted to." I stowed all three items in my shoulder bag. "No. I don't think she wanted to," I repeated.

"So what do we do now?" Octo-Cat asked.

At the same time, Charles said, "Well, this is concrete evidence, and that's always a great thing to have."

"But what do we do now?" I parroted Octo-Cat's question.

"Why, we call in the cavalry, of course," came his response.

I loved Charles's ability to stay calm and level-headed, no matter how hard the going got. Even my cat had become fully invested in pursuing our case, his complaints coming out fewer and farther between. We were now working as one, and that made us unstoppable.

Mags, hang on. We're coming!

CHAPTER FOURTEEN

Charles called Nan while I called my mom.

She picked up on the first ring. "Hey, honey. Did you find Mags?"

"Not yet," I answered sadly. "But we have a small lead. Can you and Dad meet us at the alley off Third Street? You know the one right next to the pancake place?"

"Yes, we're coming!" she promised before hanging up.

Charles wrapped both arms around me and mumbled into my hair. "It's going to be okay. We'll find her. Your Nan is on the way right now, and she said something about bringing along a friend to help with the search."

"That will be Mr. Milton," I said, my voice coming out cold.

"Who's that? I don't think I've met him before."

"Neither had I. Not until today. It just seems weird, him hanging around with all that's going on."

"Well, maybe he really likes your Nan and wants to help in order to make her happy," Charles offered with shrug as he let me go.

I shook my head, unwilling to buy that, especially given his reaction earlier. "Yeah, or maybe he's the murderer we're all looking for."

Charles tutted. "You don't really believe that, do you?"

"Yes. No… I don't know. It just seems weird to me."

"Well, if you're not sure about him, then I'm not either. Maybe we can try asking him some questions when he arrives."

"Maybe."

"Are you talking about Nan's new friend?" Octavius asked, curling his upper lip in disgust. At least we agreed on this one. "That guy doesn't have the missing parts to kill somebody."

"The missing parts?" I asked in confusion.

"Yeah, you know. The ones that boy kittens have before they go to the doctor and—"

"I got it!" I rushed to cut him off before he could add to that description.

"Still, he's rather suspicious to me," my tabby added. "Did you see a picture of him on Mr. Gable's camera when you looked?"

"The camera! That's right," I said, slapping my forehead. We'd totally forgotten to look through the images. "I'll just call Mr. Gable and see if he's willing to let us borrow that real quick."

Although the committee head was too busy to talk for long, he revealed that he'd handed the camera over to the police before begging off the call.

"See," Charles said, keeping his arms tight around me while Octo-Cat sat in the snow silently. "Someone's looking into it. We have lots of people helping find Mags."

"To be fair, I don't think Mr. Milton took Mags, but he could be the murderer. I don't know. It's just strange that a guy we've never met before has suddenly become so involved in our business."

Charles didn't say anything until Mom and Dad arrived a few minutes later.

They hugged Charles hello.

"That was quick," he said.

"We weren't too far away. Just over at the ice sculpture garden with the Officer Bouchard and the others. You'll be happy to know that they have the entire Dewdrop Springs and Misty Harbor police departments both out looking for Mags while the Glendale crew continues with the double homicide."

"Isn't that great?" Dad said with his signature oversized grin. "The more, the merrier. Also the more, the faster we'll find her. And we *will* find her, Angie."

I forced a smile. "Yeah, that's what everyone keeps saying. I sure hope you're all right."

"*Faith*. You gotta have it," Dad said, his smile stretching even wider.

"Listen," I said, dropping my voice low, making sure only the group of us could hear. "Before Nan comes by, I just wanted to say I don't trust that new friend she's taking everywhere with her."

"Are you saying you suspect *Mr. Milton?*" Mom asked, her voice hitching unnaturally high at the end of that question.

"I'm saying I don't know. But until we rule him out as a suspect, maybe. I mean, I don't know who he is. I don't know how well Nan knows him. Do you guys know anything about him?"

Mom ran her fingers through her hair as she thought. "I have met him once or twice while covering stories out on Caraway Island. He seems like a reasonably decent man."

Caraway Island. That was the one part of Blueberry Bay I seldom went. Not just because it required a ferry, but also because they didn't have much to offer other than beautiful scenery. And while ocean views and well-groomed beaches were perfectly nice, we all had those in our small corner of coastal Maine.

"Is there something wrong with Caraway Island?" Charles asked, hooking an eyebrow in my direction. He'd become such a big part of my life since moving here about a year and a half ago that I sometimes forgot he originally hailed from California. He didn't know all the little quirks of living in Glendale yet.

"For one thing, the Caraway Island Cavaliers were our high school's biggest rival," I said, ticking off the first reason on my index finger, then raising a second finger as I continued with my list. "For another, folks from Glendale often visit Misty Harbor, Cooper's

Cove, and Dewdrop Springs, and they all come over here, too. Those on the island mostly keep to themselves, like they're too good for the rest of us or something."

Geographically, Caraway Island was part of Blueberry Bay, but they didn't belong with us in any other way that counted. Perhaps that's why it felt so strange that Nan's new boyfriend—or whatever he was to her—hailed from the small, strange island.

"I wouldn't worry about it too much, Angie. I know we all have our little prejudices about those Cavaliers, but Nan likes Mr. Milton and she's a good judge of character," Mom offered, even though I wasn't sure she meant it.

"Maybe," I said looking away and still feeling so lost and defeated in all this.

"What else can you tell us? Has there been any progress?" Charles asked.

And if my parents hadn't been standing right there, I would've given him a big fat juicy kiss as a thank you for changing the subject.

"I've been staying right on the story of the *murders in the ice sculpture garden*," Mom said, making her voice every bit as dramatic as Octo-Cat's was when he was telling the story or talking about himself. "The latest is that they found the statue the ice weapon was broken from. Even though it had mostly melted by the time the police arrived, they were still able to match it to a missing piece on the sculpture of a swan."

"I saw that one!" I said. "It's beautiful."

"It was beautiful, and it was made by Pearl from the animal shelter. You know Pearl, don't you? Well, let me just say she was devastated that her art had been used to kill that poor woman. Especially considering that she'd known Zelda Benedict and they were friendly."

"Do you think Pearl might have done it?" Charles ventured.

"Oh goodness, no!" Mom hissed, looking at Charles with shock and bewilderment. "Sweet Pearl is even older than Nan and not quite as spry. I have a hard time believing she can lift that five-pound Pomeranian of hers, let alone find the strength to first break off that giant icicle and then stab it through her friend's heart. Goodness me, not Pearl."

"What's everyone talking about over here?" Nan said, approaching with her usual swagger, arm linked in that of Mr. Milton.

"Thanks for coming so fast," Charles said, not wasting a second now that we were all together. "We found Mags's things spilled out on the ground here, so we know the kidnapper headed in this direction, and right now that's all we know. But it's a good place for us to start. Can you help us search?"

"I'll get the car," Dad said with a nod. "Meet you back here just as soon as I can."

"I'll get mine, too," Mr. Milton volunteered.

"And I'll go get mine," said Charles. "Angie, I'll be right back. Okay?"

"Okay," I nodded and accepted a quick kiss on the cheek.

As my boyfriend ran off with the other two men, Mom and Nan closed in for a group hug. We'd always been big huggers, but we took it to the extreme when facing situations like this. Danger and drama were becoming far too common for us these days, and I hated that Mags had been sucked into that.

"Do you guys have any theories?" I asked, knowing they probably wouldn't but still hoping they did.

Nan tilted her head. "I still can't get over the fact that one of them was killed with an icicle and the other a bullet. That doesn't seem very well planned to me."

"It really doesn't," Mom agreed. "And there's nothing to connect Fred and Zelda other than the fact they were both victimized today."

"There is a lot to think about with the murders, and of course I want to get justice for them. But right now Mags is what's important," I reminded them. "Do you have any theories about her?"

"Only that they meant to take you instead," Nan said with a frown. "And it's not a theory I like very much."

"But they took her instead of outright killing her. That's got to be a good thing. Right?" Mom asked, looking between me and Nan waiting for one of us to offer up a bit of encouragement.

"I hope so," I said for what felt like the millionth time that morning. Until we had Mags back safe and sound, it was the only thing I had.

Hope.

CHAPTER FIFTEEN

Dad returned with his car first, and Charles arrived shortly thereafter.

"Okay," I told everyone before departing, though Mr. Milton had still not returned. "We're looking for a white cargo van. The license plate may be too muddy to read or maybe they've given the car a wash since then. The truth is we don't have anything more than that. It's a definite long shot, but right now it's all we have to go on."

"Right-o," Dad said, touching his index finger and thumb together to make the *okay* signal. "Let's go get our girl."

I opened the passenger side door to Charles's sedan, and Paisley hopped right in. He picked her up and placed her on the backseat while I sat down carefully and arranged Octo-Cat on my lap.

Although my cat was much better about riding in the car now, sometimes his claws would still dig into my thighs if the driver took turns too hard or went too fast.

As soon as I had my seatbelt pulled securely over my lap, Charles gunned it. "Which way do you want to turn?" he asked me, moving us along quickly toward the main road.

All I had now was intuition and what I hoped might turn out as lucky guesses. For whatever reason, something tugged me toward the left.

We drove slowly through the well-trafficked areas while scanning every parking lot for a sign of our white van.

"This isn't going to work," I said after a ten-minute period that seemed to drag on for an eternity. "If they were smart enough to orchestrate a kidnapping, then they're smart enough to get the heck out of Dodge."

"Maybe," Charles agreed, continuing to maneuver the streets of Glendale unperturbed, "but we still have to try."

"You're right, you're right," I said, continuing to search in silence.

Octo-Cat surprised me by pressing his two front paws to the base of the window and joining our search. His fuzzy little head whipped back and forth with determination. *Would he be the one to find her?*

If we were still searching after dark, he likely would. After all, he was the only one of us who could see well in the dark.

Oh, how I hoped it wouldn't come to that!

The longer it took, the higher the risk to Mags. We should have had her by now. She shouldn't have ever been taken.

"Mommy," Paisley yipped from the backseat. "I can't see. I can't see, and I want to help."

"Has she spotted something?" Charles asked, answering her bark.

"No," I translated without pulling my eyes away from the street. "She can't see anything back there and wants to help."

Charles patted his lap with one hand. "Oh, well then come here, girl. C'mon."

Paisley didn't need to be told twice. She vaulted from the back-seat into Charles's lap where she now stood with her paws against the door in the same position as Octo-Cat.

"There are so many cars!" she remarked. "But only one of them took Mags."

"Obviously," my cat droned, but Paisley ignored him.

Charles kept driving straight. If we didn't turn off, we would eventually wind up in Cooper's Cove. Might the kidnappers have taken Mags there?

My eyes strained and the left one began to twitch as I felt my pulse boom beneath it. My brain stayed equally busy. So much was going on, it had become difficult to keep my head straight.

Two people had been killed, but the murderer may have only meant to take a single victim. Mags was kidnapped shortly thereafter, but the kidnappers may have meant to take me instead. We didn't know if the same person—or persons—had committed both crimes or whether it was just a big ol' coincidence they occurred so close together. I had no idea who would want to take me, who would want to hurt the judges, or where Mags could be.

It all felt like far too much.

And while investigating murders was often harrowing, we weren't usually racing against a clock. The dead would stay that way, no matter how long it took us to solve the murders, but Mags could still be saved.

"I don't like it when you do that," Octo-Cat said, turning to look back at me, a sneer on his little kitty face.

"Do what?" I said innocently.

"When you get all panicky. I can smell it, and it's not a good smell."

"You mean my stress hormones?"

"Whatever you want to call them. They're pretty disgusting, and anyway, you always do so much better when you're able to look at a situation logically. The moment you start freaking out is the moment you're working with a disadvantage."

Well…

I was dumbfounded by the insight of his observation and needed a moment to decide how to respond.

Octo-Cat, however, kept going. "We've solved how many cases together now? This has got to be number ten or something near that, and each of those times no matter what happened, you figured it out. Well, usually it was me who played the most instrumental role, but you were there, and you helped, just like good assistants do. You'd be of a lot more assistance to me now if you just took a moment to get a grip already. You can treat it like an episode of *Law & Order*. First, we need to solve the crime, and then we can worry about getting justice for the victims."

He hummed a melodic beat that I believed was meant to be the *Law & Order* sound—*dun dun*—and although I didn't think everything in our lives could be likened to an episode of his favorite show, this time my cat was absolutely right.

I'd let myself become too fixated on what could happen next. I needed to shift my focus to what we already knew, what had already happened, and then go forward from there.

Taking his advice, I took several deep, steadying breaths as I reviewed the facts of both cases in my mind.

"What are you thinking about?" Charles asked from beside me, chancing a quick glance in my direction while we continued on the road to Cooper's Cove.

"I'm going over everything we know and trying to look at things logically rather than letting my worry for Mags cloud everything."

"So you're relaxing a little?" he asked with a slight grin.

"I'm still crazy worried," I admitted with a sigh, "but I need to put that aside for everyone's benefit. Octo-Cat reminded me of that."

Charles reached over and patted Octo-Cat's head while moving his other hand to the top of the steering wheel. "He's a good cat when he wants to be."

"Yes he is," I agreed, smiling over at the tabby. "Yes he is…"

"So tell me what you're thinking," Charles continued. "Any fresh insights?"

I stayed silent for a minute as I gathered all my thoughts. "I just don't see a way that the murders and kidnapping can be linked other than the location, which I believe is a coincidence."

"Makes sense," he said. "Go on."

"I don't even think that both of *the murders* were planned, so it would be a stretch to add *the kidnapping* on top of that."

"And you've made a lot of enemies over the last year and a half," Octo-Cat reminded me with a quick flick of his tail.

I told Charles what the cat had said, and my boyfriend chuckled.

"That's what happens when you're the good guy. You always ruffle some of the bad guy's feathers"

Octo-Cat perked up at this analogy, but I focused on asking the next logical question. "But whose feathers would be ruffled enough to try to abduct me?"

"*Hmm.* Let's review. First, there were the folks involved with Ethel Fulton's demise and inheritance dispute."

Octo-Cat winced. Even though I knew he was happy living with me now, he still missed his original owner every day.

Charles continued to discuss the murderers and other criminals we'd played a role in apprehending, coming up with a list of more than a dozen potential suspects.

"Looks like the cat's right," he quipped. "A lot of people have cause to be very angry with you. But who would it benefit to take you now? They've already been caught. No changing that now."

"Most recently, Octo-Cat and I solved the murder on the train and the one in the pet store."

"The folks from the train were apprehended, correct?" Charles asked, raising an eyebrow in my direction.

"Yes, they're in jail and some of the others we've caught are, too."

Charles nodded thoughtfully. "*In jail* doesn't mean *not capable.* They could have lackies working for them for all we know."

"So, what you're saying is *we can't rule anybody out?*"

He shook his head sadly. "Nope. Not a single person."

My phone buzzed from the place where I'd dropped it in Charles's cup holder after getting in the car.

"It's Nan," I cried, quickly answering the call and putting it on speaker.

"Angie, dear!" she shouted into the phone. "It's Mags! They've found her! She's safe!"

Tears welled in my eyes. "Oh thank goodness… Thank goodness." We hadn't been too late after all.

"We're on our way," I promised Nan.

"So are we. We're all going back to the Glendale police station. See you there."

CHAPTER SIXTEEN

We reached the Glendale police station in record time. Charles swore he didn't go a mile over the speed limit—being the law-abiding lawyer he was—but I'm pretty sure that when I had the chance to sneak a peek at the speedometer, we were going at least ten over.

Then again, all the police were occupied elsewhere as we made our journey toward Mags.

When we got there, Nan and Mr. Milton had already arrived on the scene, and from what I could tell, Mags had just been delivered to the station as well.

"Oh, thank goodness, you're all right," I cried, rushing to hug her as tight as I could. A giant wracking sob tore through me once I had her safe in my arms.

We'd been so close to losing each other after only just having been reunited... And I'd been dangerously close to losing her for good.

My cousin stared at me through glassy, unblinking eyes, her face devoid of any rosiness as she regarded me.

"Now, now. Just give her a moment," the delivering officer commanded. "She's had quite the shock, this one."

I gulped and took a step back, willing my cousin to speak to me —but she remained perfectly quiet as the rest of us settled in at the station.

Mom and Dad arrived about five minutes after the rest of us and hugged Mags just as tightly as I had.

"Whoa," the officer said with a kind chuckle. "I hadn't realized we'd be hosting a family reunion right here at the station."

Mom shot him a cold look, but nobody said anything more. Not until Mags delicately cleared her throat and searched the small room until she found me.

"Angie," she said, her voice emotionless, disconnected. *"Angie,"* she repeated with added emphasis. "They didn't want me. They wanted you."

"I know," I answered with a nod.

Charles pressed in close, holding Octo-Cat in his arms.

Paisley had already been returned to Nan with a flurry of licks and cuddles.

Mags reached forward now to stroke Octo-Cat's soft, striped fur. "They kept calling me Russo," she said, "and I don't think they figured out that I'm not you."

"Who is *they?* And why did they take you?" As horrible as I felt that this had happened at all, it was even worse to know for sure that it had been my fault.

"I don't know," Mags answered with a frown. "They blindfolded me in the van and tied my hands behind my back. I never got a good look at either of them."

"How many were there? Were they male? Female?" I asked, praying that this would soon make sense so that Mags's kidnappers would have to pay for what they'd done.

"I'll be the one to ask questions here," the cop growled in warning. He was one I hadn't met before, probably from one of the officers from out of town. "If you'll just give us a moment—"

Mags raised her hand and interrupted him. "No, they're my family. I want them here. Anything you want to ask me, they can hear, too."

"Okay," the officer said, nodding once although he obviously didn't agree. "Let's start with a description of your kidnappers. How many were there? Male? Female? Any defining characteristics to their voices, anything you remember hearing or smelling?"

Those were questions I was going to ask too. Some of them I already had. It seemed important to the officer that he remain in charge, so I remained quiet.

Mags shook her head slowly. "From what I could tell, there were two. A man and woman. Remember, I couldn't see anything. Only hear. And when the man pulled me into the car, I still had my things with me. That morning I bought a solid metal menorah from the nice ladies at the Hanukkah tent and I used it to thwack him over the head as hard as I could. It wasn't enough to knock him out, though. That's when he took everything away and threw it out the window."

I reached into my bag and pulled out the things we had found in the snow. "We've got everything right here for you," I said, returning them to her. "And good job getting that hit in."

A small smile flitted across Mags's face, but it was gone just as quickly as it had arrived.

"They kept calling me Russo, and I didn't correct them because I didn't want to put you in danger, and I didn't know what they would do if they found out they had the wrong person. I was so scared, Angie."

"I know," I said, my voice cracking.

"They were so angry. They kept telling me to keep my nose out of places where it didn't belong. They said bad things would happen to me, much worse than this if I crossed them again."

"But who?" I asked, unable to contain a groan.

Enormous tears spilled from Mags's eyes. "I don't know. I wish I did, so I could warn you. All I know is they were mad, and they said they'd definitely be back if you didn't fall in line. What did they mean, Angie? What have you gotten into? Is it drugs?"

"Never!" I assured her, placing a hand on her shoulder and giving it a squeeze. "This has to be related to my work as a private investigator. I've outed some pretty unsavory characters in my day."

The cop scratched his chin. "A P.I., huh?"

I nodded, and we said no more about that. "So did they just deliver the message and then let you go?" he asked after returning his attention to Mags.

"I think they planned to keep me longer, but something spooked them. Maybe the sound of sirens. I'm not sure, because it's all kind of a blur. They panicked and left. Once I was sure they weren't coming back, I got to work on the ties binding my hands. And once those were free, I took off the blindfold and made my way to the road."

"And that's where we found you," the officer concluded.

"Yes." Mags turned to me. "It's hard to believe that wasn't even half an hour ago."

"It's hard to believe a lot about today," Nan added.

Mr. Milton, who'd remained quiet until now, cleared his throat. "They took you to Dewdrop Springs. Probably means they're from there. A lot of the bad things that happen around the bay come from folks in that town."

All eyes zoomed to Mr. Milton. Nobody wanted to contradict him, but nobody jumped to agree with him either.

"It could have been anyone," I said at last. "But I doubt the kidnappers were stupid enough to return home while they had her."

"Are you saying we should rule out Dewdrop Springs?" Mr. Milton questioned, his voice flaring in irritation.

"No, but we shouldn't rule out all the other possibilities, either."

"Is there anything more you can tell us, Mags?" Mom asked, wrapping an arm around her niece's shoulder.

"That's all I know," Mags answered somberly.

I remained quiet. Mags had already been through so much. There was no point asking her to recall more when she'd already told us.

Did this mean the kidnappers wouldn't be found?

Probably at least not for now.

And who or what had scared them off? Would they really be back?

Would every moment going forward put me in peril, seeing as they could strike at any time?

They'd said they wanted me to stop, but I didn't know what I should stop. And honestly, I refused to be scared off my duties as a P.I. by some disgruntled bad guys.

More than afraid, I was angry—angry this had happened to Mags in my place, angry it had happened at all, and angry that Mr. Milton was still here.

Finally, I decided to say something about that niggling little problem. "Do you think we should limit any further discussions to family only?"

I looked to my parents for support, but it was Nan who answered. "Are you trying to suggest Mr. Milton isn't welcome?"

"I just think it would be better," I said, "if it were only us."

When Nan didn't argue in his defense, Mr. Milton became extremely flustered. "I'm only trying to help. Can't you see that?" he demanded of me.

Mags spoke up in the eerie voice she'd affected since returning to us. "Angie's right. I want him to go."

Mr. Milton looked to Nan one last time, then stormed out of the station.

CHAPTER SEVENTEEN

"C'mon," the police officer told Mags. "We need to get your statement on record before letting you go."

"Should I come with you?" Charles offered.

Mags shook her head. "I didn't do anything wrong, so I don't need a lawyer present, but thank you."

We watched her go, the rest of us remaining in the waiting room uncomfortably close to a grimy looking coffeemaker. I hung back as far as I could from the untrustworthy appliance.

If it was a coffeemaker that had first given me my ability to talk to animals, then another coffeemaker could just as easily take that power away, too. Definitely not something I was willing to risk.

"How are you feeling?" Charles asked, leaning one shoulder onto the wall beside me and sweeping his concerned eyes over me.

"I feel like a giant weight has been lifted from my chest," I said. "I know that's super cliché, but it's also like a part of me didn't even realize that I couldn't breathe until Mags was brought back safe, sound, and relatively unharmed."

"I know what you mean," Mom agreed and laced her fingers through my father's.

"I don't know if we'll be able to find the kidnappers based on the information we have, dear," Nan told me, concern etched across her aged features.

"It's not a big deal. Now that I know they're coming for me, I'll be ready," I promised.

"Maybe they only wanted to give you that warning and plan to leave it at that," my dad ventured. "Are you going to listen?"

"Of course not," Nan answered for me. "Angie hasn't done a single thing wrong."

I simpered at my parents. "She's right, you know. Now that we have Mags back, we need to focus on figuring out who killed the judges."

"What are you thinking?" Mom asked, curiosity flashing in her eyes.

"I'm thinking I'd like to talk to Mr. Gable again. He's the one who knew the most about the Holiday Spectacular. Both the festival itself and the committee who planned it."

"Don't forget he's the one who knows the most about the guests, too," Charles reminded me. "He took pictures of everyone who came through that main entrance."

"Yes, the camera!" I cried. "It's here at the police station. I never got a chance to finish looking through it."

"That officer didn't seem too keen on having us involved in his investigation," Dad grumbled. "Do you really think he'd share a key piece of evidence like that?"

Charles shook his head in response. "He might not want to, but I bet that officer Bouchard could convince him otherwise."

"Already on it." Mom held up her phone as the call connected. A moment later, a wide smile stretched across her face.

"Yes, it's me, Laura Lee. We found Mags, which you probably already heard, so now we're available to help you find the killer from the ice sculpture garden."

I couldn't hear the officer's side of the conversation, but whatever he said didn't slow Mom down one bit.

"Of course, I know you're all working on it very hard," she said, bobbing her head, "but you know how talented my Angie is, and I think she might have already figured it all out besides."

I made a slicing motion across my neck, begging her not to exaggerate our position, but it was too late.

Mom smiled even wider. "Yes, yes, we just need to take another look at those photos from Mr. Gable's camera to confirm. Would you mind letting us take a look?"

She paused while Officer Bouchard said something on the other end of the line.

"Luckily, we just so happen to be at the Glendale police station already, so if you would give the word to your colleague here, I'm sure he'd be happy to share."

I watched Mom as she marched in the direction the officer and Mags had departed and knocked on the door to the interrogation room.

Definitely not standard procedure, but Mom had never worried much about that. She would go anywhere, do anything to pursue a hot story, and this was definitely the hottest of the holiday season.

"Oh, officer!" she called through the door. "I know you're in there. I have Officer Bouchard on the line, and he has a message for you."

I stood in shocked silence as the door flung open. The officer cursed softly, then told Mags he'd be back in a moment. Sure enough, less than three minutes later we had Mr. Gable's camera in hand and free rein to look through the photographs.

"What are you hoping to find?" Nan asked me as I flicked faster and faster, taking in all the smiling faces from that morning one by one.

"I'm not exactly sure, but I'd like to see if any of the shots send up warning flares."

Although I didn't say so, I was also trying to determine who the two suspicious characters the rabbit E.B. had noted might be.

I reached the end of the photo roll and then began to flip back through in the other direction. Faster, faster, still unsure of what I was hoping to find, but knowing I was so close.

"Do you think—" my father started, but Charles held up a hand to silence him. He recognized something in my face before I'd even managed to connect the dots in my brain.

I shuffled through the pictures again, finally realizing that one very specific person was missing. "Nan, when did you and Mr. Milton join up today?"

"Why, he found me a few minutes after we arrived while you and Mags were still getting that fancy cocoa. You remember. Don't you?"

I nodded. "So he arrived before us, then?"

"Yes, absolutely," Nan assured me.

I found our photo in the lineup. We were one of the first. Only about ten folks had arrived before us, and none of them were Mr. Milton. Could he be one of the people E.B. had identified as acting suspiciously?

I wished I could ask the bunny now, but she'd already told me all humans look the same and I knew she wouldn't be able to recognize a specific person if shown a picture—not that I even had one of those since our old pal Mr. Milton had evaded the camera.

"He's not here," I told Nan, handing over the camera.

"Oh dear, don't be ridiculous." She flipped through quickly, her voice trailing off. "He probably took another entrance. There were several to choose from."

"I have a bad feeling about this," Mom mumbled.

"If you hadn't sent him away, he'd be here to answer these accusations for himself," Nan said, but I could tell she now worried about his possible involvement as well.

"He is a member of the committee, too, you know. He could have helped with information, but you never gave him a chance." This behavior from Nan was shocking. She'd always supported me, no matter what. So to see her defending Mr. Milton now sent a chill rushing right through me.

"Nan, what exactly is your relationship with Mr. Milton? I never met him before today, and he just seems a little possessive of you."

"Oh, don't be silly," Nan responded. "He's an old friend from years ago, and we simply reconnected now."

"Do you think he's capable of murder or kidnapping?" I asked.

"How could he have been the one to kidnap Mags when he was

with us the whole time?" Nan asked with a slight quaver in her voice.

"Okay. Maybe not the kidnapping, but what about the murders? He arrived before us and the victims were already dead by then."

"He would never," she insisted and bit her lip, a telltale sign she didn't quite believe the words that had come out of her mouth.

"Don't worry, Nan. I'm not saying he did it. But you are right about one thing. We need to talk to somebody on that committee."

"Should I ring Mr. Gable?" Mom offered.

"No," I said, pushing her arm down even as she had already begun to dial.

"Just like Mr. Milton attached himself to us all day, it's possible the guilty party could be lingering very close to Mr. Gable now, and I don't want to alert him that we're coming. Not until we have the chance to talk to Mr. Gable directly."

"Have you figured it out?" Charles asked, rubbing my shoulders as if I were a boxer about to go in for round two of the fight.

"Not yet, but I feel close. Mom, Dad, would you please stay here and wait for Mags? I need to go now while everything is still clicking in my brain."

"Of course, honey," Mom replied.

"But be careful and call us if you need anything. Got it?" Dad added.

Charles, Nan, and I rushed out of the station with the pets in tow just as quickly as we entered. "We'll take my car," Charles said, unlocking it remotely so that Nan and Paisley could slip into the backseat and Octo-Cat and I into the passenger side.

I took a quick moment to explain my theory to the others.

"There's definite merit to that," Charles agreed, turning the key in the ignition. "It makes sense. I just hope we're not playing our hand too soon."

"Everything will be just fine." Nan sounded more like her usual self now that Mr. Milton wasn't around.

"Are we going to catch the bad guys now?" Paisley asked with an excited whimper.

"Yes," Octo-Cat answered for me. "It's time to make the canary sing."

He licked his lips at the mention of the canary even though we weren't going to confront a snitch—we would go directly to the guilty party.

CHAPTER EIGHTEEN

W e found Mr. Gable at the sleigh same as he'd been before.
"Welcome back," he called as Nan, Charles, the animals, and I approached on foot, having parked just around the corner.

"Have you been busy?" Charles asked with a friendly smile.

"Things are slowing down now. Far fewer visitors coming into town, but we still have a lot of ticked-off vendors who want to have a word with the person in charge before they head on home."

Charles shifted seamlessly into the role of ace attorney. "Was the festival insured?"

"Of course we were. And thankfully we should have enough to cover all the fee reimbursements, but I still don't know what the future holds for us. Whether the festival is done for good or it will continue on in a different place." The weight of this uncertainty hung heavily over his shoulders. Mr. Gable appeared to fold into himself as he considered the options, both of which were far less than ideal.

"But the Holiday Spectacular has always been in Glendale." Nan also didn't want to accept that things would likely be changing, and I completely understood where she was coming from.

Traditions were special because you could rely on them being the same each year, and I hated to think that my favorite part of Christmas could be going away for good.

Mr. Gable frowned as he noted the dejected look on Nan's face. "It has been, but we were chosen to represent the entire Blueberry Bay region when things were first starting up. It could just as easily be moved to Dewdrop Springs or Misty Harbor."

"Well, it shouldn't be," Nan clucked, eliciting a smile from Mr. Gable for the first time since tragedy had struck earlier that day.

"Where's E.B.?" I asked. Might I find some time to talk with the rabbit in private about my suspicions?

"Burrowed deep in the hay to stay warm, that sweet girl."

Upon hearing this, Paisley raced over to the nativity and began to dig furiously.

I set Octo-Cat down on the seat of the sleigh, and he remained quiet, wanting to hear what would happen next just as much as I did. I still didn't know whether it would be Mr. Gable or E.B. to give me the final intel I needed, but either way, I knew we'd find the culprit soon.

"Can we gather the committee?" I asked him now.

"I suppose we could. Why? Have you figured out something that could help us?"

"I think I may have a lead," I responded with a poorly concealed smile. "But I'd really rather share with the entire committee if possible."

Mr. Gable regarded me wearily. "Most of them are still around, but at least one is otherwise occupied."

"Oh?" Charles asked, stepping closer as his interest grew.

Nan also watched Mr. Gable with wide eyes and shivering shoulders. The day was becoming colder as more and more snow fell, and we were all more than ready to go home.

We were so close now, though. I could practically taste it.

"Yes." Mr. Gable rubbed his hands together and blew out an icy puff of air. "Officer Bouchard is wrapped up in the homicide investigation, so I don't think he'll be able to put that aside for an impromptu meeting."

"He was on the committee?" I asked. Why was I only just now learning this? "That's strange, because he didn't recognize Zelda when we first discovered the bodies. And wasn't it Fred who was the last-minute addition rather than Zelda?"

Mr. Gable nodded as he turned this over in his memory. "I suppose he wouldn't. You see, Officer Bouchard only came to the meetings that pertained directly to safety and security. It's possible he either didn't pay attention to the finer details of areas that didn't concern him or that he knew about Zelda but was unable to connect the face with the name."

I nodded along, still finding it strange—especially considering Officer Bouchard served as chief detective whenever Glendale needed someone to slip into the role.

"Was it the same for any of the other committee members as well?" I asked, knowing we were mere moments from a big revelation.

"Yes, we had a couple who only contributed to certain areas just like the good officer Bouchard. Most of us were involved in all the planning meetings, though."

Nan went to join Octo-Cat on the sleigh. I worried that the cold had seeped into her bones. Even though she was in better shape than me, she was also quite old, and we'd been outside for much of the day in this frigid weather.

Charles whipped out his phone and opened the notes app. "Would you be able to give us a list of your members to help me figure out which were only partially involved, like Officer Bouchard?"

I watched as Nan settled in with Octo-Cat on her lap, glad they would keep each other warm now.

When I turned back to the men, I asked, "Mr. Gable, could you please also tell us which of the full-time members missed that last meeting, the one where Fred was added as a second judge?"

"Oh, sure that's easy. Just a second. I'll help you there, son." Mr. Gable and Charles worked out the list while I checked on the animals.

Paisley had cuddled her small, mostly black body against E.B. in the hay and was grooming her cheeks. The bunny trembled—probably afraid for her life—but I knew Paisley would never harm. She just didn't have it in her.

Octo-Cat watched the snow fall from his place on Nan's lap, following individual flakes as they floated down from the sky.

"It really is a pretty day," he said. "All the snow makes the sun shine brighter. It would be nice to take a nap if it weren't so wet —or there weren't so many murders happening around town, too."

I simpered at him and stroked his back. He always had a way of bringing things into perspective, that cat of mine.

"Angie, we've got it," Charles called me back to his side.

"Here's the full list. As you see, there are fifteen committee members in all that served this year. The ones with the stars only involve themselves in specific areas of the planning." He pointed to the names *Officer Bouchard* and *Janice Delacroix.*

"The ones with the question mark were involved in full-scale planning but missed the final meeting." He then pointed to *Bill Randone* and *Harvey Milton* on his digital list.

"Milton!" I almost choked on the name. "Is that Nan's friend, Mr. Milton?"

"What?" Nan cried, hopping down from the sleigh and coming to join us, Octo-Cat still curled comfortably in her arms. "What bout Harvey?"

"He was on the committee, but he missed our last meeting so he didn't know about the last-minute judging changeup," Mr. Gable summarized. "And you know, Dorothy, I don't think I ever would have pictured you two as a couple. That Cupid works in mysterious ways."

"Can you tell us more about Janice and Bill? I don't know those two," I asked, shaking off the reference to my grandmother's love life, especially seeing as it concerned Harvey Milton.

Charles stared at his phone while Mr. Gable met my gaze. "Janice is our go-to marketing gal. She manages social media, the website, our newsletter. Doesn't really come to the meetings, but we send her everything by email. I don't know how carefully she reads over the materials we send her way, but she has access to the full information if she wants it."

"And Bill?" Charles mumbled, not bothering to glance up from his phone.

"Bill usually came with Harvey. They both had a long trek from Caraway Island, having to catch the ferry there and back."

Something tightened in my chest. "Caraway Island?" I asked as if I'd never heard of the place before.

Mr. Gable nodded. "Yes, and they both missed the last meeting due to something unplanned. I think Bill had to work late and Harvey didn't want to take the trip over on his own. Something like that."

"Nan, did you know Mr. Milton was on the committee?"

"Of course I knew," she responded, but her face crumpled a bit as I asked Mr. Gable my next question.

Now my heart began to gallop in my chest. We were so, so close. "Did you take a picture of Bill today?" I asked.

He thought about this. "Actually, no. I don't think I saw him at all until after we were shutting things down."

If I'd have been a cartoon, a giant lightbulb would have flashed over my head at this reveal. *Bill Randone,* that was the name of our guilty party. We had it. We had it at last. Now we just had to get him.

Somehow. Someway.

"Is he still here?" I asked, my words slurring together as I worked to get them out of my mouth as quickly as possible. "Is he helping to shut things down and send people over toward the park?"

"Last I knew, he was stationed over on Third Street."

"Let's go," I said, breaking into an immediate run.

Nan pulled right up at my side and matched my pace. At some point, she must have given Octo-Cat to Charles, because he ran a few paces behind carrying both the cat and the dog as he puffed along.

Mr. Gable hadn't joined us in the pursuit, probably because he didn't want to leave E.B. on her own.

"I just can't believe all of that," Nan said. "I trust Mr. Gable, but

I also know Harvey didn't do this because he was with me the whole time. Do you think he knew about Bill?"

"There's a chance," I said between huffs. Running was still not a strong point for me, and somehow I'd managed to do it twice in one day now.

We ran another block before rounding the corner onto Third Street. And while I'd never seen Bill Randone a day in my life, I spotted him immediately because there he stood with Harvey Milton as the two carried on an animated discussion.

Suddenly they both glanced up and spotted us racing toward them. Randone immediately took off in the other direction at a sprint.

I grabbed my phone, still running, and dialed Officer Bouchard to let him know what we'd discovered and that his primary suspect was now on the run.

Nan pulled ahead, closing the rest of the distance to Mr. Milton faster than I could ever hope to move.

Then slapped him right across the face.

CHAPTER NINETEEN

I don't think I'd ever seen my Nan quite as angry as she was that day.

"You knew," she spat, her normally warm and friendly eyes saturated with a shocking coldness. "This whole time you knew and were probably even feeding information back to your friend."

Mr. Milton cleared his throat. Something I now realized he did whenever he felt nervous. "I didn't know for sure, but I suspected."

"Oh, you *suspected*," Nan repeated sarcastically. "So what were you? Warning him just now?"

"No!" Mr. Milton finally raised his voice to join in the fight. "I was confronting him with my suspicions."

"And giving him a chance to run." I jumped right into the fray as well. "Why wouldn't you have gone straight to the police?"

Picking up on our emotions, Paisley began to bark and growl and kick out her back legs like a chicken scratching at pebbles. "Bad man! Bad, bad man! No treats for you!"

Charles and Octo-Cat watched silently as the three women— two human and one dog—ganged up on a very guilty looking Harvey Milton.

"I don't agree with what he did, but I do agree with why he did it." This statement drew gasps from all of us, even Charles and Octo-Cat, who had chosen to mostly stay out of the confrontation.

"What?" Nan and I exploded in unison.

Mr. Milton shook his head. This time he didn't clear his throat, clearly feeling conviction in the words he was about to speak. "Caraway Island needs the Holiday Spectacular far more than Glendale ever did. The whole thing is a tourism goldmine, and our city is struggling. Due to the isolation, few ever manage to venture over. Each year it gets worse. Businesses are closing, and our community is becoming more and more cut off from the rest of the area. We need something… A magic bullet, if you will."

He winced. "Okay, maybe not the best choice of words."

I laughed bitterly. "The fact that you would say such a thing—even accidentally—just goes to show what a horrible person you actually are. It's like you think it's okay that your friend killed two people to try to bring more money into your city."

"Of course it's not okay," Mr. Milton responded, his gaze narrowing at me, "but we tried everything else and nothing worked."

"Everything short of murder," Nan mumbled and crossed her arms over her chest defensively.

Mr. Milton continued, keeping his eyes fixed on me. "When the planning started up for this year, Bill and I pushed for moving the festival to Caraway Island, but Gable and the others were quick to shoot us down. Bill said that Glendale wouldn't have a snowball's chance in hell of keeping the festival once a well-respected outsider got murdered on their watch. Naturally, Caraway would come to the rescue and agree to host going forward."

"And Bill told you all of this after the fact, I'm assuming." I tapped my foot in irritation. "Was this before or after your friend killed two innocent people? Oh, and the cops are already after him by the way. I spoke to my good friend Officer Bouchard while my grandmother was busy beating you up."

I thought I heard Charles chuckle under his breath, but it was hard to tell over the sound of Paisley's harried barking.

"Obviously, it was *after*. I already told you I had nothing to do with the murders."

"What about Fred Hapley?" I asked. "You mentioned shooting a well-respected outsider. But Fred wasn't either of those things. I'm sure most people tried to avoid his insurance sales pitch whenever they saw him coming."

Mr. Milton cleared his throat several times but remained every bit as angry as he had before resorting to this maneuver. "What about Fred Hapley? He got in the way. That's all. Bill missed the last meeting, so he didn't know the guy would be there. Luckily, he had a gun on him in case the icicle failed to do its job with the woman. The icicle worked, but he still found a use for the gun, anyway."

"Luckily?" Nan and I cried once again in perfect sync.

Nan reared back and slapped him across the other cheek. "I can't believe I ever considered you a friend," she said with disgust.

"If that's all, I'll just be going on my way," Mr. Milton said with one last look toward Nan as a giant frown took over his face. "It's really too bad. I liked you, Dorothy. I thought we had started something special. I can see now your affections are fickle."

"I don't date criminals," she hissed through gritted teeth.

"Believe what you want. I don't have to answer you anyway."

"No, but you do have to answer to him," Charles countered, drawing all our attention to the officer approaching from behind. It was the same cop we had run across earlier, the one who had questioned Mags and insisted on remaining in full control at the station.

Several paces back, Dad followed.

"Where's Mags?" I asked when he stopped at my side.

"Your mother took her home and sent me to find out what was going on here."

We watched side-by-side as the out-of-town officer slapped a pair of cuffs on Harvey Milton. Whether or not he planned any of it, he'd still been an accomplice by keeping his neighbor's secret.

As happy as I was to see Milton carted away, something still wasn't right. "What about the other guy?"

"Yes, what about Bill Randone?" Nan demanded.

"Bouchard's got him," came the answer. "That's right, you'll see your buddy soon enough at the station."

Milton drew on his right to remain silent, leaving the rest of us gaping until the officer escorted him from our view.

"Well, that's one way to celebrate Christmas Eve," Nan remarked with a shrug as we all burst into relieved laughter.

"I think I prefer the more traditional methods of celebration." Charles wrapped his arms around me and kissed my forehead protectively.

Octo-Cat got squished in between us but didn't utter a single meow in protest. "I knew it the whole time," he said instead.

"You did, did you?" I asked with another chuckle.

"The cat always knows," he explained, winking up at me.

Seeing as it was Christmas, I decided to let that one go. "You did good," I told him, backing out of Charles's embrace so he could breathe easily once more.

"You, too, Paisley. Good dog." I bent down and picked her up, and after having accepted a few pets and kisses from me, she vaulted into Nan's arms, completely unconcerned for her own safety.

"Whoa there," Nan cried, praising the wriggling little ball of fur.

"I'm sorry about your new boyfriend," my dad offered with a frown.

"Me, too," she said. "Luckily we weren't quite to that point yet, though."

"Think you'll ever forgive him?" Charles asked.

"Heck no," my grandmother shouted, then hacked a giant loogie onto the snow, drawing shocked laughter from all of us.

"Even though he swears he wasn't involved in the murders, he still warned his friend rather than turning him in. As far as I'm concerned, that's just as bad. I'd never be able to trust him again. Not after that stunt."

"You know what? Forget about Mr. Milton," I said. "He's not important."

"Actually, I do owe him one thing." Nan glanced from the street toward the sky, then met my eyes head-on. "I hadn't quite realized how lonely I let myself become since your grandfather passed. Of course, I have you and Paisley and…"

"And enough friends to fill a football stadium," Dad pointed out with a smile.

"That, too," she admitted her smile matching his, "but it's not quite the same as having a partner."

Charles pulled me into his side as we beamed at Nan and the touching news she'd just shared with us.

"So you think you're ready to date again?" I asked, my heart swelling with excitement for her.

"I think I'm getting there," she said with a sly grin. "One step at a time."

CHAPTER TWENTY

We spent Christmas holed up at home. Mom, Dad, and Charles all joined us at different points in the day, but mostly it was just me, Nan, and Mags sitting around our enormous Christmas tree and sharing our favorite memories from the years we'd missed out on celebrating together.

Nan, of course, dressed Octo-Cat and Paisley in their home-made holiday sweaters but held her tongue when Mags decided to wear a floor-length khaki skirt with a mint green cardigan set.

I opted to remain in pajamas, because nothing beats the comfort of flannel after a long, hard day—and the one we'd had yesterday was certainly a doozy.

That was Christmas.

On the day after Christmas, Mags finally taught us how to make candles the traditional way. Although I always loved learning some-thing new, I didn't foresee many more candle-making sessions in my future. The whole process of dipping seemed to take forever, and I had nowhere near the skill Mags did when it came to swirling colors and carving patterns.

She made it fun, though, dropping random facts in here and

there and entertaining us with a carefully curated collection of jokes.

I'd wondered if she was feeding us some of the same lines she gave her students back home. I kind of hoped she had.

We continued to eat up every moment together, but as the days passed, I grew sad knowing our time was almost up. I wished my cousin didn't live so far away because she'd very quickly become the sister I never had—and, despite everything, she said she felt the same way about me, too.

"Next time we'll have to get Nan and Aunt Lydia together with us," she said with a laugh I didn't understand, having never met Lydia for myself.

"Once we put those two together, all we'll have to do is sit back and watch while laughing our butts off," she added with a guffaw.

A couple more days passed, bringing us to New Year's Eve. Mags would be on an early flight out of town the next day. The rates, she explained, were far too good to pass up in favor of sleeping in.

I, however, balked when I saw just how early her flight was scheduled. "Are you going to be able to stay up?" I asked, having waited for the ball to drop every year since my mom had first let me stay up at the age of six.

"Of course I'm going to stay up!" she said with a scandalized gasp. "I might not even go to bed at all."

I laughed, Octo-Cat groaned, and Paisley danced, not quite knowing why. All was as it should be in my little corner of the world.

The doorbell chimed, this time to the tune of *Feliz Navidad*—in honor of Paisley's Mexican heritage, Nan had informed me, even though that little dog had never stepped foot out of Maine a single day in her life.

Nan rushed to the entryway, fluffing her hair as she went. Her normal hot pink attire had been retired for the evening in favor of a sparkly silver dress. She looked like an award show trophy, and I looked rather out of place in my polka dotted pants and Grumpy Cat T-shirt. The latter had been a gift from Mags who said she'd never known anyone who loves their cat quite the way I do.

"Come in, come in." Nan's voice carried throughout the lower floor. "So glad you could make it."

I heard her exchange European-style kisses on either side of her visitor's cheeks and a moment later they appeared. "Happy New Year!" Mr. Gable announced cheerfully, carrying E.B. in one arm and a large bag of take-out in the other.

"Happy New Year!" Mags and I wished him back.

"Something smells marvelous," my cat said, perking up from his nap. He sniffed the air and then a grin spread between his whiskered cheeks. "Could it be...?"

Mr. Gable handed E.B. to me and the food to Nan, then ran out to his car for a second load.

"Hello again, little bunny," I said, conscious of Mags's eyes on me.

"Hello," E.B. answered all the while wiggling, wiggling, wiggling that nose. Mr. Gable returned with a triangular-shaped litter box filled with hay and fresh produce. He took his rabbit back from me and set her on the ground near the area he had fashioned for her.

Paisley trotted over, head held high. "Hello again, dear E.B. Do you still want to talk about your feelings?"

Oh, that sweet Chihuahua, always willing to do whatever it took to make others happy.

"What feelings?" E.B. asked, taking a tentative hop toward a piece of lettuce while keeping one eye glued to her canine acquaintance.

"When we met you at the festival you said you were always afraid that others would hurt you. Let's explore those feelings, shall we?" Paisley tilted her head to the side, both ears perked high as she waited for E.B. to share.

The lop-eared bunny nibbled on her veggies for a spell, then said, "No one's ever asked me about how I feel before. Are you sure you want to know?"

Paisley plopped her wagging butt onto the ground. "Oh yes. I want to know everything," she said, her eyes sparkling with kindness. "Let's start with your childhood. Were you a happy baby bunny or a sad baby bunny?"

I stifled a laugh and left those two on their own.

Octo-Cat had followed Nan into the kitchen and Mags, Mr. Gable, and I now moved to join them there.

"I didn't know what to bring for our little New Year's shindig," he explained with an infectious grin. "So I stopped by my favorite restaurant and picked us up something to nosh on."

The logo for the Little Dog Diner was emblazoned across the bag, and scents of shrimp, garlic bread and lobster rolls now mingled with those of the baked goods Nan had prepared earlier in the evening.

Nan pulled each item out of the bag and set it on the counter.

The moment the lobster rolls made an appearance, my cat jumped onto the counter and twirled in three tight circles. "It is! It is! It is!" he cried as he spun even still. "It's my favorite food! Oh, Happy New Year to you, good sir."

I stifled another laugh. Sometimes it was really hard not to react to the animals in front of others, especially as I remembered E.B. using *Merry Christmas* as a curse word when last we met.

"Wonderful, thank you so much for bringing it," Nan said, and I could've sworn I saw a slight blush rise to her cheek. "Little Dog Diner is a favorite of ours, too."

"I'll get the plates," Mags volunteered.

"And I'll pour the drinks," I chimed in.

Nan plated up a nice variety for each of us, and together we retreated to the formal dining room table. None of us were big drinkers, so we shared a bottle of celebratory cider instead.

And although I hadn't known Mr. Gable and E.B. would join us, I was definitely happy they had.

"What should we toast to?" Mags asked, a sweet smile tilting her lips upward.

"Well, first of all, *to you,*" I sang out. "To you being a part of this family. To us getting to know and love you. And to you surviving the kidnapping."

We all laughed at the not-so-distant memory.

"I'll drink to that," Mags said with a giggle.

"Wait. Just you wait one second," Nan clucked. "I want your resolutions. That's right, all of you."

Mr. Gable stood. "I resolve that this year no one will get injured on my watch."

"Does that mean the Holiday Spectacular is returning to Glendale?" I asked hopefully.

"Not quite," he answered with a small sigh. "We're moving it to Cooper's Cove, but the remaining committee members, those who haven't gone to jail, elected to keep me as the head. And I of course was happy to accept."

Cheers rose around the table.

"That's awesome!" Mags enthused. "But I hope you don't mind that I probably won't be going next year."

We all laughed again. My heart remained light, mostly because I knew I'd be seeing lots more of Mags in the months to follow. In fact, we'd already begun planning a family reunion for the coming summer.

"All right, who's next?" Nan asked, looking between Mags and me and waiting for one of us to volunteer resolutions.

"Mine's easy," I said, shooting to my feet and lifting my glass. "This will be the year I get my private investigation firm off the ground."

"*Our*," Octo-Cat corrected, though only I understood. "And when do I get my lobster roll?"

Mags drummed her fingers on the tabletop. "I don't know what I want out of this year other than to try new things. New things are what brought us together, after all, and I don't think I've ever been happier than I am now."

"That's a bold proclamation given what happened on Christmas Eve," Mr. Gable quipped.

"It is," she agreed, "but it also speaks of just how much I love my new cousin and my new Nan."

Nan and I both *awwwe*d.

When the table grew quiet again, Nan rose with her drink in hand. "I live every day like it's my first, my last, my everything. That's how you make life fun, you know. But this year I'm going to be a bit more careful about who I let into my life, and maybe this year I'll even find love again."

She glanced coyly toward Mr. Gable, who blushed and looked away.

My heart did a giant happy somersault. I never would've pictured the two of them together but seeing it now made perfect sense. I wondered if they felt it, too. If they were already well on their way to something wonderful together.

Yes, the next year was looking pretty good as we dove into our meals, chatting and drinking happily enjoying the good company.

"Ahem," my cat said, jumping onto the table and flicking his tail ominously. "Aren't you forgetting something?"

Ugh. I *had* forgotten his lobster roll in all the excitement over Nan and Mr. Gable's possible forthcoming relationship.

"Off the table," I told him, taking half of my lobster roll and setting it on the ground so that he would leave me in peace.

He jumped down after it, joy sparking in his amber eyes. He moved quickly but not quite enough.

As if from thin air, Paisley appeared and snatched the treat away, racing back toward E.B. with the giant hunk of food protruding from her impossibly small mouth.

"Unhand my sandwich, thief!" Octo-Cat cried.

"I'm sorry, Octavius," she said, blinking slowly, as she regarded him. "I've been looking forward to this ever since I first smelled these things at the festival. You didn't share then, but it's okay. I forgive you."

"Angela!" my cat cried, staring at me in horror. "She took my sandwich! She stole it!"

I laughed, unable to hide my amusement any longer.

I tossed him a large shrimp, which he pawed at morosely.

"It's not the same" he mewled.

No, it wasn't the same.

Nothing was the same as it had once been.

But you know what? Ever since Mags and Mr. Gable had joined our lives, *it was better.*

I couldn't wait to see what the next year would bring.

WHAT'S NEXT?

Taking crazy cat lady to a whole new level... Binge read books 10-12 with this special boxed collection!

Ever since Angie Russo woke up from a near fatal run-in with a coffee maker, she's been able to talk to—and even worse, understand—one very spoiled tabby named Octavius.

This collection includes Retriever Ransom, Lawless Litter, and Legal Seagull. Read along as a canine kidnapping scanalizes the town, an abandoned litter of kittens cause havoc, and a militant flock of seagulls promise Angie the one thing she wants most in the world... that is if she's willing to do them a favor first. Add in a cross-country roadtrip, bizarra cameo, and an elderly romance, toss on your favorite deerstalker cap, and let's go sleuthing!

If you love kitty detectives and quirky humor, then you do not want to miss this USA Today bestselling series and your chance to binge read books seven through nine with this special boxed collection... Enjoy

PET WHISPER P.I. BOOKS 10-12 SPECIAL BOXED EDITION is now available.

CLICK HERE to get your copy so that you can keep reading this series today!

MORE MOLLY

ABOUT MOLLY FITZ

While USA Today bestselling author Molly Fitz can't technically talk to animals, she and her doggie best friend, Sky Princess, have deep and very animated conversations as they navigate their days. Add to that, five more dogs, a snarky feline, comedian husband, and diva daughter, and you can pretty much imagine how life looks at the Casa de Fitz.

Molly lives in a house on a high hill in the Michigan woods and occasionally ventures out for good food, great coffee, or to meet new animal friends.

Writing her quirky, cozy animal mysteries is pretty much a dream come true, but sometimes she also goes by the names Melissa Storm and Mila Riggs and writes a very different kind of story.

Learn more, grab the free app, or sign up for her newsletter at **www.MollyMysteries.com**!

PET WHISPERER P.I.

Angie Russo just partnered up with Blueberry Bay's first ever talking cat detective. Along with his ragtag gang of human and animal helpers, Octo-Cat is determined to save the day... so long as it doesn't interfere with his schedule. Start with book 1, ***Kitty Confidential***.

PARANORMAL TEMP AGENCY

Tawny Bigford's simple life takes a turn for the magical when she stumbles upon her landlady's murder and is recruited by a talking black cat named Fluffikins to take over the deceased's role as the official Town Witch for Beech Grove, Georgia. Start with book 1, **Witch for Hire**.

MERLIN THE MAGICAL FLUFF

Gracie Springs is not a witch... but her cat is. Now she must help to keep his secret or risk spending the rest of her life in some magical prison. Too bad trouble seems to find them at every turn! Start with book 1, **Merlin the Magical Fluff.**

THE MEOWING MEDIUM

Mags McAllister lives a simple life making candles for tourists in historic Larkhaven, Georgia. But when a cat with mismatched eyes enters her life, she finds herself with the ability to see into the realm of spirits... Now the ghosts of people long dead have started coming to her for help solving their cold cases. Start with book 1, **Secrets of the Specter**.

THE PAINT-SLINGING SLEUTH

Following a freak electrical storm, Lisa Lewis's vibrant paintings of fairytale creatures have started coming to life. Unfortunately, only she can see and communicate with them. And when her mentor turns up dead, this aspiring artist must turn amateur sleuth to clear her name and save the day with only these "pigments" of her imagination to help her. Start with book 1, **My Colorful Conundrum**.

SPECIAL COLLECTIONS

Black Cat Crossing
Pet Whisperer P.I. Books 1-3
Pet Whisperer P.I. Books 4-6
Pet Whisperer P.I. Books 7-9
Pet Whisperer P.I. Books 10-12

CONNECT WITH MOLLY

You can download my free app here:
mollymysteries.com/app

Or sign up for my newsletter and get a special digital prize pack for joining, including an exclusive story, Meowy Christmas Mayhem, fun quiz, and lots of cat pictures!
mollymysteries.com/subscribe

Have you ever wanted to talk to animals? You can chat with Octo-Cat and help him solve an exclusive online mystery here:
mollymysteries.com/chat

Or maybe you'd like to chat with other animal-loving readers as well as to learn about new books and giveaways as soon as they happen! Come join Molly's VIP reader group on Facebook.
mollymysteries.com/group

MORE BOOKS LIKE THIS

Welcome to Whiskered Mysteries, where each and every one of our charming cozies comes with a furry sidekick... or several! Around here, you'll find we're all about crafting the ultimate reading experience. Whether that means laugh-out-loud antics, jaw-dropping magical exploits, or whimsical journeys through small seaside towns, you decide.

So go on and settle into your favorite comfy chair and grab one of our *paw*some cozy mysteries to kick off your next great reading adventure!

Visit our website to browse our books and meet our authors, to jump into our discussion group, or to join our newsletter. See you there!

www.WhiskeredMysteries.com

WHISKMYS (WĪSK'MƏS)

DEFINITION : a state of fiction-induced euphoria that commonly occurs in those who read books published by the small press, Whiskered Mysteries.

USAGE: Every day is Whiskmys when you have great books to read!

**LEARN MORE AT
WWW.WHISKMYS.COM**

Made in the USA
Monee, IL
14 February 2022

15ddb694-06df-41de-8e12-fbca191319cbR01